Peaches Part II – Dead Ringers

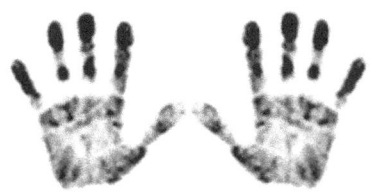

Diane Martin

http://dianemartin.weebly.com

10 9 8 7 6 5 4 3 2 1

First Edition

Edited by Dr. William A. Martin & Diane Martin

Interior Design by Diane Martin

Cover Design by Diane Martin

Printed by CreateSpace

Printed in the United States

ISBN 10: 0-9975761-3-8

ISBN-13: 978-0-9975761-3-9

Disclaimer: This is a book of fiction and not based on actual events. Any similarities to current events, characters, names and locations are purely coincidental and based solely on the imagination of the author.

My writing legacy would be my true depiction of life; exploring the entire colorful spectrum of people, both good and bad, capturing it in words and exposing it to all cultures in a respectful manner - In a way that would stand the test of time. - Diane Martin

Enjoy *[signature]*

Thank you for your support... ☺

"There are two things in life for which we are never prepared [for]: Twins."

-Josh Billings

Prologue

The splashing of water and voices, the squeaking sound of a faucet and a child fighting back tears. The loud "tick-tock" coming from the clock on the wall. Seconds turning into minutes, minutes turning into hours....hours into a lifetime. He focuses on the sound of the clock and the beating sound of his heart banging against his chest. He slows his breathing so that his heart can catch up with the clock. They are now in sync. TICK-TOCK. THUMP-THUMP. TICK-TOCK. THUMP-THUMP. The smell of soap fills the air. He looks down and watches her nipples as they grow harder as the soap washes over them. He could see her pubic hair peeking through the suds. "Wash me," she begs. He hesitates, but says, "Yes, mama." The towel washes gently over her skin, over her nipples, the curves of her breasts, down her belly, and between her legs. TICK-TOCK. THUMP-THUMP. She opens her legs, wide. She moans. "Harder, son," she begs. "Yes, mama." He obeys. She takes the towel from his hand and says, "Use your fingers....mommy likes it when you use your fingers." TICK-TOCK. THUMP-THUMP. He closes his eyes as his fingers searches for the spot between her legs. She moans, again. TICK-TOCK. THUMP-THUMP. "Harder, son." He obeys. "Yes, mama." She places one leg over the arm of the tub. "Harder, son." "Yes, mama." She grabs his head and places her mouth on his. TICK-TOCK. THUMP-THUMP. She pulls his hair. Her nails pierces his scalp. She screams. Her body trembles. Suddenly, she relaxes. Satisfied and exhausted, she pats the side of his face. "You're such a good boy," she says, as she slides further into the water. "Mommy, am I done?" he asks her. "For now," she replies. She sits up and kisses him on the forehead. "Now, be a good boy and go get your sister." TICK-TOCK. TICK-TOCK. TICK-TOCK.

"MAMA, NOOOOOOOOO!!!!" The sound of my voice startled me – awaking me from my nightmare. Soaked in sweat, I threw the blankets off of me. I climbed out of the bed, stumbling, and searching. For what? I don't know, but as I looked for it, I banged my foot against the bed post. The sound woke-up the babies. Grace whimpered for a second and fell back to sleep, but Peaches let out a loud yell. "WAAAAAAAAAA!!!!"

Flustered and frustrated, I crawled over to her crib.

"Wh…wh…Whaaaaaaaaaaa!!!!" she bellowed.

Trying to calm her, I said, "Hush sweetie… daddy's here."

"Whaaaaaaaaaaaaaaaaaaaaaaaaa!!!!!!!!!!!!!!" she screamed, again.

Panicking, I looked around her crib for her pacifier. "Shhhhhhhhhhh…" I picked her up and cradled her into my arms, but it didn't help. I bounced her up and down – hoping that it would calm her, but she screamed louder.

"WHAAAAAAAAAAAAAAA!!!"

I kissed her cheeks. "Here, honey." I tried putting the pacifier in her mouth. She sucked it three times before spitting it clear across the room. In the darkness, I looked for it, but could not find it.

"WHAAAAAAAAAAAAAAAAAAAAA!!!!!"
Her cry pierced my eardrum. I rubbed it, trying to regain my hearing. I paced back and forth in the middle of the room. Just then, I walked passed the mirror that was sitting on the dresser. I looked in its direction. My mother's reflection stared back at me. I shook my head, trying to erase the image.

My thoughts were, quickly, interrupted and I was reminded of the screaming baby in the room. "WHAAAAA!!!!!"

"Damnit, Peaches…please…you're going to wake up your sister." I held her out in front of me. She continued to cry. "Peaches, I'm begging you…please stop crying." She paused and looked at me and then let out another "WHAAAAAAAAAAAAAAAAAAAAA!!!!"

This time, Grace sat up and began to cry. I begged again. "Peaches, please stop." She let out a cry so loud it could shatter glass. "WAAAAAAAAAAAAAAAAAAAAAAA!!!!"
I began to, gently, rock her, but it only caused her

to scream more. I was so tired – so overwhelmed. The rock, quickly, became a shake, the shake turned into a tremor, and then the tremor became a jerk and I jerked her and jerked her and jerked her until there was nothing, but the sound of Grace's whimper. I looked down at Peaches' face – blood dripping from her nose. I laid her back into her crib. Her limp body laid there – stretched-out across her bed.

"HOLY SHIT…Oh my, God…OH my, GOD…I killed her." I ran out of the room to the bathroom to retrieve a cold towel. "I killed my baby," I mumbled, as the water ran in the sink. "I didn't mean to do it. She wouldn't stop crying…" I ran back into the room. Through my panic, I heard Grace crying. I gave her the pacifier that sat next to her and she fell back to sleep. I walked back over to Peaches' crib and looked in. I touched her. She still did not move. I picked her up and tried performing CPR, but she didn't respond. I laid her back in her bed. I wiped the blood from her nose and patted her forehead with the cold towel. I called out to her. "Peaches? Peaches? Baby, please wake up." She didn't respond. I fell to my knees, crying, and begging God to please help me…please help my baby. Then, I thought about their mother and how I promised to take care of them and now, only months after I made that promise, one of them lie helpless in her bed.

"Lord, please…I'm sorry. Please…I'm begging you. Don't take my baby. I'm sorry. I didn't mean to hurt her. Please, Lord…I will do anything. I will give anything…don't take my baby."

Just then, I heard a quiet whimper coming from her crib. Wiping the tears from my eyes, I stood up and looked inside of her crib. Slowly, she opened her eyes. She looked at me. I grabbed her and held her in my arms. "I'm so sorry, Peaches…please forgive me. Daddy is so sorry. I will never hurt you again."

I wiped her face, again, with the cold towel. She jerked and tried to push my hand away. I examined her, closely. She seemed okay as she stared at me, blankly. For a moment, she was fixated on my face, but then her eyes drifted behind me. Something had her attention. Suddenly, she giggled and smiled. I looked over my shoulder to see who or what she was smiling at, but there was nothing – there was no one. She turned and looked back at me – not really looking at me, but looking through me. She frowned. A chill came over the room. "Peaches?"

Something about the look on her face told me that I'd just fucked up.

REMY

"Hurt people,
hurt
people... ☹"

Chapter 1

If someone…anyone…had told me that this is what it's like to be a parent, I would have kept my dick in my pants. These kids could be the new face for "birth control." Don't get me wrong, I love my babies, but these little people are not normal. I know that that is a terrible thing to say, but I truly believe that they are in cahoots and on a mission to drive me crazy. I wasn't sure what was going on, but something wasn't right. Maybe there's something fucked-up in the "bloodline", the DNA, some rotten fruit on the family tree, or maybe there is something in the milk, but they had me so spooked, I thought that I was going to have to call someone to do an exorcism.

I wouldn't have believed it, myself, if I wasn't the one experiencing it. To think that something so little and so cute could be so diabolical and so devious. It had gotten to the point where I was afraid to play with them. Something as simple as a game of "Peek-a-boo" could end in a black-eye. And I knew that they were doing it on purpose. No one cracks you over the top of your head because you yelled, "Peek-a-boo, I see you..." unless they are trying to do some damage. I guess they didn't like playing games, but there were better ways of letting me know.

From the moment they were born, they were letting me know who they were and what to expect from them. I was the only one walking around without a damn clue, but that wouldn't be for long. I learned, quickly, that the parent and child relationship actually translated to master and slave, and they did not play. The little tyrants were demanding and when I didn't move when they wanted me to, there was a price to pay. They were forever throwing something. If it wasn't a rattle, a pacifier, a bottle, it was whatever they could get those tiny little fingers on. When they summoned me, I went crawling in, because walking in could result in a knot on my head. It was like living on a battlefield where I had to dodge bullets every day.

If someone had spoken to me, before, about reincarnation, I would have called bullshit, but these two have been here before. As what? I don't know, but you cannot convince me that someone who's only had life for such a short amount of time, who is as advanced as they are in thinking, and tell me that they have not traveled this earth before. They are well beyond their years or months, in their case. They are extremely intelligent. Smarter than some of the adults I know. They were talking early, walking early, potty-trained early, and even learning to be sneaky at an early age.

One morning, I'd awaken to the rustling sound of the plastic feet of their sleepers scratching across the floor. I knew that they were up to something. The first thing that I found concerning was the fact that they were out of their beds when I knew that I'd put them down for a nap. I had no idea how they did that, but I didn't have enough time to think about it, because as soon as I sat up to see what was going on, I'd been hit in the face and chest with diapers that were full of shit. As soon as I realized what was happening, I was confronted with two little naked booties, as they ran out of the room.

I stood, dropping poop all over the floor and followed them out of the room. It was then that I saw them helping each other back into their beds. It would have been cute if they were sleeping in twin beds, but they were still sleeping in cribs with railings. I had to find out how they were doing that. So, I cleaned them up, put another diaper on them, fed them, and then placed them in Peaches' crib to play together. I walked out of the room. I watched and waited. When they thought that the close was clear, Peaches looked at the door. I watched as she stuck her little pudgy leg over the railing, then the next one, and *Plop*, her little butt was on the floor. Grace, soon, followed behind her.

The weird thing is what happened next. Once they were on the floor, they both began to strip out of all of their clothing. They ran around the room butt-naked for several minutes before coming out of the room to look for me. I snatched them up at the door and returned them to their cribs. I redressed Grace without incident. She actually giggled through the whole process, but Peaches was not happy. She treated the moment like an inconvenience - like an intrusion on her right to be naked. She fought me with everything that she had. She kicked and screamed like I was hurting her. When I was done, I let out a sigh of relief, but Peaches was none too pleased. She reached up, grabbed my face, and dug her nails into the side of it like she was trying to pull my skin off. When I pulled her hands away, I could see that there was blood in her fingernails. I screamed and grabbed my face. It felt like it was on fire. I bolted out of the room and ran to the bathroom where I found a welt on the side of my face. After putting water on it, I returned to their room. "Look what you did, Peaches..." She looked at me, ripped her diaper off, and slung it across the room. Her eyes were so cold and dark. I stepped back and slowly exited the room.

Chapter 2

My wife is gone, my sister is gone, and my mother is gone. They had no aunties or grandparents because they were gone too. It was just me and them, for the most part. I was kinda lucky in that, every once in a while, my dad would come over to remind me that there was another world out there – one that didn't consist of dirty diapers, sleepless nights, and bottles of formula.

The relationship between me and my father was one of pure surrender. Although, he was in my life, I still considered him an absentee parent. One that I'd grown to resent for most of my childhood, but as I got older, I grew tired of hating him, because hatred was too heavy of a cross to bear, so I let it go. I realized that he was just as much as a victim as me and my sister. Sure, he should have done more to protect us, but when you're a victim too, you learn to protect your own ass. And I don't have anyone else. If I'd cut him out, I would be alone, and I couldn't do this alone.

And I don't care what nobody tells you...babies need their mothers. Sure, society will try to convince you otherwise, but there is something about them that makes them "naturally" equipped to deal with this stuff. Women are nurturers and men are not. Sure, we know how to love, and we can learn how to change a diaper, but all of that other baby shit? There's no class for that. The hospital just wrapped them up, handed them to me, and then sent me on my way and I've been a mess ever since. There is only so much a man can do on his own. Shit, it takes us years to get the "fucking-part" right, and just when you find your 'rhythm', *BOOM!* you're getting a call that changes your whole life. Then, you're faced with the decision to either be the man-in or the man-out. If you choose to be the man-in, you only have nine months to prepare for what took one minute to accomplish and you'll be dealing with it for the rest of your life, so you better learn quick.

Even after they place your babies in your arms, you're still caught-up into the whole fantasy aspect of it. Things don't get real until you find yourself standing in the baby section of some big chain department store with every other man on the planet, looking stupid as you search for a can of powdered milk that costs $50, or you find yourself in the diaper aisle trying to choose between absorbent and extra-absorbent. Only to end-up spending another $50 on a box of cotton that your baby ain't gon' do nothing more than piss and shit in.

It's a lot to think about and I think about it every day, all day, every day. I was contemplating all of this when there was a knock on the door. With one on each hip, I limped over to the door – still sore from the night before. I unlocked the door. "You're going to have to turn the knob…my hands are full," I instructed.

He walked in. "You didn't even check to see who was on the other side of the door…I could have been a murderer."

"And if you'd killed me…at least, I could finally get some sleep."

He took the girls from my arms and said, "Give me my babies, and stop talking crazy-talk. Look at grand-daddy's babies. They look absolutely beautiful."

I handed them to him so fast, I almost dropped them on the floor. Walking into the kitchen, I paused and looked over my shoulder. "You would too if you got twelve hours of sleep a day, ate ten times a day, took two baths a day, had somebody to rub lotion all over you, comb your hair, wipe your butt, and clean-up your messes all day..."

He looked at Peaches and Grace and said, "Ignore him...he hasn't gotten 'any' in a long time."

"AND I don't want 'any'...they are the result of the last time I got 'any'."

He sat down at the table. "You're kinda irritable, son...what's wrong?" He looked, closely, at my face. "What happened to your face?"

I looked at Peaches. She had a weird look on her face – like she knew that we were talking about her. "I cut myself shaving..." I said, lying.

"You need to stop buying those cheap-ass razors..."

I frowned. "Dad...language..."

He laughed. "'Ass' is in the Bible...and if you were getting more of it, you wouldn't be so irritable. Plus, as a parent you have every right to cuss. And if you don't plan on spanking them, then you better get the hang of it quick. There are only two things that kids understand...cussing and a belt...cussing is the go-to...lets them know that you're not playing with their asses...that shit is about to get real...the belt works when cussing doesn't...see watch this..." He looked at the girls and said, "Goo-goo, gaa-gaa..." The girls continued to play – like he wasn't even in the room. "Now, watch this...motherfuck a goo-goo and motherfuck a gaa-gaa..." The girls looked up, giggled, and clapped their hands. He smiled and said, "See...they understood that shit."

"I'm not going to spank my babies and plus, it's against the law."

"The government can kiss my wrinkled-Black ass...they wannabe all-up in yo' business and tell you not to hit your kids, but you don't hear a peep from their asses when some motherfucker shoots them…'cause that shit's okay…" He frowned.

I shook my head. "I'm just so tired," I said, looking at my father. "Nobody told me that it was going to be this hard."

Bouncing Peaches and Grace on his knees, he said, "Look at these little cuties…how can anything, involving them, be hard?"

My hands were shaking so bad, I could barely hold the cup of scolding hot coffee.

"Do you think caffeine is a good idea?" he asked.

"Coffee is the only thing keeping me alive." Holding the cup with two hands to stabilize it, I continued, "Daddy, you had mama…" I paused for a second and said, "I take that back."

"Yeah…she was fucked-up…" he paused for a second and said, "And I'm just going to leave that right there."

I continued. "Like I was saying…it's hard taking care of one baby…let alone two…they keep me moving…I can't take a shower…I can't eat…I can't take a shit…" My babies looked-up at me.

"Daddy said a bad word. I'm sorry…I'm just so tired."

"You're supposed to do that when they're sleep," he said, standing to place them in their play-pen.

Placing the cup down, I said, "Yeah, that sounds great…in theory…but in practice…that's a whole 'nother story. When they're sleep, I'm woke and when they're woke, I'm sleep. I'm all discombobulated." I walked over to turn on the TV. I was scanning the channels – looking for the TV show with the talking trains. "I can't get anything done."

"Well, I'm here now…go and do some of the things that you need to do…I'll watch them for a while."

Feeling like I'd just won the lottery, I said, "Really???"

He walked over to the couch and sat down. "Yes…go…I got this…me and these little angels are going to hang-out for a while."

Trying to get out of the room before he changed his mind, I said, "They've already eaten. Their diapers and wipes are over there…"

He interrupted me. "Stop...go...they're babies. How hard can this be?"

He was talking to the back of my head, because I was out of there. I ran down the hall, removing my clothes as I thought about all of the things that I was going to do. By the time I hit the bathroom door, I was already naked. I needed to wash my ass first. It had been so long since I'd last changed my underwear, they pulled at my skin like a bandage – ripping some of the hair off of my balls. *Ouch!* After stopping the blood, I, quickly, jumped in the shower. I didn't even wait for the water to turn hot. I jumped in and when the cold water hit my skin, I almost had a heart attack, but I didn't care. Even though, the water was freezing, it felt so good not to be standing over a bathroom sink trying to wash my ass before one of them woke up – which always resulted in me leaving a trail of soap in the crack of my ass. Feeling the water as it ran down my back, felt like I'd died and gone to Heaven. I never wanted to leave, but I knew that I couldn't stay in there long. For a moment, I thought that I heard one of them crying and paused to listen for the door. When it didn't swing open, I exhaled and continued to wash myself.

After I was done, I sat down on the toilet. I closed my eyes as my butt wrapped itself around the toilet seat. As I sat there, it felt good to be able to close the door, use the bathroom with both butt-cheeks on the toilet, and with both feet in front of me. Instead of having one foot out the door – ready to dart out at any moment. It had been so long that my body didn't know what to do. I had to remind myself to just relax and just let "it" flow, because when you have babies, the words "relax and flow" disappear from your vocabulary.

When I was done, I walked down the hall to my bedroom. I looked in the mirror as I threw on a pair of briefs. My skin was so ashy. It looked like I'd bathed in baby powder. I decided that since I had a minute, I would put some lotion on my skin, but I didn't have anything for grown-ups. Everything I had was for the girls, so I grabbed the pink bottle, poured half of it into my hands and rubbed it all over me. When I was done, I slid on a pair of pajamas, walked over to my bed, and climbed under my blankets. The "cold" of the sheets embraced my skin. I rubbed my feet together and snuggled against my pillow. I was on my way to "la-la land" when just as my eyes closed, my bedroom door flew open.

With one eye open, I turned and looked at the door.

"Get this girl!" he shouted, holding her up in the air – ten feet out in front of him.

He threw Peaches into my arms. "She bit the shit out of me!"

"Language, dad…" I said, holding her.

"Language my ass…she tried to take my ear off…" he rubbed his ear as he continued. "Do you feed these kids?"

I looked at his ear. "Of course, I feed them…they eat better than me."

"Well, you're not giving them enough." Looking in the mirror, he continued, "Who taught her that shit?"

I looked at Peaches. "Why did you do that, Peaches?" I asked.

He frowned. "Do you expect her to confess?"

"She's teething…it shouldn't hurt…that bad. She has a mouth full of gums."

"Those little gums hurt. Look at me…I'm bleeding."

"That's weird…"

He frowned. "Is that all you have to say? That's weird? Your baby just attacked me and all you have to say is, 'That's weird.' She better be glad that she's not taller…I would take her butt in the backyard and settle this like we used to do in the old days."

"Daddy, she's a baby…"

"She's a cannibal…instead of giving her little butt some milk, you need to go in that kitchen and fry-up some dang chicken wings and let her suck on the bones like they used to do in the south. Then, her little butt will stop taking chunks out of folks." He rubbed his ear, again. "You know that once they get a taste of flesh…there's no turning back."

"Daddy stop…she's not a dog."

He frowned. "No, she's a damn vampire. One day, I'mma come over here and find her chewing on your neck."

"You're being silly..." I paused and looked at her. "Don't listen to grand-daddy...he's just being silly." She looked at me, looked over at him, and then threw her bottle at him. "PEACHES!!"

He ducked before getting a bottle upside his head. "I'm getting the hell up out of here...something is wrong with that child."

He turned and left the room. Seconds later, he returned carrying Grace. "Here...I'm going home before I end-up in the Emergency Room...messing around with Satan's Spawn."

"I'm sorry, daddy," I said, taking Grace from him.

"Yeah, right..." He turned to leave the room mumbling on his way out. "Little heathen..."

I looked at her. "Why did you do that, Baby Girl?"

She just looked at me and smiled.

Chapter 3

I was constantly being confronted with my limitations. I was in serious need of help. Since, I had no real family, I decided to reach out to the community in search of someone who could, not provide an understanding, but a break from the stress of being a single parent. So, while shopping with them one day, I saw an ad for a babysitter and decided to give the person a call.

The day that she came over, I made sure that the house was clean and that the girls were fed and rested so that maybe they would behave themselves. When the doorbell rang, I looked out to see a young girl who looked to be in her late teens. She smiled and said, "Hi, I'm Kathy…you're looking for a babysitter?"

"You didn't bring any back-up?" I asked, looking over her shoulder.

She frowned. "Do I need back-up?"

Trying not to frighten her, I, quickly, said, "No, no, no..." and let her in.

She walked in and looked around. "You have a beautiful home."

"Thank you," I said.

She saw the babies playing on the living room floor. "Oh my goodness...they are so pretty. What's their names?"

"Grace and Peaches..." I said.

"They are gorgeous," she said, sitting on the floor next to them.

I smiled. "Thank you..." I walked over and sat on the couch in front of them. The girls crawled over to her and began to play with her. They were really taken with her.

"Have you had any experience dealing with twins?" I asked.

Handing Peaches a toy, she said, "No, but I've watched two and three kids at a time...can't be that much of a difference, right?"

"Well, twins can be a handful..." I watched as the girls climbed into her lap and hugged her.

She smiled. "I think that we will be fine...when would you like for me to start?"

Feeling comfortable, I said, "Today..." I laughed, nervously, trying to be careful not to run her away. "I'm just kidding. How about tomorrow?"

The girls giggled. "Tomorrow will be fine..." They were hugging and kissing her like they'd known her all of their lives.

While we worked out the specifics, she rocked them both to sleep. I felt so at ease and so happy. I'd found someone who could connect with them, and provide them with something else to look at other than my tired face. I was so excited. After she left, I set up everything that she would possibly need. I played with them most of the night, because I wanted them to be sleepy and not give her any trouble. After playing until about 1am, we all fell asleep. When the sun came up, I bathed them, fed them, and got ready to start my day. She arrived early. I opened the door to find her standing on the porch with a bag full of dolls. I had the girls in my arms, so when they saw her, they reached out to her. "Dolls?" I asked. She handed me the bag and she took the babies from my arms.

"Yes," she said. "The kids love them."

"Really?" I said, following her into the house.

"Yes, and it's a good learning tool. I like to introduce them to 'words' by singing, and things like that, and I do it with this little skit that I created…the babies loooooooooove it."

I smiled and shrugged. "Hey…if it works."

She placed the girls down on the couch and said, "We're going to have so much fun."

"Well, everything that you need is right here. The food is in the fridge. I've already prepared their bottles. They usually take naps…"

She interrupted me. "We're going to be fine. Please go…enjoy your day. If we need anything, I will call you."

I smiled and grabbed my keys. As I exited the door, the sun hit my face in such a way that for the first time in a long time, I felt alive. I didn't even look back at the house as I walked to the driveway. I pulled out of the driveway so fast, I left most of my tires on the pavement - almost hitting the kid that was coming down the sidewalk on a *Big Wheel*. I heard him spit out a few curse words, but I didn't stop, because I didn't care. I was free. For the first time, in a long time, I was free.

I'd stopped at the Post Office and the grocery store. I stopped by a few companies and put in a couple of applications. Since I had a few hours left, I decided to stop by my dad's house to check on him. When I knocked on the door, he peered through the blinds before opening the door.

"Where are they at?" he asked.

I sighed. "Daddy...stop..." I walked passed him – into the house.

"Shiiiiiiiiiiiiiiittttttttt, I ain't messing around with those bad-ass kids."

"Daddy...they're your grandkids..."

"Yep, and they can still be my grandkids while they are at your house and away from mine…"

"Dad…"

"I'm telling ya'…y'all young folks need to stop smoking those damn tweeds…making these dysfunctional kids…"

"Weed, dad…"

"Weeds, tweeds…y'all need to avoid all green shit. Unless it's salad…other than that, just say no…"

"Dad…y'all just got off to a bad start. Look…they've been with their babysitter all day and I haven't…" I paused and began to look for my phone. "…gotten one…" I kept searching my pockets. "….call." I realized that I didn't have my phone. "Holy shit…I lost my phone."

"That poor girl…." he said, shaking his head.

I frowned at him. "I gotta go…find my phone." I turned and ran out of the house. I jumped in my car and watched as he continued to shake his head.

As I drove down the street, I searched my seat to see if it had fallen in-between it and the console. At the stop light, I searched the floor, but there was nothing. As I got closer to my house, I began to hear sirens. "Lord, please don't let it be my house...Lord, please don't let it be my house..." I began to chant. When I turned the corner a fire truck flew passed me. "Holy shit...my house is on fire. I bet my house is on fire." As I drove closer, a wave of relief swept over me. *Whew.* "Thank God...it's not my house."

I pulled into my driveway, jumped out of my car, and ran towards the door. Just then, the door flew open. All I felt was a breeze, as a blur wearing a pair of *Nikes* flew passed me.

"I QUIT!!!!! I QUIT!!!!!!" she shouted as she ran down the street holding something up to her forehead.

"Wait!!!! What happened?" I looked inside of the house, then I turned back, and ran to the curb. "I didn't pay you!!!"

"KEEP THAT SHIT!!!!" she yelled back. Swiftly, she was out of sight.

I walked back to the house. When I walked in, I saw a trail of blood that led to the living room. There were dolls thrown all over the place. Some were missing heads while others had no arms or legs. I ran over and saw the girls playing quietly. I picked Grace up first and examined her. She seemed okay. I put her down and looked over at Peaches. I picked her up. She began to clap her hands. I noticed that there was blood on her fingers and something black in her hand. I looked closer. Wrapped around her fingers were strands of long black hair. I thought back to the vision of the girl holding her head. "Did you pull that girl's hair out of her head?"

She didn't respond. She handed me the hair and rested her head on my shoulders. I looked back towards the open door and watched as my freedom walked out of it.

I was so tired, I couldn't think straight. All I wanted to do was put their little asses in the bed, so that they could take a much needed nap. I carried them to the bathroom, turned on the water in the tub, check the temperature to make sure that it wasn't too hot, and began to undress them. Grace giggled and began to dance, naked, around the floor.

"Stop, baby, before you fall on the floor," and just like I was talking to the wall, she completely ignored me. *Sigh.* Next, I undressed Peaches. "You had a long day, sweetie. A nap will do you good."

She stared at me.

Once the tub had enough water in it, I placed them into the water. I added some shampoo to the water, so that they could enjoy some bubbles.

"You like that?" I asked, splashing the water with them. They both smiled.

I threw a couple of their bath toys into the water and sat next to the tub to watch them play. They were having so much fun. I sat back against the wall to relax while they played. Suddenly, my eyes grew heavy. I tried forcing them open, but the lure of sleep was too strong. I nodded off. I can't tell you how much time had passed, but I felt water splashing against my face. Forcing my eyelids open, I looked around the room. I turned and looked at the tub. For a moment, I thought that my eyes were playing tricks on me. I shook my head to make sure that I wasn't dreaming. I looked again. I knew that I'd put both of them in the water, but when I looked over there, there was only one sitting there. Frantically, I crawled over to the tub. I couldn't understand what I was seeing. She looked like a doll – floating across the water. "Oh my God, Oh my God, shit…no, no, no, no, no…." I snatched her out of the water. "Oh shit, oh shit, oh shit…" I said, checking her breathing. I began to do chest compressions. "Grace…Peaches…come on baby…come on," I begged. I breathed into her mouth and applied more compressions to the chest. "COME ON!!!! PLEASSSEEEEEE, BREATHE, BREATHE DAMN-IT!!!!"

Suddenly, she coughed and began to cry. She lifted her arms. "Daa-daa…" She jumped into my arms. "Daa-daa…"

I held her. "I'm here, sweetie. I'm here…"

I looked over at the tub to find the other one still playing as if nothing had happened.

Chapter 4

And for the next few years, it was pretty much the same thing. I was always on high-alert. The only time that they were out of my site was when they started school. Even then, I knew to be prepared for anything. It had gotten so bad that I was afraid to answer my phone. When I did, there wasn't any "Hellos" or any "How are you doings?" No, it was, "Let me tell you what your child has done TODAY. Emphasis on the word TODAY, because something happened every damn day. From preschool to high school – every damn day.

I will never forget the day that I dropped them off for their first day at preschool. The morning, was like any other morning - me fighting with them about everything.

"Get up, girls…"

"NO!" someone would shout from under their blanket.

"Go and brush your teeth…"

"NO!" someone else would yell from under their blanket.

The only time that they didn't say "no" was when it involved food. "Come and eat your breakfast…"

Finally, one of them would show up and I say, one of them, because for the first few years, it was hard to tell them apart. The girls looked exactly alike. The only way that I was able to tell them apart was that one of them had a birthmark in the shape of a strawberry on her left butt-cheek. But when they decided that they were too old for me to see them naked, each day became a guessing game. They used to love playing tricks on me. All they had to do was climb into the wrong bed, and they would have me all messed-up. Today, wouldn't be any different.

I looked at the little girl at the table and said, "Where's Grace?"

"I'm Grace," she said, smiling.

"Really?" I asked, curiously.

"Yep," she confirmed.

Just then, her 'look-alike' walked into the room. "Morning, daddy…" she mumbled.

"Grace?" I asked.

"Yes," she responded.

"No, I'm Grace…" the one at the table said.

"No, I'm Grace…" the other one said.

I was getting dizzy. "GIRLS!!!!!!"

They both giggled. The "one" at the table laughed and said, "I tricked you, daddy."

I squinted and said, "You did…you like that don't you?"

Peaches smiled. "Yep…"

"Cute…real cute…" I walked over to the table where I kept the mail, and began to make some name tags. When I was done, I taped them to their uniforms and said, "Daddy doesn't have the energy. Now, you're starting school, today…be nice to your teacher."

Peaches grumbled. "Why?"

"Cause I said so…" I said, pouring orange juice into their glasses.

"Why?" she asked again.

I paused and said, "Peaches…" I closed my eyes and exhaled. "Can we have one day?"

"I don't like this on my shirt…" she said, pointing at her name tag.

I opened my mouth to say something when Grace said, "I like mines, daddy."

"Okay…Grace, you wear yours... Peaches, I will take it off if you promise to be good, today."

She looked at me for a second and before I could remove it, she'd ripped it off of her shirt. "Okay…"

"Okay, what?"

"Okay…" she confirmed.

I looked-up at the clock. I didn't have time to go back and forth with her. "Okay…I'm going to have to take your word for it…now, let's get to stepping or you're going to be late."

They, quickly, swallowed down their breakfast, grabbed their lunches, and met me at the front door. The drive all the way there was uneventful. I looked at the rearview mirror to find my beautiful little girls looking out of the window – almost like they couldn't wait to start their first day of school.

When I parked, they'd already unbuckled the seat belts on their car seats. By the time I'd walked around to their side of the car, they were, anxiously, pulling on the door handle.

"Okay…okay…" I said.

When I opened the door, Grace jumped into my arms and said, "Bye, daddy."

Kissing her on her forehead, I said, "Bye, sweetie…daddy will see you soon."

She waved and ran into the crowd. I looked down at the kid without the name tag and said, "Okay sweetie…can daddy have a hug and a kiss?"

She looked around for a second. I kneeled down to her level and puckered-up. She paused and stared at me for what seemed like a lifetime. "Can daddy have a kiss and a hug?"

"No," she said.

"Daddy, can't have a kiss and a hug?" I puckered again.

She looked over at the other children and walked away leaving me kneeling with my lips stuck out. So that I didn't look like a fool, I pretended that I had food in my teeth and said, "Okay sweetie…I will see you later." I waved, but since the back of her head had no hands, I was standing there waving at trees.

I walked around my car, jumped in, and pulled-off. While thinking about the nap that I was going to take once I got home, my thoughts were interrupted by my vibrating pocket. Retrieving my phone, I looked at the caller-id. The number looked familiar, so I answered it.

Happily, I said, "Helloooooo…this is Remy…."

"Hi…I'm looking for the parents of Grace and Peaches…."

Panicking, I interrupted, "What's wrong? What's wrong?"

"There is a problem, sir…"

"A problem? What problem?"

"One of them assaulted one of the other children…"

"They haven't been there five minutes…" I said, frustrated and surprised at the same time.

"It only takes five minutes to assault someone, sir…" the voice on the other end said.

Without thinking, I veered into the other lane, spinning my car around into oncoming traffic, and sped down the road until I was right back where I was only five minutes earlier. I stopped the car and ran inside, and there she was, sitting in the principal's office. I looked down for the name tag before speaking, "Grace…what did you do?"

She didn't say anything. Suddenly, the principal walked over. Before she could say anything, I said, "I'm her father…"

She shook her head. "Your baby was being assigned a chair when one of the other children accidentally sat in her chair…well, she didn't like that."

I looked down at the name tag as she spoke. "What happened?"

"Well, she kicked the child in the stomach."

My mouth fell open. "Who kicked…what?"

"Your baby kicked another baby," she confirmed. "And we can't have…"

I stuck my hand up. "Okay, wait…not this one…couldn't have…"

The principal looked down and said, "Yep…this one…"

I frowned. "You know that there's two of them, right?"

The principal looked confused. "There's two of them?" she asked the assistant. The young lady nodded. "Yes."

I sighed. "Yes, there's two…" I looked at the little girl. "Go and get your sister." She jumped out of the chair, ran down the hall, and seconds later, we were looking at both of them.

"Oh wow…" the principal said, looking at the both of them. "I wasn't aware that we had twins…"

"Yep..."

"Well, we're going to have to do more than name tags..." she said.

I pulled the principal to the side and said, "Usually the violent one is Peaches...I know that that's a terrible thing to say, but she has a little mean-streak...Grace is the sweet one...she usually doesn't cause any problems."

"You're going to have to find a better way of distinguishing them apart, because we can't walk around waiting for one of them to hurt somebody to be able to tell them apart..."

Suddenly, we heard someone crying. I looked down at Grace who was crying and rubbing her hand, and at Peaches who was smiling and said, "You won't have to wait too long."

As I drove them home, I watched them through the rearview mirror as they played with Grace's nametag – switching it back and forth between them. I decided that I had to do something to make it easier for everyone to tell them apart.

When we walked in, I made them go into the bathroom. I squinted and said, "I send you in the school to learn…not to kick folks in the stomach. Why would you do that?"

Instead of responding, one smiled while the other one frowned.

"You can't go around kicking folks…you're going to do that one day and somebody, bigger, is going to kick you back…"

Grace giggled while Peaches, stared at me, blankly, like someone who wasn't "there" or she just didn't care.

"I tried to be nice…now, you're going to force me to do something that I didn't want to do…"

I grabbed the first one and pulled up her skirt. She struggled for a second, but then stopped. I lifted her panties, exposing her left butt-cheek, and said, "Okay…sorry Grace…"

When I didn't see the birthmark, I turned to look at the other one. "Peaches, come here."

She folded her arms and said, "No…"

I released Grace and said, "Peaches, I know that you kicked that child…what you did was wrong."

"I didn't do it," she insisted.

I turned to Grace. "Did you kick that child?"

"No, daddy…I did not do it," she insisted.

I was tired, frustrated, and sick of this shit. I looked over at the sink where a pair of scissors sat. I looked at the scissors and then I looked at Peaches. "So you're not going to tell me the truth?"

She folded her arms, defiantly. She poked out her bottom lip and shook her head.

I exhaled and said, "Okay…you give me no choice." I grabbed her and the scissors, and with one snip, one of my problems had been solved.

As her hair fell to the floor, she looked up at me. She didn't scream. She didn't cry. She picked up her ponytails with the barrettes still attached to them and looked up at me. Just then, I felt a chill and the hairs on my arms stood up. For a moment, I was scared, but I quickly remembered that I was bigger, taller, and hopefully, faster than she was.

She looked at the scissors and with the weirdest look on her face, she just walked out of the room.

Chapter 5

Later that evening, I called them to dinner. They walked into the room. Grace had her hair down - her beautiful curly-locks flowing among her shoulders. Then, Peaches entered the room sporting a short curly afro. She'd placed a ribbon in her hair to give it some personality, but the head that it was placed upon was not happy with the change. She didn't say anything, but the look on her face said it all.

They barely said anything during dinner. The twins weren't really the "talkative" type, but usually, with some prodding, I could always get them to discuss their "day." But today wasn't a day to talk about it. They didn't like me. At least not today, so I had to be satisfied with the sound of the forks banging against their plates.

When they were done, they excused themselves and went to bed. After washing dishes, I checked on them. They were sleeping, peacefully, under their blankets. I walked back into the living room and stretched across the sofa. I was surfing the channels, when I'd suddenly drifted off to sleep.

Moments later, I was awakened by the sound of something scratching against the floor. I struggled to open my eyes. "Go back to bed…" I mumbled before closing them again. I heard the sound again. I opened my eyes to find a shadow standing in front of the TV. "Go to bed…" I said. I dropped the remote onto the floor and fell back to sleep.

While sleeping, I had the strangest dream. I dreamed that I was a little boy again. I was in school. We'd taken our crayons, glue, and glitter out of our desks for arts and crafts. The teacher gave us all a handful of macaroni and told us to make something pretty to take home to our parents. This saddened me, because I knew that I had no one to give my picture to. As I stared at the blank piece of construction paper, I decided to make the picture for myself. I remember using my glue to draw some eyebrows, a nose, and a mouth. I smiled, because it looked just like me. I shook some glitter onto the paper to cover the glue. I began to use the glue to make a macaroni afro. As I looked at the picture, I couldn't help, but be proud of the work that I'd done.

Bang!!!

Something hit the floor and startled me out of my sleep. I jumped up, but for some odd reason, I couldn't open my eyes. I tried and I tried, but I couldn't get them to open. I reached up and felt something stuck to them. They were being held together with something. *What the fuck?* I tried removing it, but it began to rip my eyelashes from my eyelid. "Ouch!!!!" I needed to get whatever it was off of me. "Son-of-a-bitch…" I mumbled. I rolled off of the couch and onto the coffee table – banging my head against it. "SHIT!!!!" I crawled down the hall, running into everything, and banging my head along the way. After hitting my head the third time, I stood and felt my way until I found the bathroom. I walked in. Once in front of the mirror, I took a deep breath and as I exhaled, I ripped the object from one of my eyes. "SHIT!!!!!" I yelled. Able to see out of one of my eyes, I looked down at what was in my hand. It was a "smiley face" sticker. I looked up and realized that my whole face was covered with them. *What the hell?* I began to breathe, heavily, as I tried to remove the next sticker from the other eye. "SHIT!!!!!" I yelled again. My eye began to water from the pain. I turned and looked at the bathroom door. "Bad-ass...little motherfu...I'm going to..." I mumbled. Seething with anger, I walked down the hall, ripping the rest of the stickers off of my face, screaming in pain as the hair on my face slowly went from a beard into a goatee.

I threw the light on. "Damnit!!! Which one of y'all did this?"

Groggily, they both looked up. Immediately, they began to laugh. Waving the stickers in their faces, I said, "This isn't funny. Now, who did it?"

Peeling dried glue from her finger tips, she looked at me and said, "I don't know."

My eyes grew wide. "Stop lying, Peaches. You did this shit..."

Grace interrupted. "Oooooooo, you did it...you said a bad word...you gon' get in trouble..."

I turned and looked at her. "Lay down and go to sleep." Suddenly, I heard a loud smack. The back of my hand was stinging. I grabbed my hand and looked down. "Did you just hit me?"

She nodded her head and said, "You said a bad word...you're a bad, daddy...bad daddies get spanked."

I was in shock. "Peaches you don't hit, daddy...we've talked about this..."

She smiled and said, "You said a bad word..."

"But...but...but..." I stuttered.

Grace laughed. "You said, 'butt'...that's funny."

"I didn't say 'butt'...I said, 'but'..."

Grace laughed again. "You said 'butt' again..."

"No...wait..." I said, confused.

Finally, Peaches looked at me and rubbed her eyes. "Daddy, we're sleepy..."

I was frustrated and confused. Slowly, I removed my belt and began to swat it across my hand. She seemed completely unfazed by my gesture. She yawned, snuggled under her blankets, and closed her eyes, as if I wasn't in the room. I wanted to snatch her little butt from under her blankets and spank her, but no matter how much I believed she needed it, I couldn't. She was too little and spankings were the last result, but talks didn't work, time-outs didn't work, and sending her to her room didn't work. Peaches needed something else. A woman's touch? A mother's love? A punch in the throat? Something. Whatever it was, she needed it and fast.

The next morning, the house was unusually quiet. Reluctantly, I crawled out of bed to see what was going on. I walked out into the hallway and called out to them

"Peaches…Grace?" There was no answer. "Peaches…Grace…?" I called again, but still there was no answer. After a minute or two, I began to hear voices whispering from their bedroom. I walked in, but there was no one there. I was turning to leave the room, when I heard it again – the whispering. I walked in and stood in the middle of the room. The whispering started again. I turned in its direction and followed it until I was standing in front of their closet door. I opened it. My mouth fell open.

"Look, daddy…" She paused and patted Grace's head. "Now, we back the same." She smiled, holding a pair of scissors in her hand.

Grace smiled as she patted her lop-sided afro. "See, daddy…don't I look pretty?" she asked.

I felt defeated. I was too tired to be angry, so what was I going to do? Scold her for doing something that I'd just done to her? If it is okay for one, why isn't it okay for the other? I should have known that this would somehow blow-up in my face. I looked at Peaches as she stared at me. I kneeled down and took the scissors from her hand. "Peaches…" *Sigh*

"Yes, daddy?" she said.

"Did you cut your sister's hair?"

She didn't blink. "Nope…"

I exhaled. "Peaches, don't lie."

"I'm not lying, daddy."

"So, Grace, cut her own hair?"

"Yep…"

I looked at Grace. "Did you cut your hair?"

She stuck her hand up. "I promise not to tell a lie…stick a finger in your eye…"

"No, Grace…it's stick a finger in my eye…" I said, correcting her.

She pointed one of her fingers and rammed it into my eye. I fell backwards onto the floor. "Shit, Grace…you stuck me in the eye…"

"Oooooooooooo…" they both said in unison.

"Ooooooooooooo, nothing. You stuck me in the eye…"

"Because you told me to, daddy." she said.

Holding my eye, I said, "No, I was correcting you…you said 'stick a finger in your eye' when it's 'stick a finger in my eye'…"

Peaches walked up and stuck me in the other one.

"SON OF A BITCH!!!!" I yelled.

"Oooooooooooo…" they said, again.

With both eyes closed, I crawled over to the door and crawled down the hall to the bathroom. I closed and locked the door behind me. I stood and walked over to the sink. I was flushing my eyes with water when I heard a knock on the door. Slowly, I opened it. I looked down to find them standing there, smiling.

"Are you okay, daddy?" Peaches asked.

Squinting, I said, "No, I'm not okay…"

"Do you want me to kiss it and make it better?" she asked.

"No…" I said, as my eyes watered.

"Why are you crying?" Grace asked.

"BECAUSE YOU STUCK ME IN THE EYE!!!"

"Okay then…" Peaches smiled and turned to walk down the hall, dragging Grace behind her.

Chapter 6

$\mathbf{M}$y life was a circus and Peaches was the ring master. She stayed in trouble. Half of the shit that she did made absolutely no sense. I just couldn't wrap my mind around the "why" of it all. I mean, I understand that children get into trouble, but Peaches did shit that would make the "Children of the Corn" shake their evil little heads. She was bad as hell. If she wasn't torturing her sister or some kid at school, she was torturing me. One morning, I even checked her scalp for the "Mark of the Beast" because I was starting to believe that she is a child of the Devil.

There were mornings that I dreaded even getting out of bed, because I knew that on the other side of my bedroom door was a little girl who was waiting to make my life a living hell. Sometimes, I would open my door to find her standing there, dressed in her uniform, a large bow in her hair, and that little creepy smile painted across her cute little face.

"Good morning, Peaches…" I said, trying to get around her.

"Morning, daddy…" she said, blocking my path. "Daddy, I want cereal."

I looked down. "You had cereal, yesterday, Peaches…too much sugar isn't good for you."

She looked at me. "I want cereal."

"Again…you had cereal, yesterday," I said, moving her to the side and walking down the hall. "Now, I was thinking that today we will have something different…"

"I want cereal…" she said, stomping her feet.

I looked back. "Ummmmm, young lady…you better get your little self in this kitchen…."

"I….SAID…I…WANT…CEREAL!!!!"

I looked back, again. "What in the hell? If you don't get your butt in this…"

She ran in the kitchen. "I…SAID…I…WANT…CEREAL!!!!" Her eyes widened, as she began to ball her hands into fists.

Girl, you don't want none of this. I thought to myself as I walked away.

Suddenly, she ran passed me to block my path, again. "I said that I want cereal…RIGHT NOW!!!"

Grace was already at the table waiting patiently. I poured some instant grits into a bowl, added some water, and sat it in the microwave. When the timer went *Bing*, I removed the bowl, and placed it on the table.

"What is this?" she said, examining the contents of the bowl. "This don't look like cereal."

I kneeled-down to her level so that I could look her in the eyes as I explain the importance of good nutrition versus bad. She pushed the bowl. I shoved it back in front of her. I kneeled down again and said, "Little girl, you better wrap your lips around those damn grits and do it quick." She paused and before I knew it, she took her little hand, put it behind her back, and when it came back around, it landed on the side of my face. "I SAID…I want CEREAL!"

I raised my hand, but quickly put it down. I almost knocked her little ass across the room. My face hurt so bad. It felt like I'd been hit by a grown-ass woman. I grabbed my face – in shock. I didn't even know how to respond. My eyes widened as I looked at her.

She folded her arms across her chest and insisted, "Now…daddy."

Before I knew it, I snatched her by her arm and dragged her down the hallway and tossed her into her bed. "You better not move. You sit there until you get your shit together."

"Get your SHIT together, DADDY!!!!" she yelled.

I stopped for a moment before leaning in her face. "What did you say?"

"I said…you get yo' SHIT together, DADDY," she insisted.

The next few minutes are a blur. All I remember, before my memory loss, was me removing my belt and me snatching her little butt out of her bed. When things became clear again, Peaches was lying in the fetal position and crying. When I snapped out of my daze, I said, "Oh, I'm so sorry…daddy is so sorry." I reached out to touch her, but she pushed away from me. "Peaches, please forgive me…I didn't mean to hurt you…I'm so sorry."

She wiped her eyes and looked at me. "You hit me…"

Panicking, I said, "I know and I'm so sorry…you just pushed me…"

"I didn't push you…I slapped you."

Just then, I remembered why my belt ended-up in my hand. "What you did was wrong…you don't hit people."

"So, you was wrong too?" she asked.

She had a point, but I didn't want to hear it. "But that's not the point…"

"Then, what is the point, daddy?"

It was then that I realized that I didn't have one. At least, not a good one, so I said, "I'm sorry…"

"It's okay…" She reached out her arms to hug me. She patted me on the back before walking out of the room. I followed her into the kitchen. She smiled at me and said, "Cereal…daddy."

I looked at her. As I slid my belt through each hoop, I thought about what'd just happened. I felt like crap. I'd done the one thing that I said that I would never do and she knew it. I promised them that I would never hit them and now, I've broken that promise and I felt like shit. I walked over to the cabinet and pulled out the box of cereal. "This one?"

She looked at me. "No, the other one."

I pulled out the other box. "This one?" I asked, as I, quickly, realized that the power had been shifted from me to them.

"Yes," she confirmed. She began to dance in her chair. "I'm having cereal…I'm having cereal…" she sang, as I poured her a bowl of cereal.

Grace looked at me as I began to pour her a bowl of cereal. "Thank you, daddy."

"You're welcome, Grace…"

Grace looked over at Peaches and said, "You didn't say 'thank you' to daddy…"

Peaches looked up from her bowl and stared at Grace. Grace's face didn't change. She didn't flinch. She didn't move. Peaches whispered. "Thank you, Daddy." Grace looked at me and smiled. "It's okay, daddy."

As I watched them, I couldn't help but think about my upbringing and wonder what would have happened if I hauled-off and slapped my mother. I wonder how that would have turned out. I shudder when I think about the consequences that such an action would have brought me.

Soon guilt became her weapon of choice and she used it every chance she got. I couldn't even look at her, hard, without her reminding me that I was the mean daddy who cut her hair off and whooped her little butt. Overnight, I'd become

her "bitch" and I would remain her bitch until she
no longer needed one.

Chapter 7

I was starting to hate my life. Being a father started to feel more like a burden than a blessing. I used to look up at the ceiling and ask God, "Why me? What did I do to deserve this?" And while I'm whining like a baby, God would remind me of the night that it all happened and I would remember how good it felt when it was happening and then, I, usually, shut the fuck up and do what I have to do.

Today's crazy will involve Peaches and the school's pet hamster. Now, there are three sides to this story, but we will only hear two, because the third belongs to a terrified hamster. The teacher claims that during play-time, the kids were allowed to pet the hamster. They were supposed to all take turns playing with the animal and when they were done, they were supposed to place it back in its cage. *Simple.* Their version of the story includes the fact that they were allowed to play with the hamster, but somehow, on the way back to its cage, the hamster ended-up with a crayon shoved up his ass. Of course, they had an excellent explanation as to how it might have happened, but as usual, it did not involve them.

Taking a deep breath, I asked, "How? Why?"

Grace spoke first. "I don't know."

"You don't know…interesting…" I paused and looked over at Peaches. "Do you know how that happened to the hamster?"

"Yes…" she said.

"Will you please tell daddy how it happened?"

"Yep…you see, daddy…we were playing airplane with the hamster and we were flying him in the air like this…" she paused and waved her hands in the air. "Then, we 'cided to play doctor…"

"Doctor?" I interrupted. "From airplane to doctor…that makes sense…"

"Yep and he…" she said.

"He who?" I asked, trying to keep up with the story.

"The hamster…" she confirmed. "Well, he said, 'My butt hurt, doctor…'"

I exhaled. "He said that his butt hurt? He…the hamster?"

"Yep…so I tried…" she paused after she realized that she'd just implicated herself in the crime. "I mean…then he fell on the crayon." Satisfied with this answer, she began to walk away.

"His butt just fell on a crayon?" I asked. "Didn't have any help?"

"YEP!" She smiled. "I mean, nope…he wanted it…"

"A crayon…in his butt?"

"Yep…"

"Ummmmm Peaches…"

She stopped and turned. "Yes, daddy?"

"Something stinks…" I began.

"Did you take a bath?" she asked.

"Yes, I did…but that's not what I'm smelling."

"Huh? Then, what are you smelling, daddy?"

"I smell bullshit, Peaches…"

She checked the bottom of her shoes. "It's not me, daddy."

"Oh, but it is…" I confirmed.

The teacher looked at me. "You shouldn't use foul language around your children."

I frowned. "Cursing keeps me from drinking, getting high, or from knocking the crap out of them."

"Well, you know…" she said.

I interrupted her. "Look…I don't need parenting advice from a person who couldn't prevent my babies from sticking a crayon up a rat's butt…"

"Hamster…" Grace said, correcting me.

"Whatever…" I stood to leave the room. "So how do we fix this?"

"Normally, I would suggest a reprimand, but as I tried to write-out the discipline request, I found it difficult to put this 'one' into words…"

"Well, the least that I can do is replace the hamster…"

"That's not necessary…he's not broken…he's not dead…he's just frightened. He'll be fine," the teacher said. "You don't have to replace him…just talk to them and teach them that what they did to him was wrong."

I looked at the hamster that was cowering in the corner of his cage. "Unless he takes a crayon up the butt on a regular basis, he won't be fine. I will get a new one anyway…maybe a girl hamster who can help him find 'himself' again. In the meantime, I will take them home and have that talk with them." I looked at them and said, "Tell the teacher that you're sorry."

Grace said, "Sorry…"

Peaches didn't respond.

"Can I take them home, now?" I asked.

The teacher looked at us for a second and said, "Please…do."

On the way to the pet shop, neither of them said a word, but as soon as we pulled in front of the store, they both screamed with excitement. I'd barely gotten them out of their car-seats before they were jumping out of the car door. They took my hands and dragged me inside of the store.

"Okay, okay…let go, now…" I looked for a salesperson. "Where's your hamsters?"

"Over there…" she said, without looking at me.

"Ummmmm thanks," I said, walking away. We walked down several aisles until we found them.

"I want it…I want it…" Grace said, reaching for the glass.

"I want it…I want it…" Peaches said, but she wasn't looking at the hamsters. Pointing at the puppies, she said, "Daddy, I want it…"

I frowned. "We didn't come in here for that…we came for a hamster…and that's what we're getting.

"I said, 'I want that'," she insisted.

"No, Peaches…puppies are too much work…" I turned away from her and then, suddenly, I heard a loud *Thump!* I looked back and she was on the floor screaming, so loud, people began to flood the aisle to see what was going on.

I walked over to pick her up. "Peaches…stop it."

She stopped to look at the faces surrounding her, smiled at me, and said, "No, daddy…don't hit me…Daddy, please don't hit me…." She closed her eyes and pretended to cry.

"Wait…what…I'm not going to hit you," I paused and looked at the people who were standing around us. "Don't say that…you know that I wouldn't do that."

"Yes, you did…you beat me with a belt the other day…"

She's trying to get me locked-up. "Peaches, you don't know what you're saying…now, get up…"

Peeking out of one of her eyes, she asked, "Can I have a puppy?"

"Peaches…I said 'No'…"

She screamed louder. "Don't hit me again…"

Suddenly, the manager and a security guard walked over. "Sir, is there a problem?"

"No…" I looked down at Peaches.

"Can I have a puppy?" she asked.

Feeling defeated, I said, "Yes, you can have a puppy."

As if nothing happened, she jumped-up, fixed her clothing, and said, "Yayyyyyyyy." She wrapped her arms around my legs. "I want that one." She pointed at the glass.

The crowd slowly dispersed. A lady walked over, touched her arm, and said, "Little girl, are you okay?"

Peaches snatched away from her. "Don't touch me."

Frightened, the woman said, "I'm sorry…I thought that you needed help."

"I don't," she confirmed.

The woman looked confused. Then, she turned to me. "Maybe I should be asking you, 'Are you okay?'"

"Lady, if you only knew…:" I said, walking towards the front of the store.

Chapter 8

Purchasing the puppy seemed to work for a while. She was so good, the teachers thought that she was being medicated, but she wasn't. She had something that she could take care of and trying to meet the demands of caring for something, kept her so busy, she didn't have time to get into trouble. Things were great for several months. There were no calls from her teachers. She was nice to her sister. She was even nice to me. Things were great until…

I received another call from the school. As I drove to the school, all I could think about was what did she do now? The teacher was waiting for me at the front door with Peaches standing next to her. She didn't even bother saying "hello."

"I need you to see something…" the teacher said, as she walked down the hall.

Grabbing Peaches' hand, I sighed.

Soon, we were standing in front of the girl's bathroom. There was an "Out of Service" sign on the door.

The teacher walked in. "It's in here."

"It's?" I looked at the sign and said, "This is the little girl's room."

"It's okay…no one is going to be using this one for a while…

I stepped in and immediately heard a splashing sound under my feet. I looked down and noticed all of the water on the floor. She threw the door to the first stall open. She walked in and said, "Look…"

I couldn't understand what was going on. I didn't want to walk in and find a turd floating in the bowl. "What am I supposed to be looking at?"

"Please sir…come and see."

I walked in and looked down. The teacher folded her arms and stepped to the side. I looked closer.

When I realized what I was looking at, I asked, "Is that a leg?"

"Yes," she said. "Come with me."

Confused, I followed her to the next stall. She pointed into the bowl. I looked down. "Is that an arm?" I asked.

"Yes," she said. "Come with me."

We walked passed the next two stalls until we were standing in front of the last one. I walked in and looked down to find two eyes peering up at me.

"What is that?" I asked.

"That, sir, is the head of a doll...a doll that belonged to one of her classmates. She decided to dismember the doll and stuff her body parts into the toilet...clogging all of the toilets."

I stepped out of the stall and looked towards the door. Peaches was standing in the hallway, staring at me.

"Peaches...come here," I demanded.

"I don't want to mess-up my shoes..." she said.

Frustrated, I treaded through the water, I walked towards her. Splashing behind me, the teacher said, "This is a very serious matter…"

"I know," I said. "I'm really sorry about this."

"Why are you sorry?" she asked.

"Peaches seems to stay in trouble…I just feel like it's my fault...like I'm doing something wrong."

Shaking the water from her shoes, she said, "Sometimes, kids do things to get attention…even bad things."

"I give her attention…"

"True, but what kind of attention do you give her?"

"The kind she deserves…"

She pulled me to the side. "I don't know what you do in your household, but…something's not right…"

"Look…I'm doing my best…"

"I don't want to sound crass, but if this is your best…"

Pissed and tired of talking to these people, I said, "Look…"

"Ms. Smith," she chimed in.

"I spend so much time saying 'I'm sorry', I feel like I'm the one who's in trouble when the reality is, she did it…it's easy to blame me, for the things that she does, but once I drop her off at that door, I can't be held responsible for what she does behind it. She's your responsibility…yours. That's like me handing you the 'ball' and then you blaming me for dropping it…that's not fair. I'm apologizing for the doll in the toilet like I put her there, but where were you? Shit, she was out of your site long enough to take a doll apart and stuff it in the toilet…where were you? My daughter could have been the one in the toilet. "

She frowned instead of responding.

"Exactly…so the next time she does something on YOUR watch, call YOUR damn self…" I grabbed Peaches by the hand and dragged her out of the building.

After we got home, I decided to let the girls go out back to play just to give me enough time to think and to regroup. I was watching them when suddenly the doorbell rang. I yelled outside that "I would be back in a minute" and went to answer the door. I opened the door to find a little girl standing on the porch.

"Hi, can I help you?" I asked.

"Ummmmm, sir...I can't find my kitten...have you seen my kitten?"

I looked around and said, "Where are your parents?"

She shrugged her shoulders and said, "Have you seen it?"

"No, I haven't seen it...you should really go home...it's not safe for you to be out here by yourself."

She smiled and said, "Ummmm, okay...byyyyyyyyeeeee."

"Bye," I said, before closing the door. As I walked back to the back of the house, I couldn't help, but think about that little girl roaming from house to house by herself and how dangerous it was for her to be doing so. *Her mama needs her ass whooped…got that baby out here by herself.* I thought to myself as I approached the backdoor. I looked out into the yard, but I didn't see my girls.

Panicking, I called out to them, "Grace…Peaches????" I was in the middle of the yard when I heard a yelping sound behind me. I turned around to find the girls huddled on the side of the house. The yelping sound stopped.

Whew. Thank God. "What are you two doing?" I asked, walking towards them. They didn't respond. "Girls? Did you hear me?" Grace had something grey in her hand. I looked at it. "Oh wow, you found that little girl's kitten. Let me go and give it to her."

She pulled away from me. "No, daddy…I want it." The kitten purred as she rubbed its back.

"But Grace it isn't ours…now, hand it to me." I reached out my hands to her. "Where's the puppy?"

She didn't answer. She hesitated for a second, but then gave me the kitten. I noticed something red on its fur. *What is this?*

"Grace, did you hurt yourself?"

"No, daddy…" she said, showing me her hands, but there was blood all over them.

Peaches was still standing over something, looking at it.

Walking towards her, I said, "Peaches, sweetie…come here."

She didn't move.

"Peaches?" I walked towards her. As I approached her, I could see a red puddle forming at her feet and right next to it was the lifeless body of her puppy. I ran towards her.

She had a blank look on her face – like the light was on, but no one was at home.

"We didn't like him anymore…so we sent him to Heaven," Grace said.

The kitten purred. "Peaches…" I said, again.

Finally, Peaches spoke. "Now, he's with mommy."

The puppy rested with his eyes looking up at me. "You killed him?"

Peaches kicked a bloody rock that sat next to him. "No, he's just sleeping."

I didn't know how to respond to them. I just couldn't believe what I was seeing, so I asked her again, "You killed him?"

"No, daddy, he's sleeping," she confirmed.

Either she didn't understand what she did or didn't want to admit it, so I grabbed her hand and placed it on the puppy's chest. "Do you feel that? That's nothing, no heartbeat…no breathing…no nothing, Peaches…it's dead and you killed it."

She looked at the blood on her hands and then looked over at Grace. Grace walked over and grabbed her hand and then they both walked away, into the house, and left me standing there. I followed them inside. With blood still on their hands, they sat down to watch TV. The kitten purred. I'd almost forgotten that I was still holding it. I walked outside to see if I could see the little girl, but she was nowhere to be found. I knew that I couldn't take him back into the house for fear of them hurting it. I didn't know what to do, so I walked back into the house, grabbed a bowl and poured some milk in it and sat it and the kitten on the front porch. "It's for your own safety," I said, as I sat the kitten down.

I walked back into the house, turned the TV off, and stood in front of them. They tried looking around me. "Let's talk…"

"But Sponge…" Grace began.

Sternly, I said, "LET'S TALK." I grabbed their hands and led them to the bathroom. "Look at that…do you see that on your hands?"

"Yes," they said in unison.

"That's blood," I confirmed. "That blood belongs to someone."

They didn't respond.

I paused because, even though they'd taken a life, they were still children and may not understand exactly what is happening. So I thought about it for a second and said,

"Remember how daddy told you that stealing is wrong?"

"Yes," they said.

"Well, this blood belongs to someone else…you took this from someone…you stole it from someone."

Peaches looked confused. "Do you want me to give it back?"

"No, sweetie…you can't give it back."

Grace spoke. "Are we going to jail for stealing it? 'Cause I don't want to go to jail."

I realized that that analogy wasn't working, so I said, "You took a life…"

"Do you want us to give it back?" Grace asked.

Their minds were still stuck on the analogy. "No, no, no…you can't give it back. You took something that can never be given back. Do you think that if you walk back outside and give the puppy back his blood, he will come back to life?"

They thought about it for a second and said, "Can we try?"

"NO!!!!! YOU CAN'T TRY!!!! IT'S NOT GOING TO WORK!!!"

"Have you ever tried it, daddy?" Grace asked.

I closed my eyes and took several deep breaths.

"Daddy's sleepy," Grace said.

Frustrated, I opened my eyes and said, "I'm not sleeping…" Seeing that they think the puppy is only sleeping, I decided to explain it another way. "Okay…you said that your puppy is sleeping, right?"

"Yes…" they said.

"Okay…you see how daddy's eyes are open? That means that daddy is not sleeping, right?"

"Yes…"

"Okay…is the puppy's eyes open?"

"Yes…"

Wrong example. The image of the puppy looking up at me just crossed my mind. "Okay…the difference is, I can talk to you…I can move…I can breathe…I can…"

"Do you want us to fix that, daddy?"

I paused for a moment and shook my head, because I wasn't sure if I'd heard her correctly.

"What did you say?" I asked her.

Peaches looked at me and repeated the question. "Do you want us to fix that?"

For a second, all I could do was look at them. My eyes blinked, rapidly. Afraid, I asked, "How are you going to do that?"

Grace raised her hand like she was in school. I looked at her. "Grace?"

"You want me to go and get the rock?" she said.

"Then, you can be in Heaven too," Peaches said.

They smiled at me. My eyes moved back and forth between them like I was watching a tennis match. "Ummmmm…no…let's wash your hands and get you something to eat."

"Okay, daddy," they said. They walked over to the sink and proceeded to wash their hands. When they were done, they dried their hands and walked out of the bathroom. I sat there for a second trying to process what'd just happened when Grace peeked around the corner.

"Daddy, we're waiting for you."

Chapter 9

From that moment on, I slept with one-eye open. The girls were proving to be something that I shouldn't underestimate. They had the face of an angel, but behind those eyes was something else. They were capable of the unthinkable. Sure, they'd only assaulted a hamster and killed a puppy, but everyone knows that graduating to killing humans only took "air and opportunity." I learned not to drop my guard down around them, because underneath all of that "cuteness" was "crazy – just waiting to happen and it wouldn't be long before it did.

The next day seemed like a normal day. The sun was shining. The birds were singing. The girls awoke early to prepare for school. They ate breakfast without throwing anything at each other or at me. I didn't have a care in the world.

I went to work – singing all of the way there. Throughout the day, I checked my phone, several times, to make sure that no one had called me, but there were no notifications on my phone. For a moment, I thought that maybe it was broken, but I had a coworker call me and everything was fine. My shift was almost complete when my cellphone, finally, rang. I looked at it and recognized the number. I took a deep breath before I answered it.

"Hello Mrs. Johnson…how are you today?"

"We have a situation…" she began.

"I'm well and how are you?" I asked, sarcastically.

She huffed into the phone. "I know that you're probably at work, but we need someone to come by the school and pick up…"

"Peaches…" I said, interrupting.

"Yes…Peaches…"

"What did she do now?"

"She threatened a teacher…"

"She threatened a teacher…" Without thinking about how serious the situation was, I laughed. "What could she have said that remotely sounds like a threat?"

She huffed, again. "She told the teacher that she is, and I quote, 'is going to stick her scissors in her head and pull her brain out of her ear'…"

I dropped my phone. I heard a voice say, "Hello…hello…hello?"

I kneeled down and slowly picked up the phone. "Hello?"

"Sir, did you hear what I said?"

I sighed. "Unfortunately…I did…"

"Do you have anyone who can come and get her?"

"No, sadly…I'm on my way."

After hanging up, I went outside and sat in my car. I hesitated to start it up. I knew that once I did, I would have to pull off, I would have to go to the school, and I would have to look into the face of the woman who was just told by a second grader that she's going to give her a lobotomy.

My brain shut down. I was so numb, I couldn't even remember driving to the school. Once there, I sat in the car – staring at the doors of the school. For a moment, I thought about running. Just starting the car and driving until I ran out of gas, until the tread wore off of my tires, or until I found a cliff that I could drive off of - where no one would ever find me. But with my luck, I would survive the crash and they would wheel my ass right back here to deal with this crazy shit.

Slowly, I climbed out of the car, walked up to the door, and walked inside. Once inside of the office, I saw her, sitting there with one of the biggest smiles on her face.

"Hi daddy…" she said, waving.

"Hi, nothing, little girl…I heard what you did."

She began to sing and swing her legs. "You are my sunshine…my only sunshine…you make me HAPPY when skies are gray…"

"Do you hear me talking to you?" I asked.

Just then, a door opened. "Are you her father?"

"And if I say 'no?'"

She looked at Peaches and then back up at me. "She looks just like you…you couldn't deny her if you wanted to."

I frowned. "I don't know…you know what they say about Black folks…and how they all look alike?"

She pulled her glasses up on her face. "I see where she gets her sense of humor."

"Look…I'm sorry…I was joking….just trying to keep things 'lite.'"

"This is a serious matter, sir…"

"They are all serious matters, so I laugh to keep from crying…"

She looked over at Peaches, again. "Looks like you're going to be doing a lot of crying."

Peaches was humming to herself. "You are my sunshine…"

"Yeah…I know…"

"Let's go in here…" she said, pointing to a room.

I stuck out my hand. "Come on…child of mine…"

She smiled and took my hand. "Okay daddy…"

She sat down behind a big desk. "Normally, we expel children who threaten their teachers or anyone for that matter, but I refuse to believe that someone her age could possibly hurt another human being."

As she spoke, I thought about the puppy, the hamster, and me.

She laughed and continued, "I mean…she was very specific…stick her scissors in her head and pull her brain out of her ear? Who comes up with that stuff? Clearly, it sounds like something that she's seen on TV and she's just repeating it."

I looked down at Peaches who was staring at me. "Yeah…TV…right." I mumbled.

"And children repeat what they see…do you watch horror movies?"

"Why watch them when you're starring in one?" I mumbled.

"Excuse me?" she asked.

"Nothing…"

"I'm going to suggest counseling…"

"Counseling?" I asked.

"Yes and I'll be willing to consider placing her in another classroom...if you can prove that she's getting some counseling."

"Counseling?" I asked, again. At some point, while she was talking, I blanked-out – trying to pretend that I was on an island, far, far, away from here.

"Yes...We've found that often times, these situations 'clear' themselves up with the right approach...with the right guidance. Plus, with the 'School-to-Prison Pipeline", we try to break the cycle that puts so many of 'our' children behind bars."

"So you think that'll help?"

"Most of the time...a lot of time, children act out because they're looking for attention. What we don't want to do is counter her bad behavior with more bad behavior. It's like this...if a child acts out and you spank them, after a while, they become numb...desensitized to the pain. The discipline doesn't work anymore, so now, what do you do? Hit her harder? Doesn't work, because then she no longer cares and neither will you. As a result, everyone becomes numb. We become a society of uncaring people. We're a contradiction. We believe that we can cure most 'ills' of the world with love, but then come home and beat the things that won't change...the things that we can't fix...it's crazy. We're going to approach this with love..."

Peaches laughed. "Love, daddy...with love..."

"And what if that doesn't work?"

"Well, look at it this way. If it works, you can start putting money into a college fund, but if doesn't...the money can always go towards bail."

Chapter 10

The following Sunday, we were at church before the doors even opened. I wanted to get her there before she realized where she was going, and all hell broke loose. I didn't even give her enough time to get dressed. As soon as she opened her eyes, I scooped her up, slapped a pair of tights and pair of shoes under her nightgown and rushed her out of the house. Sure, she protested, but I was on a mission.

We sat outside for an hour, waiting for them to open their doors and as soon as they were opened, I rushed in like they were having a Black Friday sale on TVs. I grabbed three seats – closest to the front in hopes that when they began to rebuke the devil, the one inhabiting my little girl's body would get the hint and leave. I also put ample space between us just in case lightning struck. I didn't want it to get me.

They, carefully, surveyed the room. Grace was so excited about being there. The last time that they'd been there was during their mother's funeral and they were so young, they probably don't remember it. Grace seemed to enjoy watching the people while Peaches stared at the image of Christ – nailed to a cross. Her eyes were fixed on Him like she was expecting Him to climb down and say 'Hello.'

Grace picked up a Bible and began to read it. She smiled as she gave her interpretation of the words that were sprawled across the page. I looked at Peaches. "Do you want a Bible, sweetie?" She gave me a look that immediately told me that I better shut the hell up before I find myself nailed on the cross along-side Jesus.

Soon, the choir marched in singing, "We've come this far by faith…every day, I'm leaning….leaning on the Lord…" Grace clapped, as she pretended to sing with them. Peaches didn't say a word.

Service was really nice and things were going really well until they asked if anyone wanted to come up for prayer. This was my chance. I needed somebody to lay "hands" on her. At first, I asked her nicely. "Peaches…wouldn't it be nice to be prayed for?"

She folded her arms and said, "No."

Grace raised her hand. "I'll go…can I go, daddy?"

I whispered. "Look…Grace wants to go…don't you want to go too?"

She frowned. "I want to go home."

Grace stood and walked over. "Come on, daddy…take me." She began to tug on my arm.

"Come on, Peaches…it'll be fun."

"I SAID, 'NO!!!'" she yelled.

The room became quiet. Even the pianist stopped playing. Seeing that the opportunity was slipping away, I decided to drag her up there. She started kicking and screaming while Grace skipped all the way to the altar. The preacher approached us.

"Look at these beautiful little girls…God's children…" he began. "Are these your babies?" he asked.

"Yes…and I was wondering if they could be prayed for…do you have some of that oil or special water…maybe they can get 'blessed' or baptized? Yes…baptized…and you can 'dip' them twice…just in case the first one doesn't take."

He laughed, kneeled down, and looked at her. "What's wrong, baby girl…don't you know that you are safe here? We love you…God loves you…"

Without saying a word, she filled her cheeks and when she opened her mouth to speak, spit flew all over his face. Everyone around us, froze – even me. *Did she spit in that man's face?*

Stunned, the preacher removed a handkerchief from his pocket and wiped his face.

He began. "Why did you do…?"

She filled her cheeks again and when she opened it, *HACK!* spit flew all over his face. Shocked, I picked her up.

He frowned and wiped his face again. "I'm being tested…" He looked around at all of the stunned faces and said, "Lord…give me strength…"

Peaches filled her cheeks again and when opened her mouth, *HACK!* Spit flew everywhere.

He balled-up his fists. "DEVIL, YOU'RE A LIAR!!! I REBUKE THEE, SATAN!!!! IN THE MIGHTY NAME OF JESUS!"

Everyone gasped.

"Oh my God…I'm so sorry," I said, grabbing Grace's hand.

"Hold my Bible…I'm going to beat the Devil out of her." He wiped his face again. "Her butt needs Jesus…" the preacher said, as I dragged them down the aisle and out of the church. "JESUS!!!!"

Once in the car, I lit right into her. "Peaches, I can't believe you did that. I take you to church and you spit in the preacher's face. Who does that shit? Who taught you to spit in people's faces? I can't believe you did that. WHY IN THE WORLD WOULD YOU SPIT IN THAT MAN'S FACE?"

She paused for a moment and said, "Because his breath stinks..."

Grace began to laugh.

"What?" I asked.

"His breath stank like doo-doo..." she confirmed.

I have to admit that that was funny. I began to laugh too, but quickly regained my composure to deal with the matter at hand. "Then, why didn't you just say that?"

"So I should have told him that his breath smells like doo-doo, daddy?"

"No...of course not," I said.

"Should I have told you, and then you would have told him that his breath smells like somebody pooped in his mouth?"

"Yes, you should have told me, but I wouldn't have told him something like that."

"Why not? It's the truth…you have to tell the truth."

"Because, Peaches…that would have been rude."

"And what he was doing to me wasn't rude?"

Grace was laughing so hard, she had to unbuckle her seatbelt.

"I didn't want to smell that…I shouldn't have to smell that."

I thought about it for a second and realized that she was right. His breath did smell like shit and no one should be forced to smell it, but she was still wrong. "Peaches…spitting in someone's face is wrong…"

"And having to smell his stanky breath is wrong too…so now, we're even."

I didn't know what to say to her, so Grace decided to step in. "The Bible says, 'Do unto others as you have them do unto you…now, what would you have done if he'd spit back? You would have been walking around with doo-doo on your face."

Peaches looked at her and agreed. "You're right."

"The moral of the story? Don't doo-doo unto others or they will doo-doo unto you."

We all fell-out laughing. After several minutes, Peaches said, "Okay…" and smiled.

I smiled and started to turn around – satisfied that she'd learned something, but then I heard her whisper, "If he'd spit on me, I would have stabbed him in the head."

I turned back around. "What did you say?"

"Nothing," she confirmed.

I started the car and as I pulled out of the parking lot, I heard Grace say, "I would have stabbed him too."

Peaches & Grace

Chapter 11

No one can guarantee that fruit, grown on the same vine, will be sweet. Sometimes, there's some bitter fruit and I was very bitter. People seem to think that twins are alike. Sure, on the surface, but underneath, that's where you'll find the differences. And contrary to what you've heard thus far, I would like to think that I'm the good one. People just misunderstand me. What they see as bad or troubled, is just a child who's just busy – busy trying to define who I am and how I fit in the whole scheme of things.

Now, you may wonder how, when, and why someone so young could already be so jaded. Well, scientists believe that a fetus is able to feel its mother's pain and emotions. They also believe that as early as three months into a pregnancy, babies can hear sounds and noises outside of the womb, so while we were bouncing around inside of her, I learned that the world is full of crazy people. And from the moment that I saw his face, I knew that he wasn't "wrapped-tight." Something about him was "off." Now, as a baby, of course, I wasn't able to put my tiny finger on what level of crazy I was dealing with, but I knew something was going on. I used to just stare at him – watching him as he walked around with that confused look on his face and think to myself, "Poor thing…looks like somebody lost the coin-toss."

I guess I should be grateful though. At least he's trying. He could have been like a lot of men who were put into that same position and got the hell up out of there when he realized that the other player left the game early and left him holding the ball. Well, in our case, two balls, but you have to give him credit where credit is due. He tried to be both mother and father, but after a while, he realized that fathers should just be fathers and leave the mothering for somebody else.

And that's what he was – a father. He kept us safe. He kept clothes on our backs. He kept a roof over our heads and he kept food on the table, but that's it. He couldn't give us more than that because that's all he had.

He couldn't put an outfit together to save his life. Every day, we left the house looking a "hot mess." We sported every color of the rainbow, wore galoshes when it wasn't raining, and flip-flops in the snow. It wasn't until I was older that I realized that socks had mates and that we were supposed to wear them together. Until he cut my hair, I wore my hair in two ponytails with parts that had more twists and turns than the Dan Ryan Expressway. I was actually glad that he cut my hair, because now I didn't have to walk around with my hair flying every "which-a-way." He used to rub so much grease on our face, arms, and legs that during recess, we had to stay in the shade to keep from being cooked alive and if we played in the sun, you would swear that somebody was cooking bacon.

Sure, he loves us, but it's hard to know what true love is when you grow-up with only one perspective and you have to trust that the person providing that "perspective" hasn't been messed-up along the way. Without having my mama created an imbalance. The scales were titled more on one side than the other. It was two against one and we were getting used to that until he decided to even the scales.

At this point, we were a little older and attending grammar school and this made life a little easier for him. He had more time to contemplate life and to think about his relationship with the loneliness that kept him warm at night. Soon, we started to notice some changes in him. In the beginning, they were subtle. He began to shower more than twice a week. He cut his hair. He started ironing his clothes and wearing cologne. At least, that's what he calls it, but if you ask me, it smelled more like somebody sprayed air freshener in a bathroom that somebody just took a "dump" in. But that's if you ask me. He was so "different". We almost didn't recognize him.

We really knew that something was up when we had a half-day and our parents were supposed to pick us up at noon and he didn't show up. This was unlike him. He spent more time at our school than we did, so to not see him was concerning. By the time, 12:30 rolled around, I decided that it was time to go.

"We're going to get in trouble," Grace said.

"I'm tired and I'm hungry," I said, trying to figure out where we were going. "And we're the only thirteen year olds who are still standing here waiting for their daddy."

"But he always picks us up..." she said.

"Yeah, well, clearly, he had something better to do." I looked around for a second and said, "It's going to be okay...just follow me."

"Okay," she said. "I hope you know what you're doing."

Looking around, I said, "I do...now, keep up."

Suddenly, I heard her sniffing. "What is wrong with you?"

"We should have stayed at school...now, somebody is going to snatch us."

"Don't nobody want us...now, come on."

"Baaaaaaaaaaaa..." she cried.

"Stop it, Grace...you're too old. You're embarrassing yourself..."

"No, somebody's gon' snatch us and we ain't going to see daddy ever again."

Snatching her arm, I said, "Come on…we're almost there."

"No, we're not…" she cried.

Ignoring her, I continued to drag her. We roamed around for a while until we stumbled upon our house and it was a good thing because Grace was getting on my nerves. We approached the door and rang the doorbell.

I looked back at her and wiped her face with my sleeve. "See, I told you that I would get us home."

Just then, the door opened. We both turned and looked up. Confused, we both stepped back to examine the house, because we thought that we were lost. Grace began to cry again until the woman said, "Remy, your girls are home!!!" Holding tightly to my daddy's robe that was wrapped against her naked body, she said, "Come on in."

We looked at each other. *Lady, this is my house.* I thought to myself. "Come on in…Grace," she said, "Come on in…"

Grace didn't respond.

Seconds later, our dad came running down the hall wearing nothing, but a towel. "What are you girls doing home so early?"

I looked at him. "What are you doing home so early and who is this lady?"

Over my shoulder, I could hear Grace say, "We had a half-day."

Picking his clothes up off of the living room floor, he said, "Nobody told me that you had a half-day. Why didn't you tell me?"

Plopping onto the couch, I said, "Daddy, we had a half-day…" Scowling, I looked at the woman. "Now, who is this?"

The woman extended her hand. "I'm…"

I stared at her hand and she quickly retracted it. "I wasn't talking to you."

"Peaches…don't be rude," daddy said. "She stopped by…to, ummmmm, drop something off…"

I looked down at the floor. "Her panties?"

Grace frowned.

He frowned. "Peaches, go to your room and don't come out until I tell you to."

"You're sending me to my room when you're the one who left us at school…while you play with…" I frowned and pointed, "…HER!"

Gritting his teeth, he pointed down the hall. "If you don't get your butt in your room…"

I exhaled and looked at the woman. "When I come back…you better be gone."

Pointing, he screamed. "NOW, PEACHES!!!!"

Walking backwards, I stared at him until I was in my room.

Pacing the floor, he mumbled to himself. "Okay Remy…you're the adult. They are the children…show them who's the boss." He turned and looked at me.

Clearly, the look on my face indicated that I was not in the mood to hear his explanation.

Before he could speak, I said, "Somebody could have snatched us."

Grace looked at me and whispered, "I thought that you said that nobody was going to snatch us."

"Shut up, cry-baby…"

"Peaches, don't call your sister names. Now, apologize."

"No," I said, adamantly.

"You better and you better do it now…" he said, placing his hands on his hips.

"Did you apologize for leaving us at school?"

"No, I didn't…but I didn't know."

"Well, now you do," I confirmed.

He exhaled. "You know, Peaches…you can't talk to me like that."

"Okay…I'm sorry, daddy…" I smiled. "You see how I did that? I apologized."

"That's what I'm talking about, Peaches. I am your father. You don't talk to me that way."

"And how would you like for me to talk to you, daddy?"

Frustrated, he said, "Look, little girl. Before I became your daddy, I was a man…"

Grace interrupted. "You WAS a man? Does that mean that you're a lady now?"

Biting his bottom lip, he continued, "No, I'm not a lady…now, back to what I was saying…"

Squinting, Grace asked, "Are you sure that you're not a lady? You got your hands on your hips like a girl."

I laughed. "Now, all you have to do is let your back-bone slip…"

He dropped his arms to his side. "My what? No, damn-it…now, stop interrupting me…"

We walked up, formed a circle around him, and began to chant, "Little Sally Walker, sittin' in a saucer…Ride, Sally ride…wipe your weeping eyes and put your hands on your hips and let your backbone slip. Awww, shake it to the east…Awww, shake it to the west…Awww, shake to the one that you love the best…"

"You're not shaking 'it', daddy," I said.

"STOP IT! Now, like I was saying…a man can get lonely…"

Grace raised her hand. Dropping his head, he acknowledged her. "What is it, Grace?"

"You know, daddy…you should get a puppy…"

He frowned and said, "Go to bed."

Chapter 12

We were enemies. From the very beginning, I hated her. She was an intruder and it didn't matter to me that my daddy invited her into our lives, because she wasn't welcome. Something about her wasn't right and I could tell right away. You know how *Spiderman* had his "spidey-senses?" Well, this woman made my butt itch. The sight of her, literally, made me want to scratch my ass. Everything about her was wrong. She was too pretty and she was too nice and usually when somebody is too much of anything that means that they are hiding something and the prettier they are, or the nicer they are, the bigger the secrets. And from the looks of her, she had some really big secrets.

Now, it took me a while to understand it, but I think I figured out why I hated her so much. I hated her, because they never asked for our permission. Now, you may be saying to yourself, "Who the hell are you? You are a child...stay in a child's place....we don't need your permission for anything." That's where adults go wrong. You see, children grow intimate attachments to the things and the people in their lives. Once we begin to love something or someone, we don't want to share that with anyone else. That's why kids have to be taught and, at times forced, to "share". Why? Because we don't want to. Straight out of the womb, we begin to claim the things that are ours and we don't want anyone to have any or want anyone taking it away from us. Why? Because we're afraid. We know darkness, we know loneliness, and we know what it feels like to be helpless. That's why our eyes have to adjust to light, that's why we startle easy when there's loud noises, and that's why we cry when you've been away from us for too long. When you spend nine months in a place where there's nothing, but you and the sound of someone's heartbeat, and then all of a sudden, you are evicted from that place into a world that you know nothing about, you learn to cling on to the things that make you feel loved and feel safe and this bitch was infringing on that. Our sense of security was being threatened and we needed to do whatever was necessary to protect it.

The best way that they could have handled this was to sit us down and ask us if it was okay for her to come into our lives. They should have given us a chance to say "Hell no!" but they didn't. He figured that since he liked her, we should like her, but it wasn't his place to decide that. They teach us to avoid strangers, but then you come home early from school one day and there's one answering the door – wearing nothing, but a bathrobe.

A father and daughter relationship is unique and so very important. He teaches us how a man should and should not treat us. From our fathers, we learn what "real love" is and he is the first man that we will fall in love with. We love our mothers, but we "fall in love" with our fathers. Our daddies become our first real "boyfriend" minus all of the weird shit that grown-folks do. That is why it is so important, that he is careful about "cheating" on us with other women and that's exactly what it feels like when there's another woman in the picture. No woman, young or old, wants to share their "man" with anyone. We don't want to share them with our mothers, our grandmothers, or any other woman for that matter. We get jealous like everyone else and jealousy is not a very nice emotion. It has a way of making people do horrible things to each other.

In the beginning, things were okay. We only saw her every once in a while which allowed me to hate her from a distance. But then one day, they decided to take the relationship to another level, again, without asking us for our permission.

Early, one Sunday morning, I awoke to the sound of someone screaming down the hall. At first, I did not move because I thought that maybe someone left the TV on, but after a while, I realized that I needed to see what was going on. Still half-asleep, I looked around the room for something that I could use as a weapon, just in case I needed to knock the hell out of somebody. I surveyed the room and realized that the only thing that looked like it could cause some harm was my house-shoes. As I thought about how I was going to kill someone with a house-shoe, my thoughts were suddenly interrupted by the screams that were coming from down the hall.

Slowly, I opened the bedroom door. Holding the house-shoe, I walked down the dark hallway. The screams led me to my dad's bedroom. I was about to open the door, when suddenly, someone said, "Peaches...what are you doing?"

After almost pissing on myself, I said, "Shhhhhhhhhh...I think daddy is being attacked."

Her eyes widened. We heard the screams again. "Wait...give me your other shoe..." she said.

Frowning, I said, "My one foot is already cold...you want my other foot to freeze?"

Frustrated, she demanded, "Girl, give me the shoe."

"Okay..." I said, slipping the shoe from my foot. "You better not tear up my shoe..."

"Girl, shut up...now open the door..."

Confused, I whispered, "Why I got to open the door?"

Frowning, she said, "Ummmmm, you were going to open the door before I got here…"

"But you're here now…"

She pushed me into the door, the door flew open, and we saw it. That woman was attacking our father. Covered with the blankets, she was bouncing up and down on top of him, slapping his face, and screaming obscenities.

"YES! YES! YES! FUCK ME!!!!" she yelled.

Suddenly, his body began to tremble, his eyes rolled into the back of his head, and his body went limp.

We looked at each other. Grace yelled, "She killed him!!!!"

I yelled. "KILL HER!!!" And before you knew it, we were on top of her. She struggled to get us off of her.

I was swinging at her. "Get off of my daddy."

Grace yelled. "You hurt my daddy!!!!"

Fumbling, he tried to separate us.

We were whooping her ass and then, in true Tyson form, I placed my mouth over her ear and bit down as hard as I could. My father grabbed and pulled me off of her. When he did, I noticed that there was a hole in the place that once held her ear.

She screamed and grabbed her ear. "BITCH!!!! You bit off my ear!!!! You bit off my fucking EAR!!!!"

Realizing that it was still in my mouth, I spit it out – earring and all. We all looked down at it. Wiping the blood from my mouth, I said, "You killed my daddy!!!!"

Holding her ear and trying to stop the blood that was now streaming down the side of her face, she said, "I didn't kill him!!!!"

He picked up her ear. "Oh shit, oh shit, oh shit…!!!!"

Suddenly, Grace and I realized that we were the only ones wearing clothes. We looked at the woman, but then we looked at our father. Our mouths fell open. This was the first time that we'd ever seen him naked – the first time, that we'd seen a penis. We stared at it. After realizing that we were staring at him, he jumped up and grabbed the blankets to cover himself with. "Shit…oh shit, oh shit…this is bad…this is real bad," he said.

"SHE BIT OFF MY FUCKING EAR!!!! She bit off my ear…" she cried.

"Okay…okay…okay…" he said, scrambling to find his clothes. "Get dressed…I will take you to the hospital." He looked at us and ordered, "Go to your room!!!"

"But, she was hurting you," Grace said.

His eyes grew dark. "I SAID…GO TO YOUR DAMN ROOM!!!!"

We did as we were told. Moments later, we heard the front door open and then someone slammed it shut. Grace looked at me. "What do you think they were doing?"

"You know what they were doing," I said. "But we can never let on that we know 'cause then we would be in more trouble."

"It did look like she was killing him."

I giggled. "Did you hear her? Oh my God…they were naked…"

"I know…so gross…" she said. "Do you think that she'll be okay?"

I looked at her and said, "Who cares? She deserved it…now, she can get somebody else to fuck her."

While they were gone, Grace and I cleaned ourselves up and then we tried to clean-up the crime scene. There was blood everywhere. After stripping the bed of its bloody sheets, we threw the linen in the laundry, and we sat down for a bowl of cereal and to watch cartoons. A few hours had gone by before we heard the front door open again.

Covered in dried blood, he was a mess. "PEACHES, COME HERE!!!!"

Nonchalantly, I walked over to where he was standing. "Yes, daddy."

He looked down at me. "Do you know what you've done?"

I thought about it for a second before saying, "Yes…I saved your life…"

"You what?"

"I saved your life…you should be thanking me."

His eyes were bulging out of his head. "You saved my life? Saved me from what? An orgasm?" Immediately, he placed his hands over his mouth, because he realized that he'd just made a big mistake.

Confused, I asked, "An orgasm?"

He exhaled. "Forget that…you're too young to know what that is."

"But you said it like I'm supposed to know what that is…so what is it?"

He frowned. "None of your business…forget I said that…now…"

I interrupted him. "If it's none of our business then why did you do that 'orgasm' thing in your bedroom…instead of somewhere else?" I walked over and sat in the chair.

"Because that's where it's supposed to happen…"

"Are you sure?" I asked.

"Yes, I'm sure," he confirmed.

"But it's none of our business?"

Grace walked over. "You should have at least locked your door…since it is just YOUR business. That's what I do when I'm doing MY 'business' in the bathroom. I lock the door." We stared at her. "I'm just saying," she confirmed. "Maybe you should put a sign on the door…ORGASM IN PROGRESS…DO NOT DISTURB…"

My dad shook his head and continued, "Like I was saying…"

I interrupted him again. "Are you going to be doing that 'orgasm' thing a lot? Me and Grace would like to know…maybe, you can let us know in advance…so that we can prepare for it."

"It's nothing to prepare for...wait...yes... wait...no..." He started scratching his head. "How did we start talking about this?"

We shrugged our shoulders and said, "You brought up the 'orgasm' thing..."

He started waving his arms. "Forget that I said that..."

"Kinda hard to forget something like that, but I'll try," I said.

He exhaled again. "Now, Peaches...you bit Mabel's ear off..."

We frowned and laughed. "Is that her name? Mabel? Hil-ar-ious..." Grace said.

"Yes and why is that funny?" he said.

"Who would name their child after syrup?" she joked.

"No, Grace...that's maple...not Mabel, but it's still kinda funny," I said, laughing. I began to feel something burning the side of my face. I looked up to find him glaring at me. "You were saying?"

Screaming, he said, "YOU BIT HER EAR OFF!!!"

"Can she still hear?" I asked.

"Peaches, that is not the point. You hurt her…"

"Did I give her an orgasm?"

He looked confused. "What?"

"I ask because they look like they hurt too..."

He exhaled. "No, you did not."

"Good, 'cause I don't EVER wanna do that," I said, pleased that I didn't do that. "Again, daddy, I was saving your life…"

He took a deep breath and continued, "I know that that's what you thought you were doing, and I appreciate it, but daddy is a grown man…I can protect myself…"

"You wasn't doing a good job. That woman was kicking your butt…and who fights naked? What kinda fight is that? Her breasts were in your face…is that how people punch each other now?" Grace said, picking her nose and wiping boogers on the chair.

I frowned. "I hope not, 'cause we're going to need bigger boobs." I looked at Grace. "You are so gross…"

"If I'm gross then what are you...booty scratcher?" she teased.

"I don't scratch my booty..." I said, trying to deny the accusation.

"Yes, you do...yes, you do...I seen it..."

"Shut up...you are always seeing something," I argued. "Why don't you 'see' a toothbrush?"

"Why don't you see one? All of that teeth brushing and your breath still smells like feet..."

"No way...your breath smells like feet..."

We went back and forth like this for several minutes before we became aware of the heavy breathing going on next to us. We'd almost forgotten he was there. His eyes were red and he was huffing like a bull. "Peaches, don't come in my room without knocking..."

"First, we both went in there and second...even if you're screaming like a girl?"

"I wasn't screaming like a girl..."

Grace confirmed. "Sorry dad, but you did...sounded like an opera singer who was getting his butt kicked." She teased. "Oooo, aaaaa, oooooo, aaaaa…"

I smiled and nodded in agreement.

Frustrated, he said, "I am too tired to deal with this shit…"

"Maybe it's because of all of that 'orgasm' stuff…" I said, knowing that would send him over the edge. "Maybe it's not good for you…"

He sucked his teeth and said, "I give up." He walked out of the room. Grace and I smiled at each other and then went back to watch cartoons.

After I attacked her, my dad decided that it was time to take my situation to another level. You see, when talking doesn't work, an ass-whooping don't work, and when prayer fails, then and only then, will he take us to a doctor. With Black folks, it's the last resort, because they don't trust doctors. They can be a little leery of folks in white coats, folks in white robes, folks in white hoods, etc. But in order to keep their "thing" going, I had to agree to go and get "diagnosed."

After having my head "shrunk" they explained to my daddy that I have an Antisocial Personality Disorder. In other words, I don't play well with others which translates to "I'm a bitch." The tragic thing is, is that they felt that they needed to pay somebody to tell them that when I could have told them that for free.

When he felt that it was safe for her to be around us again, he invited her back over so that we could "talk." I guess he figured that enough time had passed for us to calm down. I didn't understand why he did this. Making me talk to her was like forcing me to face my demons and I didn't want to do that. Clearly, I didn't like the woman, but he felt that if he forced her on me, one day, I would come around. Where he went wrong, was that he warned us about the meeting in advance. I guess he felt that this would soften the blow…if only he knew that I was waiting for her.

Mabel made dinner. Everyone was quiet. You could cut the tension in the room with a knife, but you couldn't cut that meat. That shit was so tough, you needed a chainsaw to cut through it. After we were done choking it all down, we cleaned up, and returned to the table.

"Look at us…just one big happy family," I said, sarcastically.

My dad cleared his throat. "I think that we all got off on the wrong foot.

"The wrong ear," I mumbled.

"What did you say?" he asked.

"Nothing…" I confirmed.

He continued. "I want to take this time to clear the air." He looked around the table. "Peaches…would you like to start?"

I folded my arms in front of me. "Now, why would I want to do that? Didn't you call the meeting?"

147

He frowned. "Don't make me come over there…"

"Okay…sure…I'll start." I paused and looked at Mabel. "Can you hear me…Mabel?"

She sucked her teeth. Grace lowered her head as my dad frowned. "Peaches…apologize…"

I looked at him. "It was a legitimate question…"

"Girlllllll…don't make me hurt you…"

Mabel interrupted him. "Remy…let her speak…she's angry…and I want to know why?" She paused and asked, "Peaches…what have I ever done to you?"

I thought about it for a moment and said, "Does waking up qualify?"

Mabel looked confused. "So you wish that I was dead?"

I was about to say something, but was interrupted. "Be careful…" he said.

Mabel continued. "Does it bother you more that your mother is dead and you think that I'm trying to take her place? Or do your really wish that I was dead?"

I looked at her and said, "Can I choose two?"

Grace shook her head as she continued to stare at the floor.

She reached out and touched my hand. "I'm not trying to take your mother's place."

I snatched my hand away. "Good, 'cause we don't need a mama and I'm not looking for any friends."

"So you don't want to try to be friends?" she asked.

"Friends are chosen not forced on you…"

"I wouldn't want that…"

"Good…now…" I exhaled and sat back in my chair. "…Maple…"

"It's Mabel…" she corrected.

"Whatever…" I said.

Grace laughed, but when she realized that we were all staring at her, she stopped. "Well…it was funny."

I continued. "Mabel…I can call you Mabel, right?"

She bit her bottom lip.

Raising one of my eyebrows, I said, "If you don't want me to call you Mabel, I could call you some other names…"

"Peaches…I am losing my patience…" he said.

"Look…" she pointed. "Daddy's veins are popping out of his head," Grace said.

His eyes narrowed.

"Dad's right…we did get off on the wrong foot…" I turned back to Mabel. "I've had some time to think about all of this…"

They smiled with their eyes full of hope.

"And I've come to the conclusion that…" I continued.

"Yes," he said.

I stopped and smiled. "No matter what I think and feel…he's not going to stop seeing you. The only thing that I ask, is that…" I smiled at Grace and said, "…I never have to see you naked again…because you are gross."

The room feel quiet. Her eyes widened and her mouth feel open. Grace fell out of the chair and onto the floor and my dad stopped breathing. When he finally took a breath, he ran over to Mabel's side.

"You're not gross…you're sexy…not gross…" he said, trying to calm the situation.

I shook my head. "She probably looked real good in her hay-day…until she ate all of the hay."

His eyes turned red. "GO TO YOUR ROOM!!!"

Chapter 13

*Y*awn...

I stared at the ceiling for a few minutes before climbing out of bed. I looked over at Grace who was still sleeping and shouted, "Grace...get up!"

She mumbled something and pulled the blanket over her head. I grabbed my pillow and threw it at her. "Grace...get up!!!"

She rolled over and slipped her hand under the blanket. She felt around for a second and said, "I think I pee'd on myself."

I frowned. "That's nasty, Grace..."

"No, no...I think I...wait a minute... she pulled her hand from under the blanket. Staring at her hand, she said, "Peaches???"

I looked over in her direction. I ran over to her bed. "What is that? Did you cut yourself?"

She threw the blankets back away from her. She screamed. "What did you do, Peaches?"

Pointing at myself, I asked, "Me?"

"Yeah you…" she said, trying to see where the blood was coming from. "You tried to kill me in my sleep?"

"If I was going to kill you, you'd be dead already. Now, stop moving…you're making it worst."

"Where is it coming from?"

"It looks like it's coming from your yoo-hoo."

"My what?" she asked.

"Your yoo-hoo…your 'lady' part…" I walked over to the closet and grabbed one of her shirts. "Here, stick this in 'there'…"

"One…stick it where? Two…why are you using my shirt?" she asked.

"One…stick it in the hole where the blood is coming from and two…cause you're the one bleeding all over the place."

She lifted her gown and stuck the shirt between her legs. "I'm dying."

I shook my head. "I'm going to get daddy."

"Hurry…" she begged.

I walked down the hall and knocked on his door. "Daddy…"

"Yes," he mumbled.

"We got an emergency…"

"Everything is an emergency with you girls…"

"Grace is bleeding all over the…" I hadn't had time to finish the sentence before the door flew open and a dark figure flew passed me. I followed 'it' down the hall.

Standing next to her, he said, "You'll be okay…"

Looking up at him, she said, "I will? But I'm bleeding…"

He took a deep breath and said, "Go and get in the shower. I'm going to run to the store and I'll be back…when I get back, I'll try to explain it to you."

With a concerned look on her face, she asked, "I'm not going to the hospital?"

He smiled and said, "No, Sweetie…it'll be okay…" He stood to leave the room. "I hope."

"You hope?" she asked.

He looked at me. "Help your sister and I'll be right back…"

I frowned. "I hate looking at blood…why do I have to help her?"

"Really? You don't like seeing blood?"

"Daddy!!!" Grace screamed.

"Well, now's a good time to learn to like it…'cause you're going to see a lot of it."

"Huh?" I asked.

He shook his head. "We'll talk about it when I get back."

Slowly, Grace climbed out of the bed. Like a stream of water, blood began to run down her legs. I took the t-shirt and shoved it between her legs. "Hold it there…you're making a mess." She waddled all the way to the bathroom. She climbed inside of the tub and turned on the water. She had a really frightened look on her face.

"Daddy said that you're going to be okay...so you're going to be okay." For a moment, she smiled, but quickly went back to being afraid. Soon the front door opened. Daddy ran into the bathroom. Grace, quickly, covered herself. He emptied the bag that looked like he'd purchased everything in the "Big Girls'" aisle of the grocery store. He picked-up the first item, examined it and said, "Okay....these are sanitary napkins...ladies call them 'pads'..." he took one out of the package and opened it. "You....ummm take this...and you...ummmm...stick it to your underwear..."

Curiously, we watched him.

He stuck it to his leg and said, "They....ummmm...stay in your panties and I guess when it gets full...you change it."

"That's a diaper, daddy...why is she wearing a diaper?"

He stared at me for a long time and said, "Circle of life, Peaches...we start out wearing diapers and we 'end' wearing diapers..."

"That's scary…" I said.

"That's just the way it is…"

Grace looked down at her legs and said, "We need to hurry…"

"Okay…okay…" he took out the next item. He opened the box, pulled out a long plastic bag with something hard in it. He opened it up. As he opened the instructions, he played with the tube that was inside of it. He started to read the instructions. "Okay…it looks like you're supposed to take this thing and stick it…" He paused and continued to read. "Hold on…wait a minute…" he kept reading. "You put this where? In what?" He shook his head. "Naw, you won't be using these."

We giggled.

He pulled out the last two items. "Here's some wipes and some spray to keep you fresh…you know how to use this stuff, right?"

We stared at him.

Grace, finally asked, "Daddy, what is happening to me?"

He took a deep breath and said, "I was hoping that they taught y'all this stuff in school…but I guess it's up to me to tell you…it's called a 'period.'"

"A what?"

He took another deep breath. "It's something that your body goes through…naturally."

"So boys go through it too?" I asked.

"No…just girls…"

"That's mean," Grace said.

"I know…" he said. "It's one of the things that you have to go through before you become a woman…"

"So…this is it…I'm done? I'm a woman now?"

"No, sweetie…you still have some growing to do, but you're going to do 'this' every month…until you get old and then…I guess…it stops…or it stops when you die…I don't know…I just know that it lasts a long time. Every month, it's like nature turns on a faucet and forgets that it turned it on and then, after a week or so, it remembers and comes back to turn it off," he said.

"Every month?" I asked.

"Every month…" he said.

I thought about this for a moment and said, "But I thought that you said that it's called a 'period.'"

"It is…" he confirmed.

"Well, we were taught that a 'period' is what you use to show that you're done with something…that things are complete…this doesn't sound like it's done…" I said.

He thought about it for a second and said, "But I am…now, go and get your sister some underwear, while I put her things in the washing machine…as the machine washes the blood away…maybe I can find something that'll wash this moment away."

A few months later, I got "mine." I was glad that Grace got "hers" first. That way, I didn't have to have the uncomfortable conversation with my dad. I didn't use the pads though. I was glad that he didn't throw the forbidden tubes away and while he was at work, I snuck into his room and found them tuck way in his closet and I liked using the forbidden "tubes". It was something about them being inside of me that made me feel like I was grown. I used to love walking around my bedroom, feeling that 'string' rub against my leg and knowing that it was my little secret. And for several months, I was able to keep it that way until one day, I started to feel sick.

I was burning with fever, vomiting, and had the 'runs' something terrible. Of course, my daddy thought that I had the flu, but when he woke-up the next morning and found me on the kitchen floor, shaking and foaming at the mouth, he knew that it was serious. He rushed me to the hospital. After they examined me, they told him that I had a bacterial infection from an old tampon that was stuck-up inside of me.

"A tampon, huh?" he asked the doctor, while staring at me.

"Yes, a tampon. It's one of those things that…"

My father looked at the doctor and frowned. "I know what it is."

"Well, we found one inside of her…looks like it's been in there a while. This is not a rare occurrence. We see this all of the time…it's easy to forget that they're up 'there.'"

"Really?" he asked.

The doctor smiled. "It can happen to anyone."

My dad frowned. "Especially to disobedient children."

The doctor looked at me and then back at him. "If you don't mind me asking, where's her mother?"

"She's gone…she passed-away…" he said.

"I'm sorry to hear that," the doctor said. "So it's just you?"

"Yep…it's just me…and them," he confirmed.

"Well, tell her that it's okay to use them, but she has to remember to change them often…Toxic

Shock Syndrome is very serious…she could die…"

Tired of the whole ordeal, my dad asked, "Okay…doctor…what do we do now?"

"I'm going to write her a prescription…and just tell her to change them often and make sure that she washes her hands before inserting and removing them…"

"Oh, believe me…I'm going to tell her something…a whole lotta 'something'."

As I got dressed to leave the hospital, I couldn't help, but think about what was going to happen next. I wondered how he would punish me for disobeying him, but as we walked down the hall, he said absolutely nothing. When we stood in the elevator, he said absolutely nothing. When we got into the car, for a moment, he remained quiet, but then he pulled over, stopped the car and said,

"Peaches…I want you to remember this moment. Trying to be slick only lands you in one place and that's trouble…"

"So are you going to punish me?"

"Punish you? Nope…I will let life do that for me…" He shook his head. "You're going to find that the only things that are best done in the 'dark' are kissing, sleeping, having surgery, praying, dreaming, and dying…we do all of those things with our eyes closed…for a reason…can't be held accountable for shit that you do with your eyes closed, but the shit that you do with your eyes open? Now, that's another story. You're going to always be held accountable, one way or another, for the shit you do in the 'light.'" Then, he put the car back in drive, slowly pulled back into traffic, and never mentioned it again.

Chapter 14

You want to know what happens when you leave 'crazy' alone to monitor itself. It does crazy shit. I was on a path of self-destruction. I just didn't know it yet. I was pissed and annoyed at the world. Why? Because, I'm a teenager and that's what teenagers do. We're miserable by nature. So sprinkle in some hormones, add a dash of immaturity, and a big ass cup of all of life's other bullshit and you have a recipe for disaster.

And I was looking for a "victim", somebody, anybody, to take my anger out on, 'because misery loves company.' Then, I spotted her. She was a big girl, who was standing at the Snow Cone cart, waiting for her turn to purchase one. Teenagers love messing with "big" girls. They are the perfect target for teenage bullying. Most of them have low self-esteem and you can mess with them without worrying about retaliation. But here's the thing that I will quickly learn. Never underestimate the underdog. People who've been picked on a lot are looking for a reason to whoop somebody's ass too and there's nothing more humiliating and funnier than watching the hunter get her ass kicked by her prey.

There was a long line. I walked up behind her. It was taking her forever to choose a flavor and everyone was growing impatient. I tapped her on the shoulder and said, "There's only four flavors...we would like to get ours before all of the damn ice melts."

She looked up at me and frowned. She turned to the vendor and said, "What flavor is red?"

Frustrated, the crowd moaned. "It's too hot for this shit..."

I walked around her until I was facing her. "Bitch, are you serious? Red is red...I know what flavor it ain't...it ain't low-fat, low-calorie, it ain't diet, or skinny..."

She popped her neck. "Bitch, do I know you?"

"I would pose the same question to your waistline…when was the last time you saw it?"

Instead of answering the question with words, she cracked her knuckles and let her fists do the talking. I wasn't hungry, so I know that I didn't order a knuckle-sandwich, but she gave me one anyway. Matter of fact, she gave me ten. After that, I stopped counting. I just laid there waiting for her to beat the shit out of me, kill me, or tire herself out – whatever came first. I was walking towards the "light" when I heard someone say, "Get your big-ass off of her." There was scuffling and then, I felt someone grab me by the shoulder. "Come on…let's go."

Blinking my eyes, I tried to regain my focus. "God?"

"No, you idiot…" she said.

"What? What are you doing here?" I asked.

"Scraping your crazy butt off of the sidewalk…" Grace said. She turned back to the girl and jumped on top of her. She started punching the girl in the head. It took two people to pull her off of her. "Get your hands off of me…"

I looked at the girl who was trying to regain her balance. Quickly, she stood and ran away.

"I don't need your help...I had this..." I said, wiping blood from the side of my mouth.

Grace looked me up and down. "Really? That's amazing...I swear that I just walked up and saw someone trying to blend your face into the concrete."

"No..."

"Yes...she didn't even bother putting down her snow cone...she whopped your butt with one hand, while sipping the cone that was in her other hand...quenching her thirst while she whopped your butt."

"No, that's not what you saw. We were just getting started..."

"Looked like you were reading her palms...what did you see in her future...other than kicking your butt?"

I walked ahead of her. "You got jokes..."

Following behind me, she said, "No, I got sense. I hope that you learned something."

Rubbing my jaw, I said, "I learned that you should never get between a big girl and her snow cone."

She shook her head. "You gon' keep on and you gon' run-up on the wrong person and I won't be there to save you."

"I don't need saving…"

"At some point, in our lives, we all need saving. All I'm saying is, if you have a death wish, that's cool, but remember, when they can't find you, they'll come looking for me."

Chapter 15

I was miserable. Taking the journey from child to young adult was difficult. Not only were we dealing with the physical changes, but we were dealing with the emotional changes too. Overnight, I woke-up confused and lost. I really needed someone who could help me through this awkward stage of my life, but all I had was him. You will note that I'm now referring to my dad as "him." That is because, and this happens with most teenagers, once I became a teenager, he became my enemy. We were already on shaky ground. Especially after he brought that "chick" into our house. Now, I needed someone to blame all of the messed-up crap that's been going on in my life, and he was the perfect scapegoat.

Sure, I see how ridiculous it all is now, but as I was going through it, it didn't seem quite as ridiculous. You see, when you're going through your "shit", all you can see is your "shit" because your "shit" becomes the only "shit" that matters and that's cool until you find out that no one gives a shit about you or your "shit."

And instead of having a father who tucked me in at night, my anger did it. It poured my cereal in the morning. It helped me pick my clothes. It did everything for me and it was happy to do it. It was the only friend I had. And anger does that. It alienates you. It'll replace any chance of real love and happiness. It destroys everything and everyone around it. It kills you and all that you love or that loves you.

I didn't know what to do or how to do it and asking "him", on the rare occasions that I did, was like talking to the wall. Maybe, I should have talked to the wall. At least, the wall was always there. He'd, almost, completely given up on us. He continued to take care of us, but beyond that, we were on our own. So, I was forced to navigate through this aspect of my life, alone and you know what happens when you leave kids to their own devices. They fuck-up and they usually fuck-up bad. I relied on my peers to get me through my "Rite of Passage," so you can imagine how hard things were for me. Now, it wasn't like I couldn't hold my own against whatever life handed me, but life handed me a lot of shit and it didn't help that I was led there by folks who were just as clueless, about life, as I was.

As I got older, I went looking for love in all of the wrong places. My thoughts began to shift from books to boys. I'm not really sure what triggered the change. Just one day, I woke up and instead of wanting to knock the shit out of them, I began to wonder what it would feel like to hold one or to kiss one. They weren't so yucky anymore. I mean, they were, but in a good way. If that makes any sense and I wanted one, but I didn't know how to get one. Do you walk around with a sign hanging from your neck? Maybe, wear a t-shirt that says, "Come and get 'it'!!!!" Should I club one over the head like they did in caveman days or do you just sit and wait until God sends one in your direction? I didn't know, but I was ready.

In the 10ᵗʰ grade, I was really "crushing" on a boy named, Carlton. I allowed my cold heart to lust after a boy who didn't even know that I was even alive. Sadly, he would later become my "first." Well, I can't say that what we did qualifies as a "first" unless you file it under the first of life's many disappointments. I should have known that a boy named Carlton would cause me grief, but when you're young, you tend to think that your butt is made of Teflon – no matter how hot things get, nothing will stick to you.

I was thinking with the wrong "head." Had I used the one that sat atop of my shoulders, I would have truly looked at his ass, did the smart thing, and ran in the other direction. But such is life, right? Since shit doesn't come with a warning label, the only way that you're going to know that it isn't good for you, is by trying it and I wanted to try it – real bad.

Carlton was a nerd. If you didn't figure that out when I told you his name, now, you know. He was a beautiful shade of brown, beautiful thick curly hair, big full lips, and the longest eyelashes that I'd ever seen on a man. He belonged to all of the nerdy clubs – band, debate team, French club, and the Math club. He wore Polo shirts, khakis, and loafers. He wasn't popular. He was just Carlton.

And I wanted him. Oh my God, I wanted him. I used to dream about him every night. I used to dream that he, one day, walked up to me, said 'Hello', and then without thinking, he took me into his arms and kissed me. Unfortunately, my dreams never went farther than that because I didn't know what happens next, but for now, that was just enough.

I went out of my way to see him - any look from him, even if it was one of complete agitation over the fact that I was stalking him, was all that I needed to complete my day. So, I followed him – ducking in and out of hallways, closets, and classrooms, just to see him. I loved watching him solve math problems on the chalk board. When he was done, he would turn to us and say, "Are there any questions?" I wanted to raise my hand so bad, and say something, but was afraid that when I opened my mouth, that I would shout out, "Carlton, will you marry me?!!!" So, to avoid looking like a complete idiot, I kept it cool.

I made sure to sit across from him in the lunchroom. I loved watching him eat. The way that he would lick condiments from his face as he stared into whatever book he was reading that day. Everything he did was sexy to me. From the way that he pushed his glasses up on his nose to the way that he sharpened his pencils. He was beautiful. Absolutely beautiful.

So I waited. Seconds, minutes, hours, and days went by. I'd almost stop praying, but then one day, he walked up to me and said, "Hi, I'm Carlton." If I hadn't went to the bathroom earlier, I swear I would have pee'd on myself. The "love" was instantaneous.

"Ummmmmm, ummmmmm, ummmmm…" I said, blabbering and unable to speak.

He stuck out his hand. I looked at it. "Ummmmm…Ummmmm…"

He smiled. "Your name is Peaches, right?"

"Peaches…who?" I asked, confused.

"You…you're Peaches."

Finally, I took a deep breath and said, "Yep…that's me." *You are so stupid.* I thought to myself.

He smiled. "I noticed you watching me…"

"Me? Me? Are you sure?" I asked, nervously.

"That person that was hiding behind the tree wasn't you?"

Embarrassed, I said, "You know that I have a twin…it could have, easily, been her."

"Oh…then my mistake…let me go and talk to her…" He started to walk away.

I grabbed his arm. "I'm just kidding…it was me."

He smiled and continued, "Well…I just wanted to say 'Hi'…"

I smiled and said, "Hiiiiiiiiiiiiiiiiiii…" *You are such an idiot.* I thought to myself.

"Well, I guess I'll see you around sometime…"

"Yep…you will see me…definitely…" I confirmed.

He waved "Goodbye" and turned and walked away. I stared at his butt as he walked away.

That afternoon, I ran home and started picking out my outfit for the next day.

Grace watched me. "Is this over that boy who looks at you and frowns like he's looking at a turd?"

"For your information, he said 'Hi' to me today," I said as I pulled a strappy summer dress from the closet.

"That nerd…are you sure he was talking to you?"

"Yes…" I frowned. "You are such a hater. You're mad 'cause he didn't say 'hi' to you."

"Oh, I looked at him once…thought that he was cute, but looked again and was like, my mistake."

"Whatever…"

"Girl, please…the only thing a nerd can do for me is tell me is what a Pythagorean Theorem is."

Turning up my top lip, I asked, "What is that?"

"Exactly," she confirmed. "That's all I want from a nerd…answers to difficult questions…my man? Well, I want one with 'Bad-boy Swagger.' One of those, pants-sagging, Ebonics speaking, brothas with no job and a rap-sheet so long, he can use it to keep us warm at night when we end-up on the streets…and whose only goal is to dry-hump my leg all day."

"One of those guys who like to grab his 'junk' every two seconds like he's trying to make sure that no one stole it while he wasn't looking…?"

"Even those who eat steak enjoy ground chuck every once in a while…"

I sighed. "Well, I want a man who has dreams and goals…"

"My man will have dreams and goals….he will dream about me and his goal would be to kiss me, hug me, and maybe…"

I shook my head. "Girl, please, stop…you ain't gon' never get anybody looking like that…"

"Looking like what? You?" she asked.

"Look at those clothes…the only skin that you show is your face and hands…"

"You gotta make them work to see the rest and look who's talking? *Chewbacca*…you need to shave those hairy-ass legs if you plan to wear a summer dress…" She rubbed my legs. "The struggle is real, but it ain't that real."

I smacked her hand. "I will shave my legs when you shave that bush over your top lip…"

"Hilarious…well…Camel called…he said he wants his toe back…"

"Oh, wow…you're real funny…you're going to need a sense of humor working the pole…"

"The only pole that's going between these legs will be attached to a brotha…"

"You are so gross…"

"Maybe, but I'm not delusional and I ain't chasing nobody…"

"Me neither…" I walked over to the mirror and stood in front of it. "I'm going to make him love me."

"Love? 'Hi' is a long way from love," she confirmed.

"Oh…it's coming…watch…"

"Oh…I'm going to watch alright, and laugh, and watch, and laugh…"

"You'll see…" I stared in the mirror, not realizing that my dream would soon become my worst nightmare.

Chapter 16

For several months, the only thing that we shared was a few 'hellos' and a few stolen glances. Then one day, he made his move. I was on my way from school when he ran up behind me and said, "What are you up to?"

I smiled and said, "On my way home…why?"

"Would you like to hang out?"

Without thinking, I pinched myself. "Ouch!"

He raised an eyebrow. "Are you okay?"

Rubbing my sore arm, I said, "Yes…I wanted to make sure that I wasn't dreaming."

He laughed. "I hope not…because if this is a dream, I will have to do this all over again."

My heart began to melt.

"I would like to show you something…if you don't have anything…."

Excited, I interrupted him. "I ain't got nothing going on…me? I don't even have a life…I…" I stopped when I realized that I'd just made a fool of myself.

"Well, let's see if we can change that…starting today."

I was putty. I would have followed him over a cliff if he'd asked me to. Eagerly, I said, "Okay…" We walked through the park. Not once did I ask, "Where are we going?" He could have been a serial killer or some other type of nut-job, but I didn't care. Without thinking, I followed him as he led me through the park, and into a wooded area where there was no one, but me and him. As we walked, I glanced over my shoulder to watch the streets and any other source of life, disappear.

Finally, after an hour, we found ourselves standing in front of what looked like a cave.

"We're here," he said.

"Ummmm okay…"

He reached out and grabbed my hand. "This is my special place."

"Ummmmm okay," I said, again.

"I come here because it's quiet…"

I looked around. "Couldn't you find something closer to your house?"

"Peaches…I brought you here because I thought that you would understand."

Sadly, I didn't understand, but here he had shared something with me that he thought was special and I didn't want to be the one to tell him that it wasn't, so I held my tongue. I would say and do whatever was necessary to be a part of his life – weird-shit and all. "I do understand…this is your special place…"

He interrupted me. "Our place…"

Somebody should have stuck a fork in me 'cause my ass was done. He walked up to me, wrapped his arms around my waist, looked deeply into my eyes, and he kissed me. Startled, I stuck my arms out in front of me.

"I'm sorry…" he said.

"No…no…I'm just…"

"Have you ever kissed anyone, before?"

I waved my hand and proceeded to lie. "Yes…of course…I kiss boys all of the time…"

He frowned.

"That didn't come out right…did it?"

"No, it didn't…"

"The truth is…you're my first. I mean, I've kissed my father…"

He frowned again.

"I'm making this worse…"

Just then, he grabbed my face and placed his lips on top of mine. I closed my eyes as his lips touched mine and surrendered. When he released me, I licked my mouth, enjoying the taste of candy that he'd left behind.

"I'm sorry…I probably should have asked if you have a boyfriend…but anyone without a 'life' probably doesn't have a boyfriend."

I looked at him. My brain was still trying to wrap itself around what'd just happened. Snapping out of my daze, I said, "I don't have a boyfriend."

He held my hand. "What do you think about me and you?"

"Me and you, what?"

"You know…girlfriend and boyfriend?"

"Babababababa, dadadadadada, gagagagaga…" I babbled.

"Is that a yes?" he said, smiling.

I walked up to him, placed my arms around his shoulders, placed my lips against his, and mumbled, "Yes."

It was dark when I got home. Normally, I would care about getting home late, but tonight I didn't. I was on cloud nine and you couldn't tell me nothing because I wasn't interested in hearing it.

"Do you know what time it is, young lady?" he asked, as I walked through the door.

"I don't, but I'm sure that you're going to tell me," I said, closing and locking the door behind me.

"It's 10pm…"

"Thanks for the update, dad…I should be getting ready for bed…" I said, trying to get passed him.

"I want you in here by 7pm on a school night…"

"Will you be here?" I asked.

"Why?"

"Just wanted to make sure that this wasn't one of those 'do as I say, don't do as I do' moments…"

"Sit down," he instructed.

"Awwwww man…really?"

He sighed. "Peaches, I was worried sick about you."

I laughed. "That's funny."

Folding his arms, he asked, "Why is that so funny?"

"'Cause it is…" I folded my arms.

"Peaches, you may not believe this, but I do love you…"

"Now, that's even funnier…"

"Why is that so funny?"

"'Cause I didn't think that you loved anything, but that 'trick' that you call a girlfriend."

"That's not her name?" He frowned. "You know that's not her name…"

"Trick, Mabel, trick…what's the difference?"

He began to pace the floor. When he stopped, he said, "This isn't about her…it's about you."

I stood. "No, dad…it isn't."

"Then, what is it about?"

I sighed. "Being a parent is a full-time job. You can't 'temp'…you have to be there all of the time…you wanna be a daddy, but when I need you, you're in that bedroom brushing-up on your 'back-stroke.'"

Scowling, he asked, "What did you say?"

"You heard me, DAD. We know what you be doing in that room. You don't even bother waiting until we fall asleep. All that noise you be making. It's disgusting and in the bed that you once shared with my mama…you let that trick sweat-up my mama's sheets in my mama's bed…in my mama's house. How triflin' is that?"

"You don't know what you're talking about, little girl," he said.

"Yes, I do. We hear you in there…" Mocking him, I continued, "Oooooooo Mabel…that's it, Mabel…lick this, Mabel…suck that, Mabel…rub my balls, Mabel…stick your finger in my…"

His eyes widened. Then, he walked up to me and with the back of his hand, he slapped me across my face. "Go to bed."

Shocked, I grabbed my face. I looked at him. "Why? So you can get back to Mabel?"

He began to grit his teeth. "I said, 'Go to bed.'"

I removed my hand from the side of my face. "You know…that is the second time that you've

190

put your hands on me…you know what happens the third time?"

Scowling, he asked, "Did you just threaten me, little girl? What's going to happen, Peaches? What are you going to do to me?"

I stood up and without a tear in my eye, I smiled and said, "You know that phrase that you like to say 'about kicking a dog and how you have so many times to do so before it turns around and bite you'…?"

Squinting, he asked, "And? So?"

"I'm just saying, daddy…" I said, as I walked away. "I'm just saying…"

As I laid across my bed, staring at the ceiling, I thought about my first kiss and how "sweet" it was, but those thoughts were constantly interrupted by the image of my daddy hitting me in the face. I couldn't help, but wish that I was old enough to leave this house and never look back or wish that I was old enough to hit his ass back, but until those wishes came true, I would have to settle for what a teenager knows best, revenge.

Chapter 17

"What happened to your face?" he asked, as he examined me.

Looking away, I said, "It was nothing..."

"Never minimize abuse, Peaches...what starts off as a slap can easily escalate to something else." Carlton gently kissed the side of my face in an attempt to make it feel better. "Do you want me to kick his butt for you?"

I did a half-smile because my face still hurt and said, "Naw, I got this...it'll be okay."

"Okay..." He smiled. "Look, I have to get to class. Maybe we can go to our place later..."

"That'll be nice...I can't wait..."

"Me neither..." The bell rang, so he turned and walked away. I watched him. Daydreaming about our next kiss, I didn't realize that I was, now, late for class. When I snapped out of my daze, I turned and ran towards my classroom. As soon as I closed the door, I heard, "So you decided to join us...Ms. Peaches?"

I didn't respond. I walked over to my desk and sat down.

"Since you wanna be late...how about you come up here...first...and do your presentation?"

Oh shit...I forgot my homework. "Mrs. Daniels, I forgot my..."

She interrupted me. "I knoooooooow you're not about to say that you forgot your homework. Not my homework...so you're late and you don't have MY homework."

"I'm sorry...I had a rough night," I began.

"Oh, you had a rough night. From here, you look like you had a perfect night...hair combed, clothes ironed...you had time to do all of that, but you couldn't bring me my homework."

"I'm sorry, Ms. Daniels…can I bring it in later today?"

She stood and walked over to my desk. "You like doing stuff late?"

"No…I just…I just…"

She looked at the side of my face. "What happened to you? Looks like your mouth wrote a check that your butt couldn't cash…"

I didn't respond. She leaned into my face. "If you don't get that assignment in here before the end of the day, I'm going to slap an 'F' in my grade book so fast, they're going to add my name to the Guinness Book of World's records for…"

Finally, having had enough of her, I said, "For being a fucking bitch?"

Everyone gasped. "Did she call her a bitch?" one student asked.

"Naw, she called her a FUCKING BITCH…emphasis on 'fucking'," another student confirmed.

Folding her arms, she asked, "What did you call me?"

I realized that I was in trouble. There was no taking it back. I was going to get some "time" how much, I didn't know, but since I was going down, I might as well get some other shit off of my chest.

I stood and grabbed my books to prepare to go to the Principal's office because I knew that's where she was going to send me, but before I left the room, I said, "You see a bruise on my face and instead of asking me if I was okay, you decide to add salt to my wound…only miserable bitches do that kind of shit…"

"Get out of my classroom…"

"You can take this classroom and shove it up your big, wide, flabby, stanking ass…" As I walked out of the room, I could hear the other students snickering. "Out!" she screamed as I slammed the door behind me. I walked down the hall. I couldn't help, but think about how good it felt to curse her out. The feeling was equivalent to what I felt during my first kiss. I liked it and I like it a lot.

From the look on his face, I could tell that this wasn't going to be good.

"I hate that we had to call you, but Peaches' behavior was just…just…unacceptable," the principal said.

"It was just a matter of time," he said.

Good looking out, dad. Throw me under the bus why don't you? I thought to myself.

He continued. "She's been giving me nothing but problems since the day that she was born."

Taking notes, she said, "Well…have you considered taking her to counseling…"

"We did that when she bit off my girlfriend's ear…"

Damn, tell all of my business… I thought to myself.

Shocked, she asked, "She bit off someone's ear…"

I frowned. "You know…since you're in a 'sharing' mood, dad, why don't you tell her why?"

He exhaled. "Well, in her defense, she thought that my girlfriend was attacking me, but we were just…ummmmmm…"

The principal removed her glasses. "What?"

I smiled and folded my arms. "Yes, dad, what…what were you doing?"

He rubbed his forehead. "It's a long story…"

"I'm here to help you, so what happened?" she said.

"Tell her about the orgasms, daddy…tell her about the orgasms…" I said.

The principal's mouth fell open. Suddenly, she removed her glasses and placed them on the desk. "Sir…"

"I must apologize for her…" he began.

"Why are you apologizing for me? I wasn't the one having sex…"

Trying to turn the subject back to me, he said, "Look…that's not why I'm here…now, what do we do with her?"

"Well, we're going to have to suspend her for a few days."

I thought about Carlton. "No, please don't…"

She shook her head. "I have to…you can't just return to class after calling the teacher…" she paused for a second and continued, "You know what you called her."

"But she was 'picking'…she saw that I'd been hit in the face…"

The principal stopped me. "Who hit you in the face?"

I pointed in his direction. "He did and she saw the bruise…"

She interrupted again. "He hit you?"

"Yes," I answered. "Anyway…instead of her being sympathetic, she said something like…ummmmm…'I see that your mouth wrote a check that your butt couldn't cash…"

"Is that what she said?" she asked.

"Yes, so not only was I dealing with the fact that he'd hit me, but instead of protecting me, she made me feel like I deserved it…"

"But you did," he said, interrupting me.

I turned towards him. "You're batting a hundred, today, dad…why don't you tell her what I said that made me worthy of kissing the back of your hand…"

He looked at me and then back at her. Trying to deflect attention from himself, he said, "This isn't about me, Peaches…"

The principal looked at him. "Oh, but it is…you hit her…that's abuse…and as an administrator, I have to report all cases of abuse."

He sighed. "I didn't abuse her…I barely touched her…believe me, I know abuse."

"Well, why don't you tell her about the belt…"

The principal sighed and said, "Sir, I'm going to have to report this to DCFS…"

He waved his hands in the air. "Wait a minute…this isn't about me. This is about her.

She was the one who called her teacher a bitch…"

"I called her a 'fucking bitch'," I clarified.

They both stopped and looked at me. The principal broke the silence. "What you said was wrong, Peaches, but I believe that if it were not for the adults that you have in your life, you may not have called her…what you called her. So, with that being said, I'm not going to suspend you…THIS TIME, Peaches…now, wait outside of my office. I need to make some phone calls…."

I turned, looked at him, and smiled. "Thanks for coming up here, dad…"

Chewing on his bottom lip, he mumbled, "Wait 'til we get home."

I placed my hand against my ear. "What's that, daddy? I didn't hear you…"

He frowned. I turned to leave the room, but before I walked out, I looked over my shoulder and said, "Woof…woof…"

Chapter 18

I didn't go home, immediately. Not because I was afraid that he would hit me again. After what happened today, I didn't feel like I would ever have to worry about that again, but he was angry and I wasn't in the mood for it. Plus, I had other things and people to deal with. *Carlton.* I'd slipped him a note earlier to let him know that I would be waiting for him at the bus stop.

After getting there, I decided to get some homework done. I was completely in my "zone" when I heard someone say, "Psst...psst..." I looked up.

He waved for me to come towards the car. "Do you know how I could get to the expressway?"

I looked around for a second before placing my book down on the bench. I walked towards the car. As I approached it, I could see that he had something in his hand. He slid his hand up and down. I walked closer.

"Can you tell me how to get to the expressway?" he asked, again.

Squinting, I looked closer. I took two more steps towards the car to see what he had in his hand. When I realized what it was, he said, "Why don't you come and put your mouth on it?"

I stepped back away from the car.

"Come on…you see how hard it is…"

I frowned. "You want directions, asshole? Here's some directions…go down there…make a left….then a right and then go fuck yourself…"

"Tease…" he said.

"Pervert…" I said, walking away.

He laughed. "Your loss…" He pulled away.

Suddenly, Carlton walked up. "Sorry to keep you waiting…"

Still frowning, I said, "No problem…"

He began to help me with my books. "Hey…you want to do something different today?"

I smiled, trying to forget what'd just happened. "Sure, what do you have in mind?"

"How about I surprise you?"

"A surprise?"

"Yeah…"

"Can you tell me what it is?"

"It wouldn't be a surprise if I told you…"

As we walked, I began to talk about all of the crazy shit that'd happened to me that day. When I was done, he said, "Wow…that's terrible."

"Yep…and the day ain't even over yet."

Suddenly, we were standing in front of a house. "Where are we?"

"We're at my house," he said, walking towards the door.

I followed him. He slid the key into the door. "We can hang out here…no one's home. It'll just be us…no more crazy…"

I smiled. "I don't know about this…"

"Don't you trust me?"

"I do, but…"

"You do or you don't, Peaches…"

"I do…"

"Okay…then, follow me…"

I looked around for a second before going inside. The house was kind of dark. The only light came in through the cracks in the blinds. "You sure that this is okay?" I asked.

"It's fine," he said, placing my book-bag on the floor. He threw his keys onto the table. "Are you hungry…thirsty?"

"Not hungry, but definitely thirsty." I said, following him into the kitchen.

He looked inside of the fridge. "Looks like all we have is water and milk."

"Water would be great."

He removed a bottle from the fridge. He opened it first, sipped from it, and then handed it to me. Something about him drinking from the bottle, first – excited me. He proceeded to walk out of the room. "Follow me."

I did as I was told. I followed him down a dark hallway until we were both standing in front of a door. He turned the knob and then turned and grabbed my hand.

I looked around the room for a chair, but there wasn't any. "Please…have a seat," he said.

"There's only your bed…"

He smiled. "Are you afraid of beds?"

"No…"

"Then, have a seat."

I hesitated for only a second before I walked over and sat down. He walked over and sat next to me. He looked over at the door. After realizing that it was still open, he walked over and closed it. He turned and smiled. He came back and sat next to me. Nervously, I sipped from the bottle of water.

"You know, Peaches…I really like you." He placed his hand on my thigh.

Almost chocking on the water, I said, "I like you too, Carlton."

"I believe that what we have is special, don't you?"

"Yes, I do…"

He slid his hand between my legs. I looked down at his hand.

"Do you want me to remove it?"

I thought about it for a second and said, "No…"

"You don't mind if I open the window, do you? It's kinda hot in here."

"No…it's okay."

He walked over to the window and cracked it. A warm breeze entered the room. He walked back over and kneeled down in front of me. He grabbed the back of my head and placed his lips on mine. I closed my eyes. His lips were so soft. My racing heart began to slow down. When we were done, he took the bottle from my hand and walked it over to the nightstand. Slowly, he began to remove his shirt. My eyes widened as he slowly revealed his chest and stomach to me. My heart began to beat so hard it shook the bed. He walked back over to me and slowly climbed on top of me. My thoughts began to race. *Oh my,*

God…Oh my, God…Oh my, God…what is he doing? I thought to myself.

He lifted my skirt and slowly, slid my panties down my legs – never once taking his eyes off of me. He lifted my shirt and gently pressed his lips against my nipples. Slowly, he ran his tongue down my stomach and into my navel. My eyes rolled back into my head. He began to lick my thighs.

Snapping out of my daze, I said, "Wait…what are you doing?"

He placed his finger over my mouth. "Shhhhhh…let me do this."

"Do what?" I asked.

Slowly, he ran the tip of his tongue down the middle of my vagina. Suddenly, I felt it again. That feeling that I'd felt when I cursed out the teacher. I grabbed him by the hair and moaned. Pleased, he laid on top of me, slid himself inside of me and two strokes later he moaned and collapsed on top of me.

Confused, I opened my eyes and looked around the room. "Ummmmm…are you okay?"

"I'm fine…" he rolled off of me and onto the other side of the bed.

"Is that it?" I asked.

"Yep…"

"So we're done?" I said, sitting up.

"Yep…"

"Ummmmm, well okay…" I took his arm and wrapped it around me.

He looked at me. "What are you doing?"

"Cuddling???"

"I don't do 'cuddling'…"

"You don't do cuddling?"

Suddenly, the door opened. "Oh hey…I didn't know that you were home."

I scrambled to get dressed.

Carlton looked up. "Oh Peaches…this is my brother."

Looking for my panties, I said, "Hi…"

His brother walked in and closed the door behind him. He smiled and gave Carlton a "look." Carlton smiled back.

"Peaches…slow down…where are you going?"

"Home…"

He grabbed my hand. "Don't…stay a little while longer."

"No, really…I need to get out of here."

He pulled me back onto the bed. "Do you love me, Peaches?"

He asked. His brother remained in front of the door.

"Yes…" I said.

"Well…" he stroked my arm. "I was wondering…if you're not busy…maybe you wouldn't mind…you know?"

I frowned. "No, I don't know…"

He smiled. "Maybe you could give my brother some?"

"Some what?" I asked.

He placed his hand on my thigh. "You know?"

"Naw, I don't know…"

His brother grabbed himself and licked his lips. Carlton continued, "It won't take him long and I know that you have to get home…and it would mean a lot to me…if you let him…you know?"

Getting angry, I said, "NO, CARLTON…I DON'T KNOW!!!"

His brother spoke. "LET ME FUCK YOU!!" He started walking towards me.

"If you love me, you would do this for me."

"So…you want me to fuck your brother?"

"Yes," he confirmed.

Damn. I thought to myself. For a moment, I couldn't even speak. I felt like I'd been kicked in the chest. I realized what was happening to me. I wanted to cry so bad, but I was too pissed to do so. They were both staring at me – waiting for my answer. I knew what I needed to do, so I said, "Yes…I'll do it."

Shocked, he began to remove his clothing. Carlton jumped up. "You don't mind if I join in…I mean…you are my girlfriend."

I smiled and said, "Of course not…I want you to get yours first."

Excitedly, he removed his clothing. They moved towards me. "Kiss it for me so I can get hard again…" Carlton requested.

"You want me to kiss it?" I asked.

"Kiss mine's too," his brother begged.

"You want yours kissed too?" I asked.

"Yes…" he said, looking like he was about to explode.

I said, "Okay…" and placed my hands on each of their balls and rubbed them. "You like that?"

"Yes," they said, moving closer to my face.

I looked up at Carlton as he smiled and licked his lips. They closed their eyes in anticipation of me putting my mouth on "them," but then I tightened my grip and pulled as hard as I could. Their eyes flew open as they both screamed and stumbled backwards.

"Aaaaaaarrrrrrgggghhhh!!!" I pulled harder and they screamed louder. "AAARRRGGGHH!!!!" They both fell to the floor. Once they were down, I grabbed my stuff and ran out of the house.

Chapter 19

That night, I couldn't sleep. I spent the whole night thinking about what'd happened. It wasn't what I thought that it would be. I mean, I've never seen anyone make love from beginning to end, but I thought that it at least lasted longer than the time it took for him to stick it in. Two pumps and you're done? It takes more pumps than that to get ketchup out of the bottle in the cafeteria. Matter of fact, me saying 'two pumps' took longer than it took for him to give me the two pumps. I've never watched porno, but if all movies only lasted two minutes, they wouldn't be worth watching. Instead of making love, it felt more like a hit and run – leaving me feeling more like a victim than like a woman.

Then he had the fucking nerve to ask me if I wanted to have sex with his brother. What kind of shit was that? Was he for real? What kind of girl did he think I was? Because I fucked him, I would fuck anybody? And he wanted me to do it because that would prove how much I loved him, but what about me? Would he ask me to do something like that if he loved me? I was so hurt and confused.

When the sun came up the next day, I was trying to figure out what I was going to say to him. After I dried myself, and got dressed, I didn't bother to wait for Grace. I wanted to get to school to talk to him about what happened, because I didn't want to believe that he would do something like that to me. I was hoping and praying that maybe there was just a misunderstanding and we could somehow fix this.

I spent the whole day looking for him between classes, but he was nowhere to be seen. When the last bell, of the day, rang I walked over to his locker and waited for him. Moments later, from around the corner, I could hear him laughing. Then all of a sudden, I heard a girl laughing. As he finally walked around the corner, I saw him, walking with another girl. He grabbed her hand.

When he saw me, he turned and began to walk fast in the other direction.

I ran up behind him. I snatched him by the back of his shirt. With my eyes bucking out of my head, I said, "HEY CARLTON!!!!!"

Adjusting his collar, he said, "Ummmmmmm, hey, Peaches…"

Looking back and forth between the two of them, I asked, "Soooooooooooooooo, introduce me to your friend."

She smiled. "Hi, I'm Janet…" she extended her hand.

Frowning, I said, "Bitch, that was a rhetorical question…I don't give a fuck about you or your name."

Her eyes widened. "You don't know me well enough to be calling me a bitch…"

"Well, I know you well enough to call you a hoe, a trick, a skank…should I go on?"

She dropped her books and stepped into my face.

"Unless you're about to kiss me, you better back the fuck up."

Moving closer, she said, "I ain't gotta do shit."

I smiled. "You know what? You don't, but you will…"

"And what you gon' do?" she asked.

Carlton stepped in between us. "Girls, girls… don't fight over me."

I looked at him. "Fuck you, with your little dick ass."

She looked at me and then at him. "What do you know about his dick?"

"I know that if you blink you'll miss it," I said.

She turned her anger towards him. "When did she see your dick, Carlton?"

I answered for him. "Yesterday…"

"Yesterday…yesterday? You tell me that you got homework to do and you at home…fucking somebody else?" she said, rolling up her sleeves.

Holding his hands up. "Wait…let me explain…"

"Naw, motherfucker…you ain't got shit to say to me…"

I stepped back. She walked towards him. She swung her arm and when it landed, it landed in his eye. Before anyone could do anything, she was on top of his. Blow after blow, she hit him.

Security ran and grabbed her. He was getting up off of the floor when I said, "You are one lousy piece-of-shit." He limped away.

When it was all over, I found myself standing in the middle of the hall while everyone stared at me. I turned and ran out of the school.

When I got home, I walked passed everyone and went into my room. I slammed the door behind me.

Slowly, the door opened. Grace walked in and looked at me. "Wanna talk?"

"No Grace…I just wanna be left alone."

"Peaches, we're twins. You'll never be alone…"

I didn't respond. She laid down beside me, sat up on one arm, and looked at me. "Now, tell me what happened."

"Grace…I can't…"

"Girl, please…now, come one…tell me…"

I exhaled. "We had sex…"

Her eyes looked like they were about to pop out of her head. "You did what?"

"We had sex…" I repeated.

"Wait a minute, wait a minute, wait a minute…" She stood and walked over to the door to make sure that no one was listening. "….fucking?"

"Yes, we fucked…"

"Wow…what was it like?"

"It was horrible…"

"Dang…really? Tell me what happened."

"Well…we went over to his house…"

Her mouth fell open.

"We went into his bedroom…"

"Wow…" she said.

"I remember him taking off his shirt…"

"Yes…" her eyes widened.

"He climbed on top of me…"

"Yes, yes…" she said, salivating and waiting anxiously for the next detail.

"He kissed me all over…"

"All over?"

"All…over…"

"He went downtown?"

"Yep…tongue, first…."

"Oooooooooooooweeeeeeeee…that's nasty…okay, okay…then what?"

"He slid it in…"

She fell back onto the bed. "Oh my God…I can't take it…it's too much…really, I can't take it…okay…keep going."

"He humped…"

She screamed. "OH…MY…GOD!!!"

I continued. "He humped, again."

"OH…MY…GOD!!!!" she screamed, with anticipation. "Then, what happened?"

"Nothing…"

"Nothing?"

"Nothing…he was done."

"What?" She looked disappointed.

"Yep…he moaned a little…he twitched and that was it," I said, frowning.

"Dang…that's all?"

"That's it…" I confirmed.

"Was it good?"

"Compared to what?"

She thought about it for a second. "You got a point there…that's depressing…"

"No, it gets more depressing…"

"How can it get more depressing than that?"

I sighed. "His brother walked into the room."

The look on her face changed from disappointment to confusion. "His brother?"

"Yeah…he wanted to have sex with me too."

"What the hell? I bet Carlton kicked his ass…"

"No…" I sighed again. "He wanted me to have sex with his brother…to prove my love for him."

Now, the look on her face changed from confusion to anger. She sucked her teeth. "He what?"

"He gave me to his brother."

I was about to say something else when she put up her hand. "Give me a minute…" She closed her eyes and began to count backwards, slowly. "10, 9, 8, 7…"

"He also has a girlfriend."

Her eyes opened, wide. "WHAT???!!!"

"Yeah, I found out today…I confronted them, when I saw them together, and she kicked his butt. Plan A was to confront him and if he didn't provide the right answers, then I was moving on to Plan B…kicking his ass…but she beat me to it."

"Both plans should have involved you kicking his ass…they tried to pull a 'train' on you…"

"We weren't on a train, Grace…we were in his room…"

"Not a choo-choo train, dumbass…" She sighed. "It's like when they hook one train car up to another and…" She stopped and shook her head. "Never-mind…you don't let nobody treat you that way."

"I was hoping that I was wrong about him…"

"He gave you to his brother like a used toy that he was done playing with…ain't but one way to see that, Peaches…"

"Asked me to put my mouth on their dicks…"

Grace began to choke. "Peaches, please stop talking…now, I see why you didn't want to talk about it."

"Hey…I grabbed their nuts and his girl kicked his butt…"

"AND??!!! That's not enough and her kicking his ass is her revenge…she didn't whoop his butt for the both of you. So, what he did to you…he got away with it…it should have been me."

"What do you mean?" I asked.

"My foot would have been so far up his butt, he would have had toes for teeth…It wasn't like that dog borrowed a cup of sugar and didn't return it…you gave him your heart…your body…"

"Yeah…I did…"

"And he washed you off like you were nothing, but dried semen…"

"I guess…"

"And here you are…it'll be one thing if that's something that you agreed to, but you didn't…right?"

"Right…" I confirmed.

"So he misled you…deceived you…it's like you gave him consent to rape you…"

I thought about it for a second. "I don't think it's the same thing…"

"Maybe not, but he still took it under false pretenses…that's low…he should go to jail for that…"

"For being a dog?"

"Yep…that's fraud…people go to jail for that…I'm just saying…"

"You want me to sue him…"

"No…" she said.

"Maybe…I should just kill him…" I joked.

"It's not too late."

I raised my left eyebrow. "I was joking, Grace…"

Narrowing her eyes, she said, "I wasn't…I say let's pay ol' boy a visit."

"And then what? Kill him for being a liar and an asshole?"

"He has to learn, Peaches…people have been killed over a coat…a pair of shoes…a hot dog…I think a woman's virginity…her broken heart…her pain…her anguish…is worth more than all of that."

"Grace…I'm not going to kill that boy…even if we think he deserves it…" I paused to shake my head. "They would put us so far under a jail, they would have to mail 'sunshine' to us…that's crazy."

"No, what's crazy is that he knew what he was doing before he did it and he did it anyway…that's not right and his brother walked in the room, because he knew that he was going to get him some…they've done this before."

"You're right…" I said, agreeing.

"All I'm saying is…you're hurting…he should hurt too."

"I just want it all to be over…I learned my lesson."

"But did he learn his…?" she asked. "That's the real question."

I wasn't sure what was crazier. The fact that my sister wanted to kill him or the fact that I was agreeing with her. I needed to change the tone of the conversation. "Grace, I'll be okay…live and learn…plus, there's karma. He'll get his…"

She looked at me for a second before speaking. "Karma takes too damn long and when they mess over one of us…they mess over the both of us and I don't like being messed over." Then, she laid back on her bed. "They already think that you're crazy…let's prove them right."

"Let's go…" she said, tapping me on my forehead.

I moaned and pushed her hand away. Throwing the blankets over my head, I said, "Go to sleep, Grace."

She shook me. "Get up, Peaches."

"Is the house on fire?" I asked.

"No," she said.

"It better be…"

"Get up, girl…" she said, pulling the blankets off of me.

"What time is it?" I asked, wiping 'sleep' from my eyes.

"Time for you to get your butt up…"

I jumped up. "Have you lost your mind?"

"No…" she grabbed my cellphone and stuck it in my face. "Call him…"

"Who?"

"Carlton…"

"Grace…I'm done with him…"

"I'm not…" she said. The look on her face indicated that she wasn't letting this go until I did what she said.

I turned it on. "What am I saying to him?"

"Tell him that you need to talk to him…" she said, sitting on the bed next to me.

"About what, Grace? It's…" I paused to look at the clock on my phone. "Gurrrrlllll…it's freaking midnight."

"Perfect…" she said.

"Perfect for what, Grace?"

She huffed. "Too many questions…not enough moving…now, tell him that you need to see him…"

"He's not going to see me…especially after I grabbed his nuts…"

"Tell him that you want to give him 'some'…"

I frowned.

"No man rejects free 'booty'…he already thinks that you're easy…he will break his neck for a chance to get some more…"

"No way…" I said, doubting her.

She scrunched-up her mouth. "Call him…"

Wanting to get this over with so that I could go back to sleep, I said, "Okay, but when he hangs up in my face…" I began dialing his number. He answered on the second ring. "Hey Carlton… wait, wait, wait, don't hang up."

"What Peaches?" he asked.

"Hey…what are you up to?" I said, feeling like an idiot.

Grace punched me in the arm. She whispered. "Wave the pussy…"

I sighed and said, "Can I come and see you?"

"For what?" He said so loud that I almost dropped my phone.

To humor Grace, I said, "First…I want to say I'm sorry…I didn't mean to hurt your nuts..."

"Humph…" he said.

I continued. "I was wondering…maybe I can meet you…you know…make it up to you…"

"How?" he asked.

"Let me show you…" I purred.

His tone changed. "How do you want to show me?"

Grace whispered in my ear. "Tell him to meet you in the back of his house…"

I pushed her away and said, "Meet me in the back of the house…you know…so we can be alone…I can kiss it and make it better."

She nudged me. "HIS house…"

"Your house…" I quickly corrected.

He eagerly said, "Yes…"

I frowned. "Okay…see you soon." I hung up and looked at the phone.

"Told you…now, get up and get dressed."

"How are we going to get out of the house in the middle of the night without Daddy finding out?"

"Mabel's here…that'll keep him busy for a while." She stood, put some glue, a razor, and a roll of duct tape in her purse. "Let's hurry up and do this…we got school in the morning."

I rolled out of the bed and got dressed. We walked down the hallway and stopped by our dad's door. We heard some moaning, looked at each other, and proceeded to leave the house. I had no idea what we were doing, but I knew that Grace had thought this through. While I was the impulsive one, Grace was the planner, so I didn't even question what was happening. All I needed to know was why and she took care of the when, what, where, and how.

Casually, we followed the moonlight until it led us to his house. We didn't look like two people who were up to no good. We looked like two people who were on their way to church. Once in front of his house, she pulled me to the side. "Wait right here…"

"What are you going to do?"

"I'm going to kill him."

I grabbed her. "That was the plan? I didn't know that that was the plan."

"Well, what do you suggest?"

I thought about it for a second.

She raised an eyebrow. "You don't still have feelings for this fool?"

"No…no…"

"Good…'cause this won't be pretty."

"I just…"

"Just what?" Frustrated, she said, "This is cutting into my sleep. I have an exam in the morning…" She huffed.

"What are you going to do?" I asked again.

She frowned. "He needs to learn, Peaches…and I make a great tutor."

"Okay but…don't hurt him too bad…"

She looked me up and down. "People who are afraid to get their hands dirty shouldn't play in the mud…"

I frowned. "What's does that even mean?"

"It means shut the hell up…and I'll be back…" she said, walking towards the back of the house.

I hesitated for a moment and said, "Okay." I waited until she was in the back of the house and followed her. I watched from the side of the house.

"Hey…" he said.

"Hey…"she returned.

"So…?" he said. "What do you want?"

"Kiss me," she said.

My eyes widened. *What is she doing?*

She walked up to him and kissed him. At first, he stepped back, but then he wrapped his arms around her. I couldn't believe that she was going through with this. He dropped his pants.

Look at this nasty bastard. I thought to myself.

Just then, something happened. His eyes widened. He began to mumble. "Aaarrrghhhh!!! Let me go!"

She bit down harder.

"Aaaaaaaaaarrrrrrhhhh!"

Blood began to drip from the side of his mouth. I couldn't watch anymore. I ran back to the front of the house. I heard more screaming. I covered my ears to block out the sound. I was pacing on the sidewalk when she finally appeared out of the darkness. She returned with blood covering the front of her shirt. She wiped the blood from her mouth.

"Come on…"

"What did you do?" I asked.

"Peaches...you never have to wait for someone to be sorry when you can make sure that they are."

Chapter 20

We didn't speak. Matter of fact, after that night, he avoided me like the plague. I hated him so much, but I hated myself more for allowing it to happen. Now, I had a chip on my shoulder and the more that I simmered in my disdain for him, the heavier the chip became. My hatred for him turned into my hatred for the world and everyone who lived in it. It didn't matter that they'd never did anything to me, I hated them. I didn't trust anyone...anymore. The one time that I drop my guard, someone uses me, and tosses me to the side like some shit that was stuck on the bottom of his shoe.

I was feeling like shit and had almost made it through the day without an incident, but on my way to my Math class, he decided that we needed to talk. I was walking down the hall when he jumped out in front of me. He frowned. "Where are you going?"

"To class…" I said, trying to get around him.

"Sooooooo…when do you plan to settle your debt?"

I frowned. "Get out of my face…"

"I will when you tell me what time you're coming over…"

I looked at Carlton's brother. "Are you nuts? I don't owe you nothing…"

"Oh, yes you do…me and my brother…" He frowned. "And by the way…that shit that you did to my brother…you're going to have to pay double for that…"

"I don't know what you're talking about…now, get out of my way…"

"You thought that you would be done with us, but you'll never be done with us…"

Tired of talking to him, I pushed passed him and ran down the hall.

"WE ARE NOT DONE WITH YOU!!!" he yelled.

When I got home, I saw him sitting there watching TV. I wanted to tell him what happened, but then I would have to admit that I'd had sex with a boy. Knowing him, he would convince me that I deserved the bullshit that I was going through and that I'd brought it on myself, so I just left it alone.

He felt me staring at him. "What?"

"Nothing…" I sighed. *What a waste*. I thought to myself. I was frustrated. I walked out of the room because crying out for help in a world where no one listens is a waste of fucking time.

I was lonely and even though I knew that he was only pretending just to get something from me, the attention, even though it was fleeting, felt good and when it was gone, I missed it. So I tried to date other boys, but I couldn't. Nothing felt the same. The hugs didn't feel the same. The kisses didn't feel the same. Nothing. I guess the heart wants what it wants, even if it isn't good for you. I found myself needing to fill the "emptiness" with something else, so I began to self-medicate. Food became my drug of choice and I got "high" every two hours. From sun-up to sun-down, I was stuffing my face with something. It kept me from "feeling" or dealing with the pain that I felt inside.

Food quieted the noises that were inside of my head that told me that I wasn't good enough or worthy enough for real love. When I eat, I feel like I'm floating on air. Nothing in the world matters to me more than the plate of food that's sitting in front of me. It's as bad as any other addiction. Instead of waking up to drink, to snort, or to inject, I grab a plate of food – and another, and another, and another, to the point where I'm kneeling over a toilet trying to get rid of everything that I'd spent the whole day, stuffing down my throat. I'd convinced myself that it was all that I needed. It didn't judge me. It didn't blame me. It didn't use me. It didn't hurt me and the only time that it'd left me was when I'd eaten everything on my plate; knowing that all I had to do was refill it again.

I was addicted and my daddy was my dealer and enabler. I never ran out of my drug. He knew that something was up. Every once in a while, you might hear him say, "What happened to all of the damn food?" but before anyone could answer, he was already on his way to the store to get more.

Then, I started to gain weight. At first, it was just enough to keep me out of the small summer dresses that I had in my closet, but then it got so bad that all I could wear were spandex pants. As I began to outgrow most of my peers and I had to cut the sides of my pants until they weren't pants anymore, I began to notice that people were staring at me. At first, it didn't bother me, because I thought that the extra weight looked cute, but then I started to hear the whispers.

"Look at her...she looks pregnant," I heard one girl say.

"Looks like she ate her whole family…better check the news…they might be missing," another girl said.

Then one day, my dad walked up to me as I was choking-down some chicken wings.

"Peaches…do you want to talk?"

"Sure, dad…do you want to listen?" I asked, licking grease from my fingers.

"Can we not do this?"

"Do what, dad?"

"Fight…I'm really worried about you."

"Why? 'Cause I'm eating? Could you pass me those fries?"

He handed me the plate. "You're eating a lot…"

"And this bothers you, how?" I said, smothering them in hot sauce.

"It just isn't you."

"How would you know, dad?"

He frowned. "What do you mean? I know my daughter…"

"Then, you should know that you questioning me about my weight doesn't make me feel good…if you know me and love me, you would just accept me." I stopped to pick chicken out of my teeth. "It's just weight…"

"You do know that being overweight is dangerous…"

"Judging me, instead of loving me, can be dangerous too, dad…"

"I'm sorry…"

"No, you're not, dad…"

"How you gon' tell me?"

"Because dad, the only people who are truly sorry for the things that they say and do are babies, the ill-informed, the ill-advised, the ignorant, drunk people, and the dead…"

"The dead?" he asked.

"It's a lot of sorry people who are six feet under…" I said, licking sauce from my lips.

"I'm just trying to help…"

"And the road to hell is paved with good intentions…"

"Can we just talk? Without all of the sarcasm?"

I looked at him. "You're a man…"

"And?"

"You have a penis…you can't help me."

"Excuse me?" he asked. "You are one disrespectful-ass child…"

"True, but you just proved my point…"

"What point is that?"

"You want respect, but you don't give it…"

"You are the damn child…"

"And we don't deserve respect?"

"Sure, you deserve respect…from another child…" He smiled. "Maybe that's where the problem is…you seem to think that a person who feeds you and puts a roof over your head…have to give you something. I don't owe you shit. If anything, you owe me."

"Bill me…" I mumbled.

"I would if I thought you would pay…"

I shook my head.

"You and I? We are not equals. I gave you life…life…" He paused and said, "Inhale…"

Confused, I said, "Huh?"

"Inhale," he instructed.

I took a deep breath.

"See that…I gave you that…"

I frowned. "You gave me air, dad?"

"No, I gave you the ability to breathe…" He took a deep breath and continued, "That's some big shit…you know what you give me in return? You give me bills, headaches, ulcers, grey hair, and sleepless nights…and on some occasions, gas…have my stomach all messed-up with y'all bullshit. I can probably blame this toe fungus on your ass…I didn't have it before y'all came around…"

I shook my head. *Sigh* "Anyway, men are emotionally inept...talking to you about my feelings and what I'm going through is like talking to you about my periods. We both know

245

that I have them, but do you reeeeeaaaallllllyyyy care."

He didn't respond to my question. Instead, he paused to think about something. "Maybe this needs a woman's touch?"

"Grace can't help me, dad."

"I was talking about Mabel…"

I paused to swallow a mouthful of juice. "You want her to help me like she helps you? Sorry, dad, but the only breasts that I want in my life are mine and those in a three-piece with some mash potatoes and a biscuit on the side."

He frowned. "When did you learn to talk that way?"

"When I found out that it's the only way that you will listen to me."

"I listen to you, Peaches."

"No dad…you hear me, but you don't listen to me."

"What's the difference?" he asked.

"The fact that you don't know the difference is why you're bad at it, dad." I walked over to the counter and grabbed a loaf of bread.

"Well, let's talk now…" he said.

"You wanna throw me some crumbs and expect me to get full…thanks, but no thanks, dad. I'll just stick with these crumbs," I said, as I took a bite out of a slice of bread.

He opened his mouth to respond, but I interrupted him. "I was being facetious, dad, but don't worry your pretty little head. It's just a phase. I'll be back to 'society-acceptable" in no time."

"Good," he said. "And things will go back to normal?"

"Yeah, who doesn't love 'normal?'" I asked, as I stuffed another slice of bread into my mouth.

For months, I continued on my down-hill spiral until one day, I caught a glimpsed of myself in the mirror. My cute little waistline had completely disappeared. I had "ass" where my back used to be and my breasts had turned into two big-ass sandbags that dangled from my chest. I'd let it go too far. I had to change before I ended-up dead before the age of twenty or worst, I ended-up stuck here for the rest of my life.

Later, that evening, I was hiding in my bedroom when there was a knock on the door.

"Who is it?" I asked.

"Can I come in?" she asked.

"No, I don't want to be..." Slowly the door opened and she walked in. "The word 'no' must mean something different on your planet..."

"Your dad said that you want to talk..." she said, standing over me.

"He did? You shouldn't believe everything that he says…gotta be careful with men…they're liable to say anything."

"Well, I'm here now….do you want to talk?"

"No, maple…I mean, Mabel…but thanks anyway…" I grabbed my pillow and covered my face.

"Peaches, do you really hate me?" she asked.

I lifted the pillow and said, "Does a bear shit in the woods?"

Frustrated, she sighed and shook her head. "I'm going to let that slide…"

I frowned. "Thanks…you're so kind, but you don't have to do me any favors."

"I know I don't…"

"Then, we have an understanding…"

She shook her head, again. "Well…I guess I'm not needed here, but if you ever…"

I interrupted her. "Don't hold your breath…matter of fact, I changed my mind…PLEEEEAAASSSE hold your breath."

She opened the door. "I'm sorry that you feel that way…"

"Don't be…"

Chapter 21

The next morning, I decided that it was time for a change. I was determined to lose the weight, so I threw on a pair of gym shoes, some sweatpants, and I ran to school. During gym, I ran an extra lap and when school was over, I ran all the way home. Once I arrived home, I ran back and forth throughout the house, trying to add another mile to my regiment. I did this every day for a week and I began to notice some changes, but for some odd reason, my stomach wouldn't go down. I needed to do something else, so I wrapped my belly in plastic wrap, every day, to sweat "it" out and it worked. I was starting to feel like my old self again, but after a week of busting my butt to lose the pounds, I began to notice that something wasn't right. I looked good, but I felt like shit. My body ached all over. I was dizzy and tired all of the time and for a while, I couldn't keep anything down. I tried to ignore the pain and discomfort that it caused, but it was beginning to be too much to bear.

The following week, I rolled out of bed and dragged myself down the hall. *Knock, Knock, Knock.* Slowly, he opened the door. "What's wrong?"

"Do you have any pain-killers? I'm cramping really bad."

"Ain't it some of that 'period' stuff in the bathroom cabinet?"

"If it was, I wouldn't be standing here looking at you."

He stuck up his finger. "Give me a second." Moments later, he returned with a bottle in his hand. "Here."

"Thanks…" I said, looking at the bottle. The pain hit me again. I grabbed my stomach as I walked towards the bathroom. I grabbed three of the pills and swallowed them with one gulp. The pain hit me again. I buckled over and fell on the bathroom floor.

Suddenly, there was a knock on the door. "Come on, Peaches…I need to get in there."

"Come back later…" I screamed.

"Now, girl…I have to get ready for school," she said.

"And I have to get ready for work," he said.

On my hands and knees, I crawled over to the door and out into the hallway.

"Dang girl…you don't look good."

"Mind your business, Grace…"

"Forgive me for caring…"

"Care about yourself…" I said, as I crawled down the hall and into my room. After entering, I crawled-up into my bed and threw the blankets over my head. I fell back to sleep. A little while later, Grace tapped me on the arm. "Are you going to school?"

With one eye open, I peeked from under the blanket. "Naw…I don't feel good. It's all of the working out I've been doing."

"Well, you've been working hard…"

"I have…"

"Well, if it means anything to you, I'm really proud of you."

"Thanks…now, can you leave and lock the door behind you?"

"Sure…" she said, before leaving the room.

Minutes later, the door opened again. "Peaches…are you going to school?" he asked.

I told her to lock the door. "No, dad…I don't feel good."

"That shouldn't stop you from going to school."

"Dad…if you don't leave, I'm going to throw up all over you."

"Okay…well, call me if you need anything."

"Sure, dad…"

He left and closed the door. I closed my eyes and tried to go back to sleep, but the pain came back, but this time, with a vengeance. I rolled out of bed and onto the floor. I crawled back down the hall and back into the bathroom. I climbed onto my knees – trying to reach the bottle, when, suddenly, I felt something warm, running down my leg. I looked down and realized that I was bleeding. I'd come on my period. *Damn.* I stood to remove my clothing. I turned on the water in the shower and while I waited for it to turn hot, I decided to use the bathroom.

As I sat there waiting, the pain hit me again. I began to push. The pain hit me again, so I pushed, again. Fear grew with every push because I knew that something wasn't right. I tried thinking about everything that I'd eaten, tried to remember the last time that I'd had my period, and I tried thinking about anything that I may have done to cause this type of pain, but each thought was met with more pain. This happened several times until I pushed one last time and all at once, everything came out. Suddenly, the pain stopped. I felt so relieved. I closed my eyes and rested my head against the wall. Just then, I heard a faint cry coming from inside of the toilet. Afraid, I sat there for a second, but then I heard it again. As I stood, I looked down and saw something moving inside of the bowl. I fell backwards – realizing that there was a rope dangling from inside of me and there was something tied to the other end of it.

Frantically, I yanked it out of me. I fell onto the floor when I heard the cry again. I placed my bloody hands against my ears trying to muffle the sound, but it got louder.

I crawled over to the toilet and looked inside of it. I realized that my bowel movement had eyes, a mouth, she had hands, and she had feet.

Frightened, I reached in and pulled her out. She screamed. "Waaaaaaaaaaaa!!!!"

"Oh my God, Peaches…what have you done?" I thought to myself.

She continued to cry. "Please stop crying…please stop crying," I begged, but she didn't stop. I noticed that we were both covered in blood. I reached into the shower, turn down the temperature, and we climbed in. The water seemed to soothe her. She stopped crying. Gently, I washed the blood and debris from her little body. After we rinsed off, I held her close to my chest. Slowly, she fell asleep.

I exited the shower and walked down the hall towards my bedroom – leaving a trail of blood behind me. I laid her and the sac that was attached to her on my bed and went back to clean up the mess. When I was done, I returned to the room. She was resting quietly on the bed. I stared at her. "A baby? It's a baby." I stroked her hair. "How did this happen?" Then, I thought back to Carlton. "Wow…a baby." I climbed into the bed next to her. "What am I going to do with you?"

She made a gurgling sound. I placed my finger into her hand and she tightened her grip. I placed my nose onto her cheek and inhaled. She smiled for a second before she gurgled again. She closed her eyes and fell back to sleep. I stared at her for a moment, but the exhaustion from bringing her into the world took a hold of me and I fell fast asleep. A couple of hours later, I woke up and noticed that she was no longer brown, but a dark shade of blue. I picked her up and noticed that her body was cold. "No…wait…no…" I said, panicking. All of a sudden, the front door opened. "Oh shit!!!!" Nervously, I looked around the room. Quickly, I wrapped her in some clothes and slid her under my bed. The bedroom door opened.

"What are you doing?" she asked.

Pretending to be looking for something, I said, "I was looking for my house-shoes."

Grace giggled and pointed. "They're right there…"

I looked up. "Oh wow…there they are." I picked them up, sat on the bed, and slipped them onto my feet.

"Girl, if they were a snake, they would have bit you in the butt."

"Yep, you're right. Good thing…they aren't." I laughed, nervously.

I couldn't sleep. I tossed and turned all night. I opened my eyes and stared at the ceiling. I tried closing my eyes, again, but then I heard it.

Waaaaaaaaaaa…

I looked around the room.

Waaaaaaaaaaa…

Frightened, I grabbed the pillow and covered my head.

Waaaaaaaaaaaaa...

Slowly, I removed the pillow, leaned over the side my bed, and looked under it. My heart was beating so hard and so fast, I thought that it was going to jump out of my chest. The noise stopped. As I climbed back onto the bed, I looked up to find Grace staring at me. It was so dark, I couldn't see anything but the whites of her eyes.

"What are you doing?" she asked.

"Ummmmmm...nothing...I thought that I heard something..."

"If you don't take your butt to sleep, you will hear something...my fist upside your head."

I giggled, nervously. "Okay...okay..."

She laid down. I spent the rest of the night listening, again, for the sound of my baby crying.

The next day, I got ready for school like I normally did, but once at the bus stop, I pretended to leave something at home.

"Hey…go on ahead of me…I'll be there soon…"

She shook her head. "You really need to get your life together."

"I know, right…" I said, pretending to look through my book-bag.

Once back inside, I looked back to make sure that I wasn't followed. I ran to my bedroom and locked the door. I kneeled down and pulled her from under the bed. I sat down on the floor and held her. I unwrapped her, slightly, exposing her face. She looked so peaceful – like she was still sleeping. I rocked her and sang to her. *Twinkle, Twinkle, little star…how I wonder what you are…up above the sky so high…like a diamond in the sky…twinkle, twinkle, little star…how I wonder what you are…* "Did you like that?" She didn't respond. Not like I expected her to, being a baby and all.

The singing was making me hungry. I stood and walked over to the door. First, I placed my ear on the door – listening for any sound or movement.

When I didn't hear anything, I peeked out of the door and proceeded down the hall. Once in the kitchen, I placed her on the table. I grabbed a bowl, some cereal, and the milk and sat down to eat. After I was done, I placed the bowl in the sink, picked her up, and walked over to the front-room to watch some TV. I grabbed the remote.

"What would you like to watch?" I asked her. Pretending like she responded, I said, "Cartoons it is."

We watched cartoons for several hours before I became tired. I turned off the TV and went back to my bedroom. I locked the door and laid her next to me. I fell fast asleep. A couple of hours later, I heard someone banging on the bedroom door.

"Open the door, girl!!!" she yelled.

Startled, I jumped up. "Wha…wha…?"

"Open the dang door!!!" she demanded.

I grabbed her, wrapped in her up in my sweatshirt, put her into the laundry basket, and covered her with clothes. Scrambling, I grabbed everything that had blood on it and threw it into the basket on top of her. I opened the door and tried to walk pass her.

"What happened to you? Why didn't you come to school?"

Dazed and confused, I said, "Wow…what time is it?"

"Really chick? Clearly, you missed another day of school."

"I must have fell asleep…"

"You must have…" I heard her say. "I picked up your homework from your teachers so that you don't miss anything." She followed me out into the hall.

"Hey…thanks for getting my homework," I said, rushing passed her. She followed me down the hall and into the laundry room.

"Girl, you missed it. Your boy got dumped today in front of everybody…some girl came to school with blisters all over her mouth…she tried to choke the crap out of him. It took three teachers to pull her off of him."

Nervously, I said, "Ummmmm yeah...that's a shame."

She frowned. "Something like that should make you happy."

"It does...it does..."

"Why are you acting funny?"

"I'm not...I'm just standing here listening to you."

She looked at the basket. "Aren't you going to put your clothes in the machine?"

I looked at the basket. "Yeah...ummmmm, sure."

With one eyebrow raised, she said, "Then do it...I want to finish telling you about my day."

"Ummmm okay...why don't you go in the room...I'll be in there in a minute."

She knew that something was up. "Put the clothes in the machine, Peaches."

Becoming angry, I said, "Why are you so concerned about my damn dirty clothes?"

She folded her arms. "And why are you being so defensive? You're holding that basket a little too damn hard…"

Trying to collect myself, but doing a horrible job at it, I said, "Just let me wash my clothes…can a person wash her clothes in peace?"

She leaned against the wall. "Okay…go ahead."

"GO GRACE!!!!" I demanded.

"No…" she said.

"GO GRACE!!!!"

"NO!!!!" She grabbed my arm. "What are you hiding?"

I tried snatching my arm away from her. "Nothing…now, go…" I let go of the basket to push her out of the room, but then the basket fell onto the floor. A little hand stuck out from among the clothes. She kneeled down. "What is that?"

"Nothing…nothing…" I said, trying to pick everything up from the floor.

She pushed me and the bundle fell from my hands. "I can explain…"

She looked down at the floor. "What the hell?" She fell to her knees and scooped the baby up into her arms. She began to cry. "Is this real…is this a baby?"

"Grace…let me explain…"

"Peaches…what have you done?!!!!"

"I didn't do anything…" I paused and said, "I mean, I did, but it's not what you think."

"Peaches…I'm holding a dead baby. Is she yours?"

"Yes," I mumbled.

"How did this happen?"

"Grace…"

She interrupted. "So this is why you stayed home…to deliver her?"

"No…I didn't even know that I was pregnant."

"How do you not know that you have something growing inside of you?"

"I don't know, but I didn't. Grace, I swear…"

She pulled at the cord and the sac that was still attached to her. "You didn't cut the cord?"

"Cut the cord? How was I supposed to know to do that? Grace…I never had a baby before…I didn't know what to do."

She frowned. "Look at your fucking stomach…do you see a cord?"

I looked down. "I swear…I didn't know. When she came out, I panicked…I wasn't thinking."

"Some stuff is just basic…you shouldn't have sex if you don't know what you're doing."

"But I did know…"

"What? How to have sex or how to get knocked up?" She raised the baby up into my face. "Look at her…"

Wringing my hands, I said, "I know…I know."

She ran her fingers through her hair and began to kiss her little fingers. She began to cry.

"What am I going to do, Grace?"

She began to cry harder. "We're going to have to tell daddy."

Grabbing her, I said, "No…you know what he would do to me? Please Grace…there have to be something else that we can do?"

She looked at me with tears in her eyes. "What would you like to do, Peaches…toss her into the washing machine, wash her away like a stain on your fucking clothes…like you were about to do."

"No, Grace…I wasn't going to do that."

"That's what it looked like…"

"I panicked…"

"This is not good…this is a baby."

"Then, what should we do with her?"

"I don't know…"

I looked down at her. "I don't know what to do…"

She looked down at my baby and said, "We're going to have to bury her."

"How? Where?"

She stood and held the baby close in her arms. "Let's wrap her up, first…her little body is so cold."

 After wrapping her up in one of my summer dresses, we placed her tiny body into a shoe box. We lined the box with pillowcases and made a pillow out of one of my bras. Grace thought that it would be a good idea to wrap the box up in wrapping paper, so that when she gets to Heaven, God knows that she's a gift and not something that we'd just thrown away. We grabbed a shovel and headed out into the back yard. After digging a hole, we placed the box inside of it. I was about to throw some dirt on top of the box, when Grace stopped me.

"What's her name?"

"Huh?" I asked.

"You have to name her…what's her name?"

"Grace…please…dad will be home soon."

She snatched the shovel from my hand. "You name her, damn-it. You owe her that much."

I looked down into the hole. "Her name is…" I thought about it for a second and continued, "Her name is…Genesis…."

"The beginning," she said.

"Yes, the beginning," I confirmed.

"I like that…" she said, crying again.

We both looked into the hole and said, "Goodbye, Genesis."

I took the shovel and began to cover the hole with dirt. When we walked back in, daddy was standing in the kitchen. "Hey girls…"

We didn't respond. We just looked at him and continued down the hall.

Grace showered and climbed into bed. I didn't shower. Instead, I stood and stared out of the window – into the darkness. I watched as the moonlight lit up the backyard. As I replayed the events of the day in my head, as I replayed the actions that led to this moment, I couldn't help, but hate myself for what I've done. I was so miserable, but then I remembered the moment that we shared in the shower – her warm little body, pressed against my chest – her heart beating against mine. I remembered the sweet smell of her skin. She was so beautiful. Suddenly, my thoughts were interrupted by a knock on the door. "Are you ladies coming to eat?" he asked.

Grace didn't respond.

"No, dad…we're not hungry," I said.

"Okay…well, be careful. I wouldn't want you to starve yourself to death."

Grace began to sob, softly. I turned back towards the window.

The next morning, I awoke to find that I'd fallen asleep, sitting next to the bedroom window. I looked over at Grace who was sitting up in her bed and watching me. I walked over to her bed.

"Thank you…"

"For what?" she asked. Her eyes were swollen from crying all night.

"For helping me…"

She frowned. "You're unbelievable…"

"What do you mean?"

"A dead baby…" she said, shaking her head.

"I didn't mean to do it, Grace…"

"And, yet, here we are…" She was pissed. "You're such a selfish, bitch!"

"What??!!!"

"Yes, you heard me…selfish bitch…"

"Don't call me that…"

"I will call you whatever I want to. All of your life…all you've thought about was yourself. You, you, you…" She began to prance around the room, pointing at herself. "Look at me. I'm Peaches. I'm special. Hey world, look at me."

Then, she stopped and narrowed her eyes. "Do you want the world to see you now...baby killer?"

"How can you say that?" I asked.

"I can say that because I've watched you, Peaches...all of your life...it's always been about you trying to be the center of attention and it's because of your selfishness that a little baby...a helpless little baby...lost her life."

"I didn't mean to do that, Grace...I'm sorry."

"What did you think was going to happen?"

"I didn't think..."

"Of course, you didn't."

"I didn't mean to do it. You have to believe me."

"I have no choice since the dead can't talk." She shook her head. "And look at you now...look at us...you've made me an accomplice to your bullshit."

"I'm sorry..."

"You know what, Peaches? Save your damn 'sorries' for that little girl in the ground." She walked out of the room, slamming the door behind her.

Chapter 22

Shit only got worse after that. You're probably wondering how could things get worse than that. They did and it didn't take long either. The interesting thing about bad decisions – they're kinda like a snowball that's rolling down-hill. When they're small, you can get in front of them to prevent them from getting bigger, but if they're big? All you can do is step back and wait for things to go BOOM!

Losing a baby to illness is hard, but losing one to stupidity can leave a person fucked-up and I was - fucked up. Everything that mattered went into that ground that day - my baby, my relationship with my sister, and my self-esteem. I was all alone and I deserved it. I went into a self-loathing campaign that would carry me into the next four years of my life.

Peaches no longer existed. A girl who killed her baby had moved in and took her place. I gave up on myself. I no longer cared about my appearance, no longer cared about goals, and I no longer cared about life – especially mine. I could no longer live with the person that I'd become. I wanted to die, but was too lazy to kill myself.

It was during the ball drop that the snowball got bigger. "5,4,3,2,1…HAPPY NEW YEAR!!!" Everyone yelled, but me.

My dad opened up a bottle of sparkling grape juice for me and Grace and he opened a bottle of champagne for him and Mabel.

After filling our glasses, he said, "I would like to make a toast…to love, life, wealth, and happiness…"

Grace frowned and walked out of the room. I would have followed her, but I didn't feel like dealing with her. So I was stuck with these two.

"Come on…toast…" They held out their glasses. I exhaled and lifted my glass.

"Yayyyyyy!" they shouted.

They paused and looked at me. "Yay!" I mumbled.

They kissed each other. She grabbed his hand and led him to the bedroom. I sat at the table, thinking about 2015. I poured myself another glass of juice. "Happy Fucking New Year!" I sat the glass down and walked over to turn the TV off. When I returned, I noticed that I'd sat my glass down next to theirs. I looked at them for a moment and then took a sip from one of the other glasses. The bubbles tickled my nose. I giggled and finished the glass. I picked up the bottle and filled the glass again. After finishing this one, I decided to by-pass the glass and went straight from the bottle.

The next thing, that I remember, I was butt-naked and sleeping on the hood of the car. I heard someone say, "PEACHES, PEACHES…Girl, wake your ass up! What the hell are you doing?"

Squinting, I said, "Huh?"

"Girl, look at you…what are you doing?" he said.

I looked around and said, "Who moved my bed outside?"

"Look around you…your bed is in the house…your naked ass is outside…how did you end-up out here?"

I lifted the bottle that I'd spent the whole night holding on to like a teddy bear. He took it from me. "You drank the alcohol? You know better than that…"

I grabbed my head. "Dad, why are you screaming?" My ass squeaked as I slid off of the car.

"You're drunk…"

Grace walked out of the house and walked passed me. "You're such a loser…"

"Take your butt in the house and get ready for school. We will deal with this later…"

"Dad…I don't feel well…"

"Oh, you won't pull that shit again…now, GO!"

I couldn't go back to school. I was too ashamed of myself. Instead, I went and sat in the park until school let out. This went on for a while until the school realized that I wasn't sick and wanted a meeting with my dad. The day that we were supposed to go, I decided not to attend. I wasn't interested in participating in any attempt to save me from myself. So instead of waiting around to hear his mouth, again, I spent the day walking the streets until I ended-up at the local mall. While sitting on the bench and feeling sorry for myself, a young man walked up to me.

"Hey…is someone sitting here?" he asked, cheerfully.

I frowned. "What about 'me' says, 'friendly?'"

His smile quickly disappeared. "Damn, I was just trying to be nice."

"Well, go and be 'nice' somewhere else," I said, looking passed him.

"Since you don't own this bench, I'm going to plant my ass…" He sat down next to me. "Right here…"

"Sit at your own risk…"

"Risk of what?"

"At the risk of being cussed out."

"Damn…what crawled up your ass and died?"

I exhaled. "Look…this is how this works. You don't say shit to me and then you don't get cussed out."

He laughed. "You are too cute…why you wanna be so mean?"

He was getting on my nerves. So I stood to walk away. I looked back and he waved at me. I frowned and kept walking.

Being a bitch can make you hungry, so I decided to go and get something to eat. It was only after I ordered that I realized that I left my lunch money at home. I looked at the server and said, "I'm sorry, but I don't have any money."

A voice said, "Don't worry…I got this." I turned to see the 'pest' standing behind me. He handed the cashier some cash and said, "Keep the change."

The server smiled and gave him the receipt.

I looked at him and said, "Thanks."

"No problem."

I took the food and proceeded to walk away. He ran up behind me. "Hey…do you want some company?"

I sighed. "Thanks for the food, but I feel like shit right now…just want to be alone."

"Maybe that's why you feel like shit…"

"Huh?"

"Because you're alone…"

I looked him up and down. "You want to analyze me?"

"No…I'm waiting for a friend…"

"A friend?"

"Yep…a friend," he confirmed.

"And you want to talk to a stranger while you wait for a friend? Makes sense…"

"Who better to talk to?" he smiled.

I took a deep breath and said, "Sure, but I won't be good company…"

"That's okay…"

I looked around for a second and said, "Let's sit over there…"

"After you…"

Slowly, I walked over to a bench in the middle of the mall where there was a lot of foot traffic.

He began. "So who are you up here with?"

Biting into the sandwich, I mumbled. "Why?"

"I'm just trying to make small talk…"

"I'm here by myself…"

"Shopping???"

"No, just hanging out." I took a bite out of the pickle.

"What's your name?"

"Why?"

"I'm just trying to make conversation…"

"It's Betty…"

"Betty? That's an interesting name…"

"Yep…" I took another bite from the sandwich.

"So, Betty…what's up?"

I didn't respond.

"Betty?"

"Huh? Oh…me…Betty…"

He raised one of his eyebrows.

"Look, lying is too exhausting…my name is, Peaches…"

"So you lied? That's terrible…"

"Yep, it is. That should make you want to walk away."

"No, I'm having fun…Betty…"

I took another bite out of the sandwich and looked around the mall.

"Well, I'm Gage…" he smiled.

I opened the bag of chips and threw a couple in my mouth.

He cleared his throat. A young lady walked towards us. She smiled, waved, and when she approached him, she leaned in and kissed him on the cheek.

He looked over at me and said, "This is Peaches."

"Hi Peaches…" she said.

Suffering from a weird case of déjà vu, I looked away. They were about to walk away when he turned and said, "Well, Peaches…enjoy the rest of your day…I hope that it gets better."

I took another bite out of the sandwich and looked away. When I was done, I noticed that it was dark out and time for me to go home and face the music. The walk back home was a long one, but when I walked in, I was surprised to see that he wasn't waiting for me. I have to admit that it was a little disappointing, but I was glad that I didn't have to deal with him. When I walked into the kitchen, I noticed that a plate of food was waiting on the counter with a note that said, "We'll talk in the morning." I grabbed the plate and sat at the kitchen table. It was so quiet in the house, I could hear myself chew. When I was done, I placed the plate in the sink and proceeded down the hall.

I opened the door. Grace was already in the bed, asleep. I walked over to her bed and stood over her. She didn't move. I sighed and began to remove my clothing. Once in the bed, I found myself staring at the wall. My thoughts were all over the place, but I silenced them. It'd been a long day. All I wanted to do was go to sleep.

The next morning, I looked over to find that Grace was already gone, but on her bed sat my dad who was waiting for me to wake up.

"What am I doing wrong, Peaches?"

Rubbing sleep from my eyes, I asked, "Is that a trick question?"

"Come on, Peaches…I do everything for you girls…I can't do any more than that."

"Well, dad…if you can't do any more…and you've done all that you can…nothing that I say will get you to do more than that."

"Peaches, I don't know why you treat me like I'm your enemy."

"Dad…I'm just going through some stuff, right now…that's all…"

"But you're not going to school…"

"Right now, school is the last thing on my mind."

"Well, it should be your first…you only have one job, Peaches…and that's to be the best daughter that you can be and that requires you going to school."

"I hate that school and I hate those people at that school."

"You don't have to love them to do what you have to do…when you graduate, you will never see them again. Look at it this way…pretend that you're on a drive…"

"Really? You're going to do this now?"

"Peaches…listen…you know the trees that you see as you travel down the road? You will only see those trees again if you take that same road again…"

"Huh?"

"Peaches, there is a whole world out there. You want to take the 'road less traveled'…"

"Isn't that how people get lost…taking roads that are less traveled?"

He huffed. "The point is…you want to get the hell up out of here. There's nothing here for you…Chicago is great, but there's nothing really here. You don't have a record. You don't have any kids…"

"Not now…" I said, thinking about Genesis.

"Yep…not now. You have a long life ahead of you. You can live your life…see the world…and then one day, you will settle down with someone who will love you forever, and you can have kids…make me a grand-dad…" He smiled.

I started to cry.

He came over and wrapped his arm around me. "Now, let's get up and go to school…okay?"

I didn't respond. He stood to leave the room. I thought about what he said and decided to get up and go to school, but when I arrived there, I just couldn't do it. I just couldn't walk through those doors, so I turned around and walked to the mall.

Once there, I grabbed the same seat near the water fountain and looked around. Suddenly, I heard a voice over my shoulder. "Hey Peaches…"

I didn't want to be bothered so I pretended not to hear him.

"Peaches," he called.

I stood up and began to walk away. I was halfway across the mall when I heard it again. "Peaches!"

I flipped around and said, "Dang dude…can't you take a hint?"

"What 'hint' is that?"

"That I don't want to be bothered…you chasing me like I owe you money," I said, trying to catch my breath.

"I was…I was…" he stuttered.

"Were you waiting for me?"

"Kinda…"

"Can you, please, stop?"

"Ummmmmm…."

"Now, go and find somebody else to stalk," I said, walking away. I walked over to the food court. Just as my butt hit the seat, he said, "I was just thinking…"

My eyes widened. "Do I need to call somebody? What the fuck do you want?"

"I'm just trying to be nice…" he said, with a pitiful look on his face.

"I'm just trying to be by myself."

"Okay…then I won't bother you."

"Good…" I dropped my head on my arms, pretending to go to sleep. I was peeking through my arms when I saw his legs standing next to the table. I looked up. "This is my fault for forgetting my 'Stalker Repellent.'"

He smiled. "You know…you kinda remind me of someone."

"Do I remind you of a person who doesn't give a fuck?"

He laughed. "No really…you do remind me of someone."

"That's great…okay…I remind you of someone…got it." I placed my head back on the table.

"Are you hungry?" he asked.

"If I say 'no', will you walk away?"

"Probably not…"

I sighed. "Then, I guess I'm hungry."

He smiled. "I'll be right back."

Chapter 23

The next day, I got up, got dressed, and left for the mall. I was out on the sidewalk when I dropped my bus card. I looked down to pick it up when someone walked up. I looked up to find him standing in front of me.

"What the hell?" I asked, surprised that he was standing in front of me.

He smiled. "You live over here too? Wow…what are the odds?"

"Bullshit…I've lived here for most of my life and I've never seen you."

"Well…I don't live here…I have family over here."

"Really?"

"Yep…"

I looked him over. "Well…that's nice." I turned to walk away.

He ran up behind me. "So…you're going to the mall?"

"Are you going to the mall?" I asked.

"Yes…"

"Then, I'm not going to the mall."

He frowned.

I closed my eyes. When I opened them, he was standing there with the biggest smile on his face.

"Ummmmm…"

"Gage," he replied.

"Gage…yeah…Gage…look, I'm going to the mall, but I want to go by myself. Is that okay?"

"Sure, but you don't mind if we ride the bus together…I mean, we are going to the same place."

I sighed. "I can't prevent you from riding the bus."

"But you can prevent me from sitting next to you…I hope that you won't do that. I would really like to sit next to you."

"Why?" I asked, becoming more annoyed.

"It's a bus ride, Peaches…I'm not trying to marry you."

I thought about it for a second and said, "Sure…okay."

When the bus pulled up and the doors swung open, he said, "After you."

I climbed on. I was about to use my bus card, but he said, "Put that away…I got this." He swiped his card twice and followed me to the back of the bus.

When he sat down, he accidentally sat down on the side of my thigh.

"Sorry about that…"

I didn't respond.

"Was that your house? I saw you come out of it."

"You know what's a lost art?" I asked, annoyed.

"Ummmmmm…no…"

"Minding your own business…I remember a time when people did that? What happened to those days?'

"I was just asking…"

"Don't…" I frowned. "And why do you wanna know?"

He shrugged. "No particular reason…just making conversation. Seems like a nice house…"

"Houses are only as nice as its occupants…"

"I guess…soooooooooo…why are you going to the mall?" he asked.

"Do you have to talk?"

He huffed into the palms of his hands. "Why not? My breath stink?"

"When I agreed that you could sit next to me, I thought that you would look out of the window or something…"

"So you want me to look out of the window…like some kid or maybe a dog?"

"Dogs don't ride buses…unless they're one of those seeing-eye dogs…and even they know how to sit q-u-i-e-t-l-y."

He frowned. He looked out of the window for a minute and then asked again, "Sooooooo…why are you going to the mall?"

"Since you can't seem to shut up…I'm ditching…okay?"

"Ditching?" he asked. "Ditching what?"

"I wish I could ditch you…"

Ignoring me, he continued. "I'm going to pick up my little sister…"

"And I'm supposed to care?"

He frowned. "You ain't gon' ever get a man acting like that."

"And I ain't looking for one…" I sighed.

"You know, Peaches…the walls that we build to keep out pain and sadness also keeps out love and happiness."

"How philosophical of you…did you read that on the bathroom wall or did you just pull that out of your ass?"

He sucked his teeth. "You know…I could be like most people and not give a shit…"

"And oh, what a world this would be…" I sang.

The bus pulled into the mall. He stood to let me walk out first. We stepped off of the bus.

"Peaches…I don't know why you're so mean to me. You don't even know who I am…I've never done anything to you…And I promise you, once you get to know me, you're going to say, "Wow, you're just like a brother to me.""

"I wouldn't go that far…"

"Give me a chance…you won't regret it. At least, not in the beginning."

"But in the end?"

"You're going to say, 'Wow…wow…'"

"Wow?" I laughed – something that I hadn't done in a really long time.

"Wow…" he confirmed.

"Okay…I can't wait for the 'wow' part…"

"Me neither, I just can't wait…" He smiled. "You want to get something to eat?"

I hesitated and said, "Sure."

We walked over to one of the restaurants, grabbed some food, and had a seat. As he spoke, I couldn't help, but notice how "plain" he was. He wasn't cute, but he wasn't ugly either. His clothes were nice – a cross between 'hood' and 'burbs'. I watched him eat. He didn't eat like a man or like one that I was accustomed to. I was used to them taking large bites out of their food like most carnivores. He didn't do that. He nibbled like a girl trying to make a good first impression. He was a little "dainty", but I wrote it off to good home-training. Me? I wasn't playing nor pretending. I ate my food like a person who had someone standing over her waiting to snatch her plate.

"Look at me…running my mouth…this was about you…"

When he said that, something "softened" inside of me. "Naw…I'm okay…I'm just hanging out…"

"I'm glad…"

"You bought me lunch two days in a row…I can pay you back, if you want."

"Naw…it's cool. I can afford to buy you something to eat."

"Thank you…"

"But I wasn't always able to…"

"You had a hard life?" I asked.

He began to breathe heavily. "Hard is an understatement."

"I'm sorry…"

"You should be," he said.

"Excuse me?"

He slowed down his breathing. "I'm just saying…we should all feel sorry when a child struggles…especially, to no fault of his own…"

"You're right…"

"But you look like you've had a good life," he said.

"Looks can be deceiving…"

"Yes, they can," he said. "Yes, they can…"

Chapter 24

The weatherman called for sunny skies and yet, I could tell that a storm was coming and it was waiting for me in the kitchen.

"I got a call from your school, again," he said. When I walked into the house, he was waiting for me. I rolled my eyes into the back of my head. "You know, dad…you know how you feel when we tell you that a bill collector called?"

"Yep…"

Rolling my eyes back forward and frowning, I said, "Well, that's how I feel when you tell me that the school called…"

"If your ass was at school, they wouldn't call…"

"And if you paid your bills, bill collectors wouldn't call…"

"Don't worry about my bills…" he said.

"Don't worry about…" I began, but then said, "Never-mind…"

He frowned.

"I just know how much you hate it when they call and you hate it more when we tell you that they called…it's annoying and yet, here you are…"

"I'm going to pay my bills…when are you going to take your ass back to school?"

Grabbing some cookies, I tried to pretend like I didn't hear him. "Can I just eat?"

He walked over and stood next to me. "I asked you a question…"

"I heard what you said, dad…" I stood to walk over to the refrigerator.

"I can pay bills if I wasn't buying food…"

Pouring the milk into a cup, I said, "You want me to pay you back for the cookies?"

"And how will you do that without a pot to piss in and a window to throw it out of."

"Wow…that's real classy, dad…I'm trying to eat and you're talking about piss." I shook my head. "Maybe you would like for me to throw it up and put them back in the box…talking about piss while I'm trying to eat."

"All I'm saying is…I do everything for y'all…"

I began to clap. "There's nothing more special than a parent who brags about meeting his parental duties. You want an award for doing what you're supposed to be doing?"

"No…"

"How would you feel if every time you look up, I'm bragging about being a kid?"

"You couldn't brag…look at your life…they don't give awards to kids who ditch school."

"And he leads with an upper-cut…" I paused and shook my head. "Dang, dad…if I'd known better, I would have come prepared."

"For what?"

"This afternoon beat-down…" I shook my head. "I didn't ask to be here…the least you can do is let me eat in peace…"

"Ummmmm, I feed you, clothed you, put a roof over your head…I don't have to give you any 'peace'…just like I don't have to stay out of your business. Matter of fact…you ain't got no damn business. As long as the state is in my business, yo' business is my business and right now, I want to know why your ass ain't been going to school?"

Slurping the milk, I said, "Dad…"

He interrupted me. "And what the hell is going on with you and Grace?"

"Nothing's going on with me and Grace…"

"Something's going on, Peaches…I'm sick of this shit. You think that I'm stupid. Don't run game on me and don't piss on me and call it rain…"

"Again with the piss, dad?"

"Look…I've tried to be patient with you, but just like I don't owe you 'peace', I don't owe you 'patience'…now, if you want to be a failure, that's fine, but do it somewhere else. I'm not going to continue to throw money, time, and love…into a pit…"

"Is that how you see me, dad? As a pit…"

"I look at you and I don't know what I see, but I know this much…no fool continues to invest in something that does nothing but fail. I want a return on my investment…so get your shit together."

I'd, suddenly, lost my appetite. I stood to throw my food into the garbage. He walked over and stood between me and the garbage.

"Until you start buying food…you don't throw shit away." He stuck out his chest and began to breathe heavily. I took the cookies back to the counter and finished them.

"Now…I don't want my phone ringing, today…unless, somebody's calling to tell me that I won a million dollars…and since we both know that the odds of that happening are slim to none, my phone better not ring…do we have an understanding?"

"Sure," I mumbled.

"That didn't sound like a 'yes'…" he said.

I sighed. "Yes…"

He turned and walked out of the room.

"Asshole," I mumbled to myself.

I wasn't thinking about his ass. He can threaten me until his teeth fall out, but I wasn't going. I don't know why he thought that shit was going to work on someone who has been pushing the limits since she pushed herself out of her mother's womb. I waited until he left and I went back to the mall.

When I walked into the mall, I found him waiting for me. He had the biggest smile on his face. "Hey Peaches..."

I walked up to him. I realized that he was the only person willing to tolerate my bullshit, so I decided to give him a chance. "Hey Gage..."

When, I approached him, he leaned in and wrapped his arms around my shoulders. I loved how his face felt against mine. He was warm and he smelled good. When he released me, he paused to look me in the eyes. "Hungry?"

"Naw, I'm still trying to 'digest' breakfast."

"What did you have to eat?"

"A bowl of bullshit…with a side of 'getting on my gad-damn nerves'…"

"Sounds delicious…" he joked.

"It would have been if I wasn't on a no-bullshit diet…"

He laughed.

"You wanna talk about it?"

This time, I decided to share. Just to see what he would say. "I'm thinking about dropping out…"

"Out of school or life?"

"Out of school…"

"Based on the time that you spend at the mall…seems like you've already made up your mind."

"I could say the same about you…" I said.

"Naw, sweetie…don't let the baby-face fool you…I'm twenty-one."

"You're a MAN?"

He looked down at his crotch and said, "I hope so…"

I giggled. "I mean…you know what I mean."

"Why don't you want to go to school?"

"I hate that school…"

"Most people hate school…even the people who get paid to be there, hate school."

"Exactly…" I said.

"But if all your dad is doing is trying to make you go to school, so that you can be somebody, you're getting off easy."

"But…something bad happened…I just don't want to go back…and look at those people."

"Kids have short attention spans…what was gossip today is 'silence' tomorrow…we tend to think that people really care about what's going on in our lives…only those who don't have a life are the ones looking for one. I wouldn't sweat it…you would have had to really do something crazy for them to care about it this long."

"I did…"

"You want to tell me?"

"Naw…I'm good…"

"Secrets kill, Peaches…"

"Oh…believe me…I know that they do."

"Life is about steps, Peaches and school is one of those steps."

"Are you about to start preaching?"

"No…only because I left my collection plate at home, but your dad is right…it's hard enough, out here, without an education…why would you want to complicate your life over something that takes a short time to do?"

"Ummmmmm…the minimum is twelve years. Criminals get less time than that…"

He stopped and took my hand. "Do what your dad asks of you…you only have a couple of years left…I promise…you're going to be happy that you did."

"And why do you care if I go to school?"

"Because…"

"Because what?"

"Because if you go to school, I don't have to worry about you breaking in my house and stealing my TVs…" he laughed.

"You have your own house?"

"I have a lot of stuff, Peaches and maybe…one day…AFTER you get out school, you can come over…and see my stuff. All of it…"

"All of it…" I joked.

"All of it…" he confirmed.

I smiled. "Bribery…I like it, but it only works if what you're offering is something that I want."

He moved in close and placed his lips against my cheek. "Go to school, Peaches…if not for you…do it for me."

That was sweet. Still thinking about the kiss, I said, "I will."

Chapter 25

The next morning, I was up so early, I woke up the birds. I looked over at Grace who was still sleeping. After saying my morning prayer, I stood and walked over to the closet to find something nice to wear to school. Considering that it was my first day back, I wanted to look good. As I began to pull things out of the closet, I felt something burning a hole in the back of my head. I turned to find her looking at me.

"I'm sorry if I woke you up," I said.

"I'm just making sure that you're not wearing anything that belongs to me."

I was so glad that she was speaking to me that I bit my tongue and said, "No…I would never do that without asking you."

"See that you don't", she said, before pulling the blankets back over her head.

Since we were "talking", I decided to say, "I miss you."

She didn't respond.

I began to walk over to her bed when the door flew open. "What did I tell you?" He said walking into the room.

"Dad, can you knock? We're not little girls anymore," I said.

"You ain't got nothing that I've never seen before…'cause you got some hair where none used to be doesn't give you the right to tell me not to walk into a room that I'm paying for."

I just looked at him.

"Now, didn't you and I talk, yesterday? I swear that that was you at the table. I KNOW that it wasn't Grace because I NEVER have to talk to Grace…"

"Yep, daddy…you never have to talk to Grace…"

She removed the blankets. "Keep my name out of your mouth."

Feeling cornered, I said, "I can say what the hell I want to say…"

She stood. "No, you can't…"

"Yes, I can…"

"No, you can't…" she walked over and stood in my face.

"Get out of my face, Grace…"

She pushed me. "Or what?"

I looked at her and then over at my dad who wasn't intervening. I realized that I was on my own.

"Grace…don't touch me…"

"Why not? You let other people touch you."

"She let who touch her?" he asked.

I looked at her. "She doesn't know what she's talking about…"

She stopped, smiled, and stuck her finger in the middle of my forehead. "Stay out of my face, little girl." She turned and walked out of the room.

He looked at me. "What was that about?"

"Who knows? And y'all think that I'm crazy."

Constantly looking over my shoulder, I spent most of my day, trying to find out what I needed to do to get caught up and once I did, I, immediately, got started. And when my day was done, I spent the afternoon with Gage. He was so proud to hear that I'd return to school that he decided to reward me.

We'd just finished eating when he handed me a gold box with a beautiful gold ribbon wrapped around it.

"Wow…what is this?" I asked.

"Open it," he encouraged.

I looked at it for a second before ripping it open. My mouth fell open as the light bounced off its contents. I pulled it from the box. It was a beautiful gold locket.

"Open it," he said.

I opened it to find a picture of a key. "Oh wow…that is so cute…what does it mean?"

He smiled and took my hand. "I know that this is soon, but I want you to know that I'm serious…if you graduate. I mean WHEN you graduate…you can come and stay with me."

"Stay with you?"

"Yeah…then you'll be legal and by that time…I would have shown you what I'm really about."

My eyes began to fill with tears. "I've never had anyone speak to me that way…"

"It's nothing…believe me."

If he only knew how bad I wanted to climb over the table and hug him, but something in me wouldn't allow me. I'd already trusted somebody and that got me hurt and I wasn't in any rush to get hurt again. "I'm really glad that you walked up to me that day."

"Peaches…it was something about you…like maybe, this is meant to be….well, not maybe…this was definitely meant to be."

"Meant to be what?" I asked.

He touched my hand. "The universe has a unique way of bringing people together…the way that it led me to you…who knows what it's got planned for you…I mean…for us." He stood to clear the table. "Now, what do you want to do next?"

"Whatever you want to do…" I said, looking at the necklace.

"Here…let me put that on for you." He walked over, placed the chain on my neck, and leaned down to kiss me behind the ear. "How about we end the night with a movie?"

My heart was so full, I couldn't speak.

"Is that a 'yes?'"

"Yes."

He smiled as we walked away.

He let me choose the movie. It was some "chick-flick" about a woman who lost a man, found him, lost him, found him again, and then they lived happily-ever-after. I wish I could tell you more about the movie, but we started kissing during the beginning credits and didn't stop until they turned the lights on. It was then, that I realized that there may be hope for me.

This time he offered to give me a ride home. As we walked through the parking lot searching for his car. I stopped by every rusty and dented car in the lot, but he kept walking until we found ourselves standing in front of a Cadillac, jet black, with matching rims. He walked around and opened the door for me. Once inside, he adjusted the seat for me.

"I wanna make sure that you're comfortable…"

I smiled. "What about your sister?"

"Today, is about me and you…she's an adult. She'll be fine."

He started the car and pulled off. The quiet roar of the engine made me feel right at home. He turned on some music that, softly, filled the cabin of the car. The leather seats embraced me - felt like a warm hug. All I could think about was the fact that, soon, I would have to get out. When he pulled in front of my house, he said, "Let me get your door."

When he came around, he leaned in and kissed me on the cheek. Over his shoulder, I could see someone peeking through the window.

"If you want, I can swoop by here, pick you up, and take you to school…"

"That would be so nice…" I stepped out of the car.

"Then, it's a date…that way I can make sure that you get there."

I laughed. "I'll be standing on the curb." I waved as I watched him jump in and pull off. I turned and looked at the house. As I approached the door, I noticed that it was already open. I walked in and found her waiting for me.

"Another one," she began.

"So we're talking?"

"I'm just trying to plan my life…just in case you mess up again."

I sat across from her. "Grace…I messed up. I was young…"

"Did you have some birthdays that I'm not aware of? You're still young…" she reminded.

"This time it's different…we're not having sex. He cares about me…he respects me. He even got me to go back to school…"

She huffed. "Some stranger walks into your life and now, you've changed. When the people who love you…who's been here for you…couldn't get you to do nothing."

"It shouldn't matter who convinced me…"

"Oh, but it should…cause when that one walks away, we will still be here."

"I don't know what you want from me, Grace…I'm trying."

"You're always trying…this time, try to get it right. I can't bury another dead baby."

Suddenly, my dad walked in the room. "A dead baby? What is she talking about, Peaches?"

I jumped up and stood in front of her. "She's not talking about anything."

She pushed me out of the way.

"Enough!!!!! GRACE, what dead baby?" he asked.

She looked at him and looked at me.

It was time to stop this. "Dad...she was my baby....I had a baby."

"Baby? When the hell did you have a baby?"

"A year ago," I confirmed.

He stumbled backwards onto the couch. "A year ago? Stop lying."

I looked down at the floor. "I'm not lying."

"Where the hell was I?"

"You were at work, daddy." Grace and I sat down across from him.

He placed his head in his hands. "I can't believe this shit..."

We didn't respond.

"A gad-damn baby…Where?"

"I had her in the bathroom…"

"The bathroom? How?"

"Daddy…please…"

"I'm just trying to understand what the hell happened…"

I took a deep breath. The whole time that I told the story, he listened without saying a word. When I was done, he asked. "Where is she?"

Hesitating, I said, "Out back."

"Out back, where?" he asked.

We both pointed towards the back door. He turned and looked. He took a deep breath and said, "You have got to be fucking kidding me."

We didn't respond.

He sighed, shook his head, and said, "I want to see her."

We took him out back to her resting place. He looked at the ground that was now covered in grass and weeds and said, "All this time, I've been stepping on my grandbaby's grave?" He kneeled down and touched the ground. He looked up at me and shook his head. "I can't believe this shit."

I opened my mouth to speak, but he interrupted me. "Don't talk…don't fucking say a word."

With tears in his eyes, he turned to Grace and stuck his finger in her chest. "YOU…you were in on this…"

She looked down at the ground.

"You helped hide this from me for an entire year. What does that say about you? She died and then you killed her again by throwing her away and hiding her like she was nothing."

"No, daddy…I wanted to tell you but…" she said.

"But what? You chose to keep your mouth shut? Some secrets are worth keeping…surprise birthday parties…where you hide Christmas gifts…shit like that, but this…this is serious…do you understand that?"

"Yes…" she said.

"I can't believe this shit…right under my fucking nose…Do you know how many times I've been back here…cut this grass…barbequed…sat in my lawn chair and my grandbaby was back here all this time?"

We didn't answer.

He kneeled, again, over her grave. "Get out of my fucking face…"

We turned and walked back into the house. We looked out of the kitchen window into the backyard to find him sitting next to her grave. He was talking to the ground. That night before we went to bed, we looked out to find him still sitting there and when we woke up the next morning, we looked out to find him lying next to her grave, asleep. We went to school and when we came home, we'd found that he'd planted flowers around her grave.

Finally, he walked into the house covered in mud. He looked at me, but didn't speak.

I cried all day long. Grace became frustrated. She sat up in her bed. "Shut the hell up!"

I wiped the tears from my face. "Grace, he doesn't want me here."

She laid down and placed the covers over her head.

"He hates me. You hate me…" I wiped the tears from my eyes.

She looked up. "Peaches, you just don't get it…when we were kids…doing something stupid might have been cute, but we're almost adults…the shit gets old." She placed the cover back over her head.

I covered my face and spoke into my hands. "I made a mistake."

She sat up again. "Own your shit, Peaches…own it. That's the only way…"

"But I have…"

"Well…in this case, I guess it's not enough…" She turned her back to me.

I was so upset. I had to get out of there. I grabbed a sweater and walked out of the house. I decided that the safest place to hide my tears would be the library. There, I didn't have to worry about anyone bothering me and I really needed to sort things out. Once there, I walked inside and grabbed a seat in the Adult Fiction section. I grabbed a random book off of the shelf and sat in the middle of the floor to read it. At first, I just stared at it, but then decided to open its pages. I was so engrossed in its contents that I didn't realize how late it was. The librarian approached me. "We're closing...you need to come up to the desk if you're checking out something."

"Oh no...thank you...I'm just going to head out..."

"Okay..."

I put the book back and she walked me to the door. Locking the door behind me, she said, "Be safe..."

I waved. "Oh, I'm fine...thanks..." Once outside, I couldn't help but notice how quiet it was. *Better take a shortcut...* I thought to myself. I walked two blocks and noticed a crowd of boys on the streets. I didn't feel like dealing with their nonsense and decided to take the alley. I was a block away from the house when, suddenly, I heard a dog barking. I looked to see where the noise was coming from. I began to walk faster when I heard a bottle roll across the pavement. I started to run when someone stepped out of the darkness and into the alley.

"Hey Peaches…" they said.

Shit. "Who is that?"

They walked and stood under the street light. "You didn't think that we forgot about you…did you?"

I turned to run in the other direction. They ran behind me and when they caught up with me, they grabbed me.

"Hey girlfriend…" he said.

I looked over his shoulder. "Carlton, what do you want?"

His brother tightened his grip. "Don't talk to him…talk to me…"

I pushed him away from me. "Get out of my way…"

He jumped in front of me. "Why? We just got here and there's still that little matter of...you know..."

I frowned. "Fuck you...I'm going home..."

"No...you're not..." He grabbed Carlton. "And you owe my brother an apology."

"I don't owe him anything, because I didn't do anything to him."

"Oh, yes you did..." He grabbed Carlton and pulled him under the streetlight. "Show her..."

"No," he said.

"Don't make me kick your ass...show her," he demanded.

Carlton hesitated, but then he opened his mouth.

"I can't see anything..."

"You trying to be funny, right?" his brother asked. He grabbed Carlton by the face and forced his mouth wide open.

I jumped back. "What happened to his tongue?"

"You took a chunk of it when you came to the house that night..."

"Damn, she messed him up…kinda hard to kiss with half-a-tongue…"

He frowned. "You think that shit's funny."

"No…I don't…"

Then, he grabbed Carlton by the pants. They wrestled for his zipper. Finally, his pants fell to his knees. His brother pointed at his penis. "And like that wasn't bad enough…you had to do this…"

Curious, I leaned in to see what he was pointing at. "Where's his hair," I asked.

"You know what happened to his hair and now, the shit won't grew back…looks like he got a damn hairless Chihuahua stuck in his damn pants. What is he going to do with that unattractive shit? Huh?"

"Ummmmmm…he could join a circus…maybe, a freak show?"

"ORRRRRRRRR…since you did the shit, you can be the one to like it…for the rest of your life."

"You have lost your damn mind...I wouldn't fuck him again if his dick had the cure for Cancer in it and I was knocking on Death's door."

"Well, that's a shame..."

"I guess it is...and on that note...good-bye..?" I said, walking away.

"No, 'good-byes' for you..." He walked towards me. "You still have work to do..."

I looked around until I found a large rock on the ground. "Come closer and I'm going to finish where I left off..."

He walked closer. "It's two against one..."

I looked at my hand. "Yep...it's two against one..."

When he was within arm's reach, I swung as hard as I could. I felt my hand hit something and then there was a loud *thud!* I looked down. The whole side of his face was bloodied. I looked up at Carlton and said, "Your turn..."

He turned and ran off, leaving his brother on the pavement. Still holding the brick in my hand, I walked away, leaving him there too.

When I got home, the whole house was dark. I walked into the bathroom, sat the brick down on the sink, and washed my hands. I decided to wash the brick to remove any evidence. When I was done, I went into my room and waited for the knock on the door.

Chapter 26

The last two years in that house were a blur. We all did what we had to do and that's it. Except for a few "niceties", we didn't speak. I couldn't wait to get out of there. The closer we got to the date, the more anxious I became. I was like a prisoner waiting to be released. As I got closer to my graduation date, Gage and I agreed that I would come and stay with him for a while and he would help me get on my feet. All I had to do was make sure that I didn't fuck up again and I was "home-free."

And when we graduated, our dad didn't even bother to show up. It was like the day never happened. The day after graduation meant more to him, because now he could start counting down the days until eviction. His desire for us to leave became evident when I walked out of my bedroom one morning and instead of saying "good morning", he said, "You still here?"

"Yes, dad…sorry to disappoint you," I said, rubbing 'sleep' from my eyes. Because Grace and I wasn't 'really' speaking…accept for the occasional "Kiss my ass", I didn't even know that she was gone, so when she walked in the house, she scared the shit out of us.

"Where have you been?" he asked.

"I was out job hunting," she said.

He looked at me. "Job hunting…you hear that, Peaches? Grace went job hunting."

Grabbing a bowl from the cabinet, I said, "Are you trying to tell me something, dad?"

"I'm not trying to tell you anything…I'm telling you, you need to find a job."

"Dad, I won't be here too much longer…"

He walked over. "Peaches, don't tease me…"

Frowning, I said, "I have a plan."

"If that plan includes getting the fuck out, then it sounds like a damn good plan…"

I sighed.

"And, exactly, what is this plan of yours?"

"I have a friend and he said that once I graduate I could come and stay with him…"

"Really? So you work hard all of these years just to go and shack-up with some man you barely know?"

"I know him, dad. We've been dating a while."

"Really? And you just gon' move in with him?"

"Yes, dad…"

He looked at me. "You go from one fucked-up thing to another…why don't you try some normal shit. Oh, I forgot…you're not normal."

"You did it with mama…"

"I loved your mother…"

"Well, I love him…and…I think he loves me."

"You think? That's some shit you should know before you start moving in with folks. I don't want you packing your stuff up, getting me all excited, just to get over there and find out that it wasn't what you thought it was and wind-up back here. I got plans for that room…"

"Wow, dad…don't give me too much love…"

"I'm just saying…I've done my job. Now, it's time for y'all to grow-up and get out."

"Why don't you say what's really on your mind, dad…"

"I'm saying it…you ain't listening…"

Suddenly, Grace interrupted. "As much as I enjoy these loving family moments, I'm going to get back out there…"

He turned. "You see that, Peaches…she's going to get back out there…"

I, suddenly, lost my appetite. I sighed and put the bowl down. "I'm going to get out of here too."

"You are? Praise Jesus…" he said, sarcastically.

After showering and getting dressed, I decided to go to the mall to look for Gage. I was ready to end this madness and move on with my life. I was walking out of the front door when I noticed, Grace's purse on the ground. I looked around, but she was nowhere to be seen. This was strange, even for her. I picked it up and went back into the house.

"Back already?" he asked.

I frowned. "Grace dropped her purse on the ground."

"She probably decided to hang-out with her friends. She'll be back for it."

"Dad, a woman never, just, leaves her purse…something's not right." I looked through it. "Everything is still in here except for her favorite pictures…"

"Well…if they're her favorite, she'll be back for them. Now, those jobs won't find themselves."

I frowned and walked out of the house.

Grace & Peaches

Chapter 27

After driving around for thirty minutes, we arrived in front of a two-flat that was located on the Chicago's south-side. The man pulled around to the back of the house. He parked it and stepped out of the car. He looked around for a second before walking around to my side of the car. He opened the door, looked in, and smiled. I wanted to run, but the woman sitting next to me was holding a knife. "Don't even think about it," she said.

Afraid, I said, "What do you want?"

"You," she said.

"Me? For what?" I asked, fighting back tears.

She leaned over to whisper in my ear. "It's a surprise."

"What are you talking about?" I asked.

The man held out his hand. "See…I kept my word."

"What word?" Panicking, I said, "Look, I don't know what this is about…"

"Get out of the car," she said.

"Please…please…let me go," I begged.

He leaned into the car. "If I have to drag you out of this car, it's going to hurt and I don't want to hurt you. Now, come on, sweetie. We have so much to talk about."

"Well, can we talk about it here?" I asked, frantically.

The woman said, "Bitch, I'm hungry. You need to get out of this car."

He stuck out his hand again. "You don't want me to beg. Now, come on."

The woman placed the knife against my throat. "Get out."

I looked at her and back at him. Realizing that I had no choice, I slid across the seat. He took my hand. "I've been missing you."

As we walked towards the house, I kicked off one of my shoes in an attempt to distract them, but they knew something was up. This angered them. She picked up the shoe and hit me in the face.

"Arrrrrrrrggggghhhhh!" I grimaced in pain.

She raised the shoe to hit me again.

He caught her arm. "Don't go messing up her face. She has to look good for the camera."

Chapter 28

That night, I couldn't sleep. I couldn't believe that he refused to call the police – insisting that she was just out celebrating, but I knew that he was wrong. She wouldn't do that. She wouldn't just up and leave without saying a word. Now, me? Yes, in a damn heartbeat, but not Grace. So I spent the whole night dialing her phone. "Grace, call me…" Dialed again. "Grace, call me when you get this message." Dialed again. "Grace, stop fucking around…call me, please." She never returned my call and when she didn't walk in the door, I was pissed.

I banged on his door. When he didn't answer, I walked in his bedroom, unannounced. She jumped up and tried covering herself.

I frowned. "Ain't nobody looking at you…where's my daddy?"

She pointed towards the hall. I walked out and slammed the door behind me. I opened the bathroom door and found him sitting on the toilet.

"The fuck, girl…don't you know how to knock?"

I ignored his question. "Grace didn't come home."

"Are you sure?" he asked, trying to cover himself.

I crossed my arms. "I sleep right across from her. I would know if she came home."

"Okay…I will call the police."

I waited for him to make the call.

"Can I wipe my ass?"

"As long as it doesn't take all day…" I slammed the door and walked down the hall to wait for him.

When he walked in, he said, "We're not calling the police."

"What? Are you serious?" I asked.

"Yes…your sister is eighteen. She's an adult…"

"She's an adult? What are you talking about?"

He pulled a shirt over his head. "Who am I to bother her if she wants to stay out all night until the next day?"

I was confused. "Because something could be wrong? She left her purse."

"What could be wrong, Peaches? She was in front of the house…who would snatch a grow-ass woman right out of her front yard?"

"Crazy people…that's who," I insisted.

He frowned. "I love my daughter, but really…who would want her that bad. Now, I'm sure that if we give her some time, she will just pop up like nothing happened."

"I can't believe you…"

He turned to walk out of the room. "She's not a baby anymore and neither are you."

I stood and walked towards the door. "Then, I will look for her."

"Sure, but you might want to change your clothes first."

I left without a plan or a clue. I barely got passed the front yard before I realized that I didn't know anything about her. I didn't know who her friends were, what places that she liked to hang out at – nothing. I decided to walk around, hoping that I would just run into someone familiar and after hours of nothing, I went back home.

When I walked in, he said, "Did you find her?"

"No, I didn't," I said frustrated.

"Peaches, you have to trust me. I had a sister. She did what she wanted when she wanted. If my parents called the police every time that she decided to be 'grown', the police would never have left our house. They would had to move in. I remember, one time, she left for a whole month…a whole month…and when she came back, that bitch…" He paused for a second and continued, "I know that it's not nice to speak ill of the dead, but she was a bitch. Anyway…the point is… parents have to step back and let their kids make their own mistakes. We have to allow them space to leave the nest…"

"Even when they can't fly?" I asked.

"That's the only way they'll learn. Now, watch…give her some time. She'll be back."

"I hope so…"

"She will and you and I will look back on this day and laugh."

I walked down the hall to our bedroom. I sat down and looked at her bed. I walked over and decided to make it for her. When I threw her blankets into the air, I caught her scent. I gathered her blankets and held them. I inhaled, deeply. I missed her so bad. "Grace, please come back home."

The next day, I went to the mall. Even though I wasn't up to seeing him, I thought that maybe he could help me find my sister, but he was nowhere to be found. I went back every day for an entire week, but he never returned. I prayed that nothing happened to him, but the truth is, I really didn't care. I needed to find my sister.

Chapter 29

I could no longer fight back my tears.

"Don't cry, sweetie," she said. "You want a sandwich?"

"I want to go home," I begged.

"And I want abs like Janet Jackson, but you don't see me crying. We have to all accept what God has given us and this, girlfriend, is what God has given you."

"Please…please…please…I'm begging you…"

"Girl, stop, cause it ain't gon' happen."

He walked into the room. "Follow me…"

"No…I don't want to," I said.

He walked over to me. "Don't be rude. When you're in somebody else's house, you follow their rules and the first one is, you do what I say, when I say it or that pretty lady siting behind you is going to cut you from the rooter to the scooter."

"The what?" the woman asked, laughing.

"I don't know…it's one of those things that folks from the south say."

"The south, where? South loop?"

"No, the south…Mississippi…"

"Sounds like some shit they would say," she said.

They stopped to look at the "elephant" in the room and remembered that they had something to do. "Let's go…" he demanded.

I stood and began to follow him.

"I'm so glad that you're here with us…I wouldn't have had it any other way."

I didn't respond.

He turned on the light in the hall. "My sister owns the first floor…so we have all of this to ourselves." He continued. "I know that this is new for you, so…look around…Mi Casa es Su Casa."

"What does that mean?" I asked.

"It means 'get comfortable cause you're going to be here a while…'"

"Why?"

He ignored my question and continued, "Now, they are all completely furnished. I like to keep them that way…you just never know when someone might want to stop by and sleepover…"

"Sleepover…" I heard her say from behind me.

He continued. "Just in case…"

"In case, of what?" I asked.

The woman giggled. "Let me give you all some space…"

"Don't pay her no mind…she's special and not always in a good way…"

He took me on a tour of his home. It was absolutely beautiful. From the hardwood floors, to the marble counters, everything was new. As he took me from room to room, he explained why the rooms were furnished the way that they were.

"This room…I like to call my playroom…it's when someone comes over and they want to …you know? Play..."

We proceeded to the next room. "This is one of my favorite rooms…" He smiled.

This room was completely dark. "Why is it so dark in here?"

"This room is for reflection…I like to come in here after I've had a long day and…reflect." He smiled.

The next room, was absolutely beautiful. There were bright white lights dangling from the ceiling over a king-sized bed that was draped in a red comforter and white satin sheets. The walls were painted black to match the black nightstand and dresser. Underneath the bed was a beautiful white carpet. He walked inside. "This is my room."

"This is nice," I said, nervously.

"Yeah…it serves its purpose."

"And what purpose is that?"

He smiled. "Come on…let me show you your room."

"My room?" I asked.

"Yes…there's a room just for you."

We walked down the hall to a room that was all pink. From the floor, to the walls, to the bed – everything was pink. It looked like someone painted the walls with vomit.

"You like it?" he asked.

I didn't know what to say to him. It dawned on me that he'd been planning this for a long time. What he had planned, I didn't know, but it was clear that he wasn't letting me go anytime soon. My survival instinct kicked in and I decided that I had to do what I could to get the hell out of here even if that meant being nice to his crazy ass.

"Yes….it's…beautiful."

"Just like you," he said.

"You did this…just for me?"

"For you," he confirmed.

I wasn't sure how to react.

"A 'thank you' would be nice."

"Oh, I'm sorry…my head was somewhere else…thank you."

He smiled. "Okay…get settled in…remember, you graduated today…today, is a big day for you…in more ways than one."

He walked out of the room and locked the door. I walked over and sat down on the side of the bed. *I have to get out of here.* I thought to myself. I looked around the room. As soon as I heard the sound of his footprints fade down the hall, I jumped up and began to search the room. I opened all of the drawers, looked inside of the closet, looked under the bed and there was nothing. I ran over to the window and tried to open it, but it was nailed shut. I tapped on the window and realized that it wasn't glass, but a type of hard plastic. I looked around the room for something to cut it, but there was nothing. I walked over to the bathroom and noticed that they'd hung up a nightgown on the door. On the sink was a towel, a toothbrush, a bar of soap, and a bottle of lubricant. I ran and tried to open the door, but I couldn't. Frustrated and defeated, I walked back over to the bed and began to cry. I was so tired. My eyes grew heavy. I did everything that I could to fight it, but the exhaustion was overwhelming. Suddenly, I lost the fight and drifted off to sleep.

Later, when I woke up, I found him standing over me. "Hey sleepy-head…" he said.

Startled, I jumped up. I didn't want to agitate him, so I said, "Hey…I'm sorry…I must have fallen to sleep."

"Yeah…you were knocked-out."

"This is so embarrassing…I've never done this before."

"Done what? Sleep?"

"Fallen asleep in a stranger's house."

"But we're not strangers…"

"What do you mean? I don't know you…"

"Don't do that…" he said. "You will hurt my feelings…especially, after all we've been through."

"Who? What are you talking about?" I asked.

He sighed. "You've hurt me…"

I hesitated, but reached out to touch him. "I'm sorry…I didn't mean to."

"Don't worry…you'll have more than enough time to make it up to me." We stared at each other. There was an uncomfortable silence in the air. The woman peeked her head in the room. "Dinner's ready…" she chimed.

He turned and said, "Let's go eat."

I stood and began to walk towards the door, "Oh, okay…if you say so."

He kissed me on the cheek. "I say so…"

As we proceeded down the hall, I tried to see if there were windows in any of the other rooms. From where I was standing, I couldn't tell if they were glass or plastic. He caught me looking.

"You don't plan on leaving us…do you? I would hate for you to do so…cause then I would have to look for you, again…find you…maybe find you in that nice little house of yours…with that wonderful fucking family…" He took a deep breath and continued. "But the next time, I won't be so nice."

Afraid, I said, "No…no…no…I wasn't thinking that. I just can't get over how nice your house looks."

He wrapped his arms around me. "You're going to love it here." After dragging me into the kitchen, he said, "Have a seat." He sat down next to me. "Smells good, Charlie…what are we eating?"

She walked over to the table and sat a plate of food in front of us.

There was something "oozing" all over my plate. "Excuse me…ummmmm, what is this?"

Charlie put her hands on her hips. "It's called, 'Free Food'…now, put some in your mouth and shut the fuck up."

Still afraid, but not willing to eat whatever this was on my plate, I said, "I'm not trying to be rude…"

She interrupted me. "But you are…"

I continued. "But it's bleeding…"

She frowned. "You wanna cook, bitch? I come in here and try to prepare something special for you and you wanna bitch cause it's bleeding…you're not supposed to cook your meat all the way through…the nutrients are in the blood."

I frowned. "There's other stuff in blood too."

She grabbed a knife and placed it against my throat. "In a minute, it won't be the other thing bleeding at this table."

The man, finally, spoke. "Charlie…stop it…she's new here. Let our guest get settled in for a second before you kill her."

"Kill me?"

He smiled. "Just kidding…"

She agreed. "Yeah, kidding…" She grabbed a plate of food and sat across from me. "Now, let's say grace…" They grabbed each other's hands. They looked at me, waiting for me to join them. I looked at the knife sitting next to them and then lifted my hands. She began. He stopped her. "We have a guest. Let's have her say it…"

"Well, she better hurry up before my food gets cold."

"You want me to say 'grace'?" For a second, I wanted to laugh. Watching them was comical, at best. Soon fear was replaced with hatred and disgust.

"I want you to hurry the fuck up…" she said, growing impatient.

Fighting them was useless, and I didn't give a fuck anymore, so I bowed my head, and said, "Our heavenly Father, we thank you for this food we are about to receive...except for whatever this red shit is on my plate."

She jumped up. "THAT'S IT!!!!! GET YOUR UNGRATEFUL ASS UP AND GO TO YOUR ROOM!!!!"

I stood up and walked towards the front door. There were three deadbolt locks on it.

"Where do you think you're going?" he asked.

"She said, 'Go to your room'…my room is at my house."

"You know what? You are making me tired…real tired…" she said. "Now, walk your annoying-ass down the hall before I get up and cut you."

I proceeded down the hall.

"And don't try no dumb-shit…'cause even though I'm tired, I always have the time and energy to fix dumb-shit…"

As soon as I walked into the room, someone ran up and locked the door behind me. The room was dark. The only light, in the room, was coming from the street light outside. I sat down on the bed. I'd been sitting there trying to figure out how I was going to get out of there when the door opened.

They both entered the room. The man turned on a light. He sat down in a chair across from me. "Where's the necklace that I gave you?"

"What necklace?" I asked.

He frowned.

"Ohhhhhhh…that necklace," I said, trying to think of a lie. "It was so pretty…I didn't want to break it…"

Pleased with my response, he smiled.

Nervous, I said, "Ummmmm…so when can I go home?"

"You're at home, Peaches…"

"Peaches?" *I should have known.* I thought to myself. "I'm sorry, but I'm not Peaches…"

"You just said that you had my necklace…now, how would you know about the necklace if you're not Peaches?"

"I was lying…I have no idea what you're talking about."

"Like you did when we first met…what was that name that you gave me?" He paused for a second and said, "Betty…yeah, that's the name…"

"Okay…look…I'm not lying…I'm her sister…"

The woman spoke. "Yeah right…Peaches."

"Seriously…look at me…" I, quickly, realized that that was a dumb thing to do. "Is this about, her? Do she owe you money? Did she hurt one of you?"

Ignoring me, he walked over and sat next to me. "We've all had a long day." He wrapped his arms around my shoulders, pinning my arms against me.

"What are you doing?" I began to wrestle with him.

"I'm going to give you a little something to help you sleep."

"Look, I'm not tired…" I tried to pushing away from him.

The woman walked over with some pills in her hands. "Open wide…"

"No," I said, trying to get away from them.

She sat the pills down and grabbed the knife. She pulled up my skirt and ran the blade down the inside of my thigh. She made a small incision on my leg.

"This can go in your mouth or in your vein…now, me, I prefer the vein, but I don't want to put any holes in your arms.

"Noooooooooo…" I begged.

She cut me again. "If I stick this in a little further, I could cut that main artery and leave you here to bleed-out…nice and slow. Do you want to bleed-out?"

I mumbled, "No…"

"Then, open your mouth."

I saw the blood running down the side of my leg. With tears in my eyes, I, slowly, opened my mouth. She placed the pills inside and handed me a bottle of water. I swallowed them. They felt like rocks going down my throat.

"Open, so I can make sure that you're not 'cheeking' them…"

Again, I opened my mouth. She looked inside. "Oooooooo…I'm going to like you."

He continued to hold me. My eyes grew heavy. I tried keeping them open, but I couldn't. The next thing I knew, everything was black.

Chapter 30

Memories of us playing in the yard flashed before my eyes. We were young, happy, and at home, together.

"She's sleeping like a baby,'" he said.

"She's so cute. At first, I didn't like her, but she's growing on me…" she said.

I tried opening my eyes. When I was finally able to open them, I saw them standing over me. He looked at her. "Close your mouth, Charlie…you're drooling all over the place."

She wiped her mouth. "My bad…"

He turned back to me and shoved a picture in my face. "Who are they?"

Groggily, I mumbled. "How…how did you get that?"

"It's what's left of your purse," she said.

I tried sitting up, but realized that I couldn't move my arms or legs. "Wait…what the fuck is this? What are you doing to me?"

"I thought that it would be better that we establish the rules…or better yet, an understanding of how things are going to go on from this point forward."

I looked down. "Where are my clothes?"

She exhaled. "Bitch, this ain't no game show, so stop with the damn questions…" She looked at her watch. "Matter of fact, can we hurry this up? My 'soaps' are coming on."

He shoved the picture in my face again. "Who is this?"

"It's my mama and her sisters….now, can I have my damn clothes?"

Frustrated, she said, "Another damn question…I'm telling ya'…one more question…I swear…I'm going to cut your fucking tongue out."

"Chill Charlie…" He turned back to me. "Their names?"

"Regan, Raven, Ivy, and Grace..." I blurted out.

"They all look so much alike. Especially, these two." He stared at it for a while. "Are these two twins?" He stuck the photo in my face again.

"Yes…" I said, trying to get out of the restraints. "It's fucking cold in here."

"It's hot as hell in the oven…you wanna go in the oven?"

He looked at her.

"That's all I'm saying…" she turned and left the room.

He turned back to me. "They're beautiful. They look just like you…you could be their twin," he said.

"I already have a twin…"

His eyes widened. "You never told me that you had a twin!"

"I haven't told you shit!!!"

"You're fucking with me, right?"

"No, I'm not!!!"

"I know Peaches when I see her."

"You don't know shit...obviously..."

"You're just trying to fuck with my head..."

"I'M NOT LYING TO YOU!!!!!"

He stood and walked over to the door. "Charlie!!! Charlie!!!!"

She walked in the room, frowning, and fixing her clothes. "What the hell is wrong with you? You scared the shit out of me. I was on the damn toilet. Almost made me piss all over myself."

"Get the tape..." he demanded.

"Awwwwwww...sucki, sucki, now...should I take a shower?"

He pushed her. "Get the damn tape."

She ran out of the room. He walked back over to the bed. "I know what you're trying to do, but it won't work. Now, you need to prepare yourself.

What's going to happen next is going to change all of our lives, but mostly yours."

"Why? Why?" I tried pulling at the restraints again.

She ran into the room, wearing a black negligee, and dangling a roll of tape from her hand. He grabbed the tape and said, "Not yet…I want her to simmer…"

She started to touch herself. "But I'm about to come to a boil."

He pushed her out of the room. "Then, take a cold shower…" He ripped a piece from the roll and placed it over my mouth. "I would place a piece over your eyes, but I wouldn't want you to miss anything."

Later that night, I heard the door open. In the darkness, I saw a shadow sweep across the room.

It climbed on top of me and said, "Welcome home…"

I tried to say, "No," but my mouth was taped shut, so I tried pulling my hands out of the ropes. I tried kicking her, but couldn't.

She said, "Shhhhhhhhhh…trying to hurt me is only going to cause you to hurt yourself." She kissed my cheek. "Stop moving…you're not going anywhere…" She laid on the side of me. I began to cry. She licked the tears from the side of my face. "I know that I was hard on you earlier, but it upsets me when he brings other girls home."

Huh?

She cupped my breast and bit me on the tip of my nipple.

I jumped.

"He always bring home something new…like I'm not good enough. I'm pretty, right?"

I couldn't respond.

"It makes me so jealous…now, the others? They were nothing. He flashed a smile and they followed him home like he had a $100 taped to his ass, but you were different. He looked for you…just had to have you." She bit me again. "You know what that means for me, right? I'm going to get your leftovers. I take care of him…I love him…and he will fuck you like I don't even exist and then come and climb in my bed like I don't know what he's doing." She slid my nipple into her mouth and began to suck hard like she was trying to rip the skin from my breast. I began to cry harder. She climbed back on top of me. "You know what they say about a woman scorned?"

Don't do this. Please, don't do this.

"Oh, but wouldn't it be funny if I took you right now…be the first to open you up? That would really fuck with him…knowing that someone took a bite out of his precious little Peaches."

No, please!!!!

She slid her hand between my legs and slid her finger inside of me. "Oooooooo, you are so tight. Are you a virgin?"

Please, I'm begging you…please…don't…

"Oooooooo, I would so love to be the one, but a man can tell when someone else has been 'pissing in his territory.'"

I closed my eyes. I didn't want to look in her face. I realized that there was nothing that I could do to stop what was going to happen next. I decided to lay still, so that she would do what she had to do and get it over with, but then I felt something rub up against my leg. *What is that?*

"You're not so fucking special…what's so special about you?" She slid her tongue between my legs. "Your shit taste like all of the other shit that he's brought home."

My thoughts began to race. She grabbed her knife. "I should split you open…" She ran the blade over my stomach and looked me in the eyes. "You think that it'll piss him off if I slice you from ear to ear?"

I stared at her.

"You have no idea how tempted I am to just end this shit, right now, but that would be no fun and believe me…I plan to have fun." She looked at me and pulled the tape from my mouth. "Look at me doing all of the talking…"

As soon as she removed it, I said, "I swear, bitch…I'm going to kill you…"

She laughed and laughed – so hard tears fell from her eyes. "You're going to kill me…that's cute." She stood to walk out of the room. Her robe fell open.

I looked at her. "What is that?" I asked, as it dangled between her legs.

She walked over, leaned in and licked my face. "His pleasure and your pain… and don't worry, sweetie. You will experience both. The best is yet to come."

Chapter 31

The next morning, I felt someone untying my hands. They untied my feet. "Come on…" he said. When I stood, he looked at the bed. There were spots of blood on the sheets. "Charlie!!!" he yelled.

She ran into the room.

"What is this?" he said, pointing at the bed.

She looked at the bed, looked at me, and then back at him. "It's a girl thing…give her to me and I will clean her up."

He snatched her by the arm. "Charlie…"

She exhaled. "I just talked to her…I promise."

"Talking causes bleeding?"

She sighed. "I'm sorry…"

He began to stroke her hair. "I know that this is hard for you, but we cannot take pleasure in this…"

"No?"

"No," he confirmed. "We have to stay focused…remember, this is not about rape, torture, or murder…"

"It's not?" she asked.

"No, there's something 'greater' happening here. Yes, we will hurt her, but we must not forget why we're doing it…"

She smiled. "Okay, daddy…"

He kissed her and said, "Get her ready so that she can eat…"

"Okay…"

She dragged me into the bathroom. She ripped the tape off of my mouth. "Got me washing your ass…who the fuck do he think I am?" She turned on the water. I was cold. I screamed. "Suck it up…" She washed me. When she was done, she dried my skin.

"Can I at least have some clothes?"

"You don't need them…takes too much time and effort to keep taking them on and off." She dragged me back into the bedroom.

"But can I…"

She slapped another piece of tape on my mouth. She shook me. "Now, listen to me. We're going to go in there and we are going to eat and the only time that I want to see your mouth moving is when you're chewing. You open it and I'm going to stick something in it…do you understand?"

I nodded my head, "Yes…"

"Now, let's go."

As we walked down the hall, I could hear him talking to himself in the kitchen. When we walked in, he turned and pretended that he was singing a song. *If I could wear your clothes, I'd pretend I was you and lose control…*

She pushed me into a seat. She walked over to the refrigerator and pulled some items out of it. He stared at me the whole time. When she was done cooking, she sat a plate in front of me. She ripped the tape from my mouth. "I hope that you like pork."

I frowned and mumbled. "I don't eat swine."

She looked up at him.

"That's not nice…my sister cooked us breakfast…the least that you can do is eat it. Remember…beggars can't be choosers…"

"I didn't ask for this shit and that's your sister?" I asked. He frowned and turned to her.

"Hey…remember that talk that we had…about…umm, eating and umm…friends… and ummm, chewing???"

I looked down at the plate. "I don't care what you say…I'm not eating this shit."

She jumped up, ran over to my side of the table, and grabbed the meat off of the plate. "Oh you gon' eat, bitch…" She grabbed my face and stuffed it into my mouth. "Chewing…less talking…more chewing." I held the food in my mouth. Feeling accomplished, she walked back around to her chair. She fixed her hair. "Now, see how easy that was?"

I filled my mouth with the food and all of the spit that I could muster up and spit it all in her face. "Eat your own pig…pig…"

She wiped her eyes. She looked at her hair. "My weave? Oh hell naw, bitch…" She lunged across the table – landing on top of me." I hit my head against the floor. We started wrestling. He stood up and walked over.

"Get off of her," he demanded, as he pushed her off of me.

She scrambled to her feet. "Get out of the way, Gage…that bitch needs to know who she's fucking with."

He pulled me to my feet and stood between us. He took my arm and began to drag me down the hall. I snatched away from him and looked at them. "You're, both, going to pay…I promise you."

"Sure, Sweetie…but right now, it's your turn," he said.

That night, my stomach began to rumble. At first, I thought that it was from hunger, but no, this was something else. It rumbled louder. I felt a sharp pain in my stomach. "Oh shit…the pork." I said, as I realized what was happening. The pain hit me again. "Help!" I screamed. "Help!" No one responded. I wanted to buckle over, crawl to the bathroom, but I was back in my restraints. "Help!" I screamed, again, but still there was no answer. I tried screaming again, but instead of words, food came rushing out and as it came out of my mouth, it came rushing out of every other hole in my body. Every time, that I tried to scream, it came out and it did until I thought that there was nothing left. I was covered in my own waste. Finally, the door opened and she walked in the room.

"What do you want?" She paused when she saw what happened to me. "You shitted on yourself?" She began to look around the room. "I cannot believe that you did this…you know, what…I've tried so hard to be nice. Now, you've gone too far." She walked out of the room and when she returned, she had a small black thing in her hand. She climbed on top of me. "I hate to do this, but you really need to learn." She stuck something against my leg and then *ZAP!* It felt like I'd been struck by lightning. My body became rigid as the current rushed through it. *ZAP!* She did it again. I had no control over my body. I became stiff as a board. *ZAP!* The remaining fluids left my body. She looked down and frowned. "I should make you lick this shit up." She zapped me again and held it for more than a minute. The smell of burnt hair filled the room. It felt like my heart was going to explode. I began to foam at the mouth. She removed the device and said, "You can't die, yet…he would kill me if you do…" She slapped my face and when I moaned, she continued, "Now, take your ass to sleep and don't make me come back in here." She walked out of the room – slamming the door behind her.

Peaches

Chapter 32

We create our own monsters. They no longer wait for us under our beds or in our closets, they are right in our heads – wreaking havoc on our thoughts – creating memories of shit that never happened. They control us – control our every move until the day we die and all of this shit ends, permanently. The only thing we can do is do everything we can to keep the monsters at bay, but until then…

When she left, a part of me went with her. I didn't realize how much I loved her until I was no longer able to tease her, no longer able to rely on her, and no longer able to hold her. I know that it's hard to believe that I loved her, but you have to remember who taught us how to love. A man who never knew love himself.

And when he refused to look for her, I didn't know what to do. Even when he finally called the police, he'd convinced them that she'd just run away. I tried telling them that she would never do that, but they believed him over me. So I was the one left to stare at an empty bed every day.

The sadness and loneliness was so bad that it'd become all that I had. Often times, I would find myself talking to her – hoping that where ever she was, she would hear me. Every day, I would call her cellphone. No one would answer, but I would sit and listen to her message. "Hey…this is Grace…leave a message…" It was nothing special, but it was hers.

Getting up every day took every ounce of energy that I had. I just didn't give a fuck about anything anymore. I stopped eating, barely slept, and the only time I washed my ass was when I could actually smell myself. Now, that I was the only twin at home, I let my hair grow out. I didn't do anything with it along with the rest of the hair on my body. The hair under my arms had gotten so long you could style it. If she were here, she would talk about me like a dog. I, desperately, needed to do something with myself.

After showering and cutting the bush that had grown between my legs, I proceeded to groom the rest of my body. When I stepped out of the shower, I felt ten pounds lighter. I walked over to the mirror and began to wipe the water from it when I caught a glimpse of the uni-brow and matching mustache that was growing across my face. *Gross.* I pulled a razor out of the medicine cabinet. I was cutting my eyebrows when I accidentally cut myself. Normally, when I cut myself, I brush it off, but this time it felt weird – something about this time was different. I watched the blood form within the hairs on my forehead. As it began to drip onto my face, something about it intrigued me. I watched it bleed until the blood began to clot. When I looked at my face, I looked like something out of a scary movie, but then an eerie feeling swept over me. What if Grace is dead? The whole idea was overwhelming – the thought that she was gone forever. For the first time, that felt like a real possibility.

I was looking at my wrists when I began to think about it. What it would be like to be gone too – to just end it all. How simple life would be. So, I picked up the razor again. At first, afraid, I hesitated, but then I remembered what my life was like with her and how bad it would be without her. I took the razor and placed it against my skin. I closed my eyes and imagined her smiling at me and pulled it across my arm. At first, it felt like a paper cut. It stung a little bit. I bit my bottom lip until the pain eased up. I waited for the stinging to stop and for death to take hold, but that didn't happen, so I did it again. For a moment, it didn't hurt and fear was suddenly replaced with control. I was in control over my life and over my death.

When I opened my eyes and saw all of the blood, it freaked me out. I scrambled around the room looking for something to stop the flow, but before placing the towel on my arm, I stopped. Watching the blood ooze down my arm and into my hand was actually soothing. I wanted more, so I decided to do it again. This time applying a little more pressure. As the blade slid across my skin, I felt a rush. It was like an "out of body experience" like I was watching the whole thing from across the room. In that moment, I was so high that it made me forget about everything even Grace.

Soon, I wouldn't need a reason. I was cutting myself every day. It was the "cutting" that gave me pleasure – that gave me peace. The whole process of waiting until I was alone. Rubbing alcohol on my arm and blowing on it until it dried – the cool sensation of it on my skin. I just loved how the light bounced off of the blade right before I applied it to my skin. The waiting for the pain. The waiting for the blood as it starts off warm and turns cold as it ran down my arm. And it was mine, all mine. Not something that I had to share, but mine. My bloody little secret.

Chapter 33

Then one day, for no particular reason at all, I felt down and was feeling so sad – like I wanted to crawl in a hole and die, when a voice in my head said, "Get your ass up and get out of here."

"No, I wanna die," I responded.

"Well, if you're going to do it, then do it and stop feeling sorry for yourself," the voice said.

I became annoyed. "You don't tell me what to do…"

"I'm waiting," it said.

"Fuck you," I said, as I got up, grabbed my keys, my cellphone, and left.

It was so hot outside and the long sleeve shirt that I was wearing didn't help. Water was pouring off of me like I was sitting in the oven. I was being cooked alive. The only thing missing was the butter to baste my ass with. I was by a convenient store when I decided to duck behind it to pull my sleeves up to get some relief from the heat. It was only then that I realized that the shirt had adhered itself to the dried blood on my wounds. Acting as a Band-Aid, my shirt and my skin became one and when I pulled my sleeves up it ripped the scabs off of my cuts. "SHIT!!!!!!" I yelled.

A young man riding pass on a bike heard me. My scream frightened him and he stopped, quickly, banging himself against his handlebars. "Son-of-a-bitch!!!!!" he yelled.

I pulled my sleeves down when I heard him. I was about to walk away when, while rubbing "himself", he looked up and said, "Are you okay?"

I looked back. "I'm fine…" I said.

Still buckled over, he said, "Okay…"

I proceeded to walk off when I looked back and saw that he was still bending over. I looked down at the dried blood on my sleeves, decided to fold my arms to hide them, and walked over to where he was. "Thanks for…" As I thought about the next word, I realized that the only time I used it was when I was pointing out that no one really did it. "…caring." I continued.

He huffed as he rose up. "Not a problem…just heard you scream…now, I won't be able to make babies."

I giggled, but then felt bad about almost castrating him. "I'm sorry."

He laughed and smiled. "I'm just joking…I'm young…I'll heal."

I frowned. "Good…well…okay…"

He stuck his hand up. "Whoa…are you sure that you're okay?"

"I'm fine…" I looked around and said, "I do need to get out of here." I dropped my arms.

He saw the blood on my shirt.

Feeling embarrassed, I put my arms behind me. "I've taken up enough of your time."

With a concerned look on his face, he said, "My name is Isaac."

Realizing that he wasn't trying to let me go, I said, "That's great, Isaac."

He raised one of his eyebrows. "And your name?"

I was sweating in places I didn't even know I had skin. My underarms were wet, my back was wet, and my thighs were wet. I looked down to find that there was so much water pooling south that it looked like I'd pee'd on myself. "Look…it's hot as hell out here and I'm not looking to make a 'Love Connection'…"

He broke-out in laughter. "Sister…me neither. I was just trying to be friendly…"

"My name is Peaches, okay?" I said, agitated. "You wanna know my address, phone number, and blood type too?"

"I only asked you your name," he said, confused.

"Just feels like you trying to get up in my business…" I said, annoyed.

"You would think that someone with a name like Peaches would be….ummmmmm…sweet."

I rolled my neck. "And you would think that someone named Isaac…" I suddenly realized that I didn't have a come-back for that. "Well…whatever…" I said, defeated.

Frustrated, he said, "You know what? I'mma let you go. You look like you have a lot of 'inner shit' going on…"

Damn, is it that obvious? I thought to myself.

He continued. "So I'mma leave you to go and work that shit out…go take your meds."

"Fine…" I said, stomping away.

"Fine…" he said, climbing onto his bike. "Have a good fucking day."

Looking over my shoulder, I yelled. "No…you have a fucking good day."

As I stomped off, I don't know why, but I began to laugh. *Have a good fucking day.* The more that I thought about it, the more I laughed. Before I knew it, I was laughing so hard, I had tears in my eyes. He must have thought that it was funny too because he turned and rode up on the side of me, laughing.

"That was some funny shit…" he said.

"That was…" I agreed. "We sounded like a married couple…or like people who've been dating for a long time…"

"Or like some folks who should be fitted with a straight-jacket…and thrown into one of those padded rooms," he joked.

"I know, right." I wiped the tears from my eyes. "That was terrible…At times, I could be such a bitch."

He smiled. "I like that…"

"What? That I called myself a bitch?"

"Yeah, it means that you're not messed up…there's nothing worse than a bitch who doesn't know that she's a bitch or one who knows, but won't admit it…"

"I take it you deal with a lot of bitches…"

"You'd be amazed…" he laughed. "But really…you're not a bitch. There's a big difference between a bitch and a woman with an attitude. An attitude can be adjusted…turned off and on…but that bitch-shit is engrained…can't fix that."

"So I have an attitude?"

"Yes, most definitely…a bitch would have left me and my swollen nuts to fend for ourselves…but you stopped…you care…"

"Ummmmm…okay…thanks?"

Concerned, he said, "I saw the blood on your shirt…"

Feeling embarrassed again, I looked down at the ground.

He lowered his head to catch my eyes. "It's okay…I promise you."

I looked up at him.

He smiled. "It's hot can we find some shade before we turn into two chocolate puddles on the sidewalk?"

I smiled. "Sure, Isaac."

We walked down to the store and sat on the cinder blocks that sat near the parking lot.

He stood up. "Could you keep an eye on my bike?"

Using the bottom of my shirt, I wiped my forehead. "Sure…"

Raising an eyebrow, he asked, "You're not going to steal it, right?"

I frowned. "It's too hot for all of these questions and too damn hot to be stealing bikes."

He laughed. "Okay…I'll be back."

I stared out into the street until he came back. When he returned, he was carrying two bottles of cold water. He rubbed one across his sweaty forehead. "You want a bottle of water?"

"Can I get one without the body fluids?"

He laughed. "Are you always like this?" He handed me the bottle of water.

"Like what?" I asked, opening the bottle and taking a sip.

"You know…funny?"

"Don't you mean crazy?" I asked, taking another sip and thinking how good the water felt as it cooled me from the inside.

"Naw…I don't mean that…" He sat the bottle down, pulled his shirt over his head, and proceeded to wipe his face with it. I fell backward after feeling like I'd just been slapped in the face with the tightest six-pack and the most beautiful pecs I'd ever seen - other than the ones in my dreams. You wouldn't think that I was thirsty with all of the salivating that I was doing.

He smiled. "You like what you see?"

His ego was inflated, so I decided to take a little air out of his "balloon." "You're alright."

"Just alright?" He wrapped his shirt around his shoulders and sat down next to me.

I giggled and took another sip from the bottle.

"So Peaches…" He paused and took a sip from the bottle. "You wanna talk about it?"

I looked down and saw a rock on the ground. I kicked it. "You will never understand."

He looked out into the parking lot. "Try me…"

Thinking that I may never see this guy again, I figured what do I have to lose? "I have a twin…"

"A twin?" he interrupted. "Your family was twice blessed…huh?"

I laughed. "I don't know about that..."

"Sure…twins are a blessing from Heaven…what I would do to have a twin…I would get away with so much stuff…"

"You can't when the world thinks that you're the evil one…"

"Are you evil?"

"You know, Isaac…I don't know what I am…" I sighed. "And the good one is missing…"

He looked truly concerned. "What do you mean by missing?"

"I mean that she's gone…it's been a few weeks now and no one's looking for her."

"Why?"

"My dad thinks that she just ran off to be with some friends or to be with some boy, but I know that that's not true…something's wrong. I know it. I'm the one who needed to run away…not her."

"Then, go to the police…"

"We did, but they're not taking it seriously because my voice is being overshadowed by a motherfucker who doesn't care about us."

"Why do you say that?"

"It's true…he doesn't love us…"

"Love is subjective, Peaches…what he thinks is love…what you think love is…what I think love is…it's all relative…"

"Love feels good and I've never felt that with him…"

"What about your mom?"

"She's dead…"

"I'm sorry to hear that, but that might explain some of it…"

"What do you mean?"

"When it comes to love, men and women are different…it's like comparing apples to oranges…they're both fruit, but they have to different functions and two different ways of accomplishing them. Men are raised to be hard and women are raised to be soft and if there's no woman around to teach him that, then what do you expect...you can't get blood from a turnip."

"So all these years...I've been hating him... for no reason?"

"I'm sure you had your reason...now, was it a good reason...that's the question?"

I smiled.

"Do you want me to help you...you know...find your sister?"

I laughed. "How can you help me?"

"You'd be amazed at what I can do."

I was flattered. "That's sweet, but any intervention would drive a bigger wedge between us and I don't have anywhere else to go...right now."

He took my hand. I snatched my arm away, but then something made me give it back to him. Slowly, he pulled up my sleeve. "Damn!!!"

I snatched my arm away, again. "You ain't gotta act like that..."

"I've just never seen anybody or met anybody who tried to kill themselves before and from the look of all of those cuts, you've failed a lot."

I frowned. "I don't want to kill myself."

"Then, why cut yourself?" he asked, confused.

I shook my head. "You wouldn't understand..."

"No...no...I want to. This is just some new shit...I've never heard of folks cutting themselves for the 'fun' of it."

I thought about what he said. "It's not really fun...well, I guess it is..." Flustered, I said, "I don't know how to explain it."

He thought about it for a second. "Hey...when I do shit that I can't explain...I try explaining it and when I can't explain it, I stop doing the things that I can't explain...does that make any sense?"

"For some strange reason, it does..."

"Does it feel good?" he asked.

I shook my head. "It's going to sound stupid…"

"Hey, we're young…stupid is what we do."

"Well, it hurts, but it feels good too. If that makes sense."

"Like sex?" he asked.

"I don't know…I guess…It's more like…I guess it's kinda like being a heroin addict or an alcoholic…the first 'hit' feels real good. It feels good even though it causes you pain…and somehow…even though you know that there will be pain…at some point, you begin to look forward to it…anticipate it…then, at some point, the body becomes numb to it and you can't feel the pain anymore…but you keep doing it…pushing the limits…it's like a tiger…always hungry…no matter how much you feed it…until, one day, you over-feed it…"

"Wow…ummmmmm…okay…"

I continued. "Like seeing the blade go into the skin…the blood as it rushes out…knowing that it could one day kill you, but you do it anyway, because the body needs it…"

He had a strange look on his face. "You've put a lot of thought into this…"

"Not really…not until now…saying it out loud sorta makes you…think about it."

Confused, he asked. "That's a big risk…it's like playing with matches and hoping that you don't get burned."

"True…not to mention that the process requires a certain level of fortitude, resolution."

"Fortitude? Resolution? It's too damn hot for big words…but I like it."

"You pick-up a few things when the only friend you have is a book." *Sigh* "Killing yourself requires a certain level of 'follow-through' and the only thing I'm capable of completing, successfully, is fucking-up…"

He wiped sweat from his forehead. "Maybe you're being tested…"

I laughed. "Isaac…life ain't nothing, but one big-ass test…and at some point, the 'teacher' is going to call 'time' and we're going to have to put our pencils down and get our grade…pass we move on or fail and we stay right here until we get it right."

"You're trying to get out of taking the test?" he asked.

I laughed. "Maybe I was just trying to get a note from God, so that I wouldn't have to take it."

"Even those with notes eventually, still, have to take it…one way or another…"

I laughed. "I've never really thought about it that way, Isaac."

"Also, think about this…your sister is out there somewhere…if you're dead, who will look for her?"

I didn't respond.

"All I'm saying is, Peaches…you made it this far for a reason…maybe just for this moment right here…but whatever the reason…there is a plan…"

"That's deep..."

"And it gets deeper…believe me…"

We smiled as we spent the rest of the afternoon watching the cars go by.

I couldn't stop thinking about him. I hadn't realized what I was doing to myself...really doing to myself until today. My secret became my shame. Hearing myself compare my behavior to that of an addict made me realize how sick I was and how sick the behavior was. I was cutting myself to forget about her absence, while, singlehandedly, erasing my own existence.

I had to find her. Even if she's dead, I want to know and if they wouldn't listen to me because I was young, then I would become a person that they would have to listen to. A person that the world could no longer dismiss.

Chapter 34

A year had gone by. I couldn't stand being in the house with him. Watching him move on with his life, while my sister was out there, alone, was unbearable, so I decided to get out of there. I went on to college, but I never stopped thinking about her or the boy who saved my life. I'd spent most of my time on this planet running through life without a helmet on and the only two people who tried to keep me from hurting myself, were gone. I had to get them back – one way or the other.

College was tough at first, but I was focused. I never wanted to go back home until I was in a better position to help myself, to help her, or to find him. It was in my second year of college that I decided to go back. To be honest, I never really expected to see him again, but I wanted to try.

For days, I went back to that convenient store and waited in the parking lot. While I sat there, I thought about how weird and funny it would be, if he'd rode past on a bike – the same bike, carrying an older version of himself. How fun it would be to catch up and to ask him if maybe, he thought about me or missed me like I'd missed him.

Then, on the last day, just when I was about to give up and return back to school, I'd become thirsty and decided to walk inside. I walked over to the cooler and pulled out a bottle of water. As I held it, I thought of him and smiled. I turned to walk over to the register when suddenly the door opened. With the cool breeze that drifted in was the man that I was looking for. When he walked in, he smiled. My heart swelled. I would recognize that smile anywhere. I smiled back.

He walked up to me and said, "Hey Ms. Peaches."

I giggled. "Hey you."

He slid his arms around me. He nuzzled his face against mine. "I'm glad that you're still here."

I melted into his arms. My heart swelled. "Yeah…I'm still here." We stood in the middle of the floor and held each other for what seemed like a lifetime. We held each other so tight, that when he started to release me, I wanted to grab him and never let him go. We giggled.

"So how have you been, Ms. Peaches?" He looked at my arms. "Looks like you're healing nicely."

I looked down at my arms and said, "You can't see the part of my body that's truly healing…"

He smiled. "Let me pay for that water before they think that you're in here shoplifting and maybe, if you're not busy, we can sit on the ground and talk."

I laughed. "I have a car now…we can sit in there."

He laughed. "I got one too…we can sit in mine."

"Alright, Mr. Isaac…whatever you say."

He walked over to the register, but the young man behind the counter said, "Will you, please, stop…" He laughed.

Isaac laughed and said, "Thanks."

The young man said, "No…thank you."

He handed me the bottle and pointed to the door. As I walked outside, I didn't expect to see the bike, but I definitely wasn't ready for what happened next. I looked to my left and then I slowly looked to the right. "Dang…is this you?"

He smiled and said, "This thing? It's nothing."

"Ummmmm…it's better than the two-wheeler I saw you on not too long ago."

He laughed. "Yeah, I guess it is."

As we approached the car, slowly the front door opened. A man stepped out. "You ready to go, sir?"

The fuck? I thought to myself.

"What's wrong?" he asked, as he took my hand and led me to the car.

"Ummmmm…" I said, confused.

The man opened the back door. I looked at him and then back at Isaac. "What the hell is going on?"

He shook his head. "Get in the car…please."

I looked at the man and then I stepped into the car. The man closed the door. Isaac walked over to the other side. The man followed, closely, and opened his door. Isaac slid in next to me. The man closed the door.

I had a confused look on my face.

"Why are you looking like that?" he asked.

"What's going on, Isaac?"

"What do you mean?"

He ignored the question and asked, "Where's your car?"

I frowned. "I'm ashamed to show you."

"Stop being silly…which one is it?"

Hesitantly, I pointed towards the "hooptie". "It's the car over there with the plastic as the window."

He looked over there and smiled. "I love the duct tape…nice touch."

"Hey…it runs…" I folded my arms in front of me.

"Adam…call inside of the store and tell them to keep an eye on the car with the duct tape."

"Yes, boss…" he said.

"Yes, boss?" I asked.

He shook his head and smiled. "Drive Adam…"

"Yes, Sir…"

"Sir?" I asked, looking like a crazy person. I was starting to think that I was still at home in my bed, dreaming.

"You're so funny, Peaches."

"Me? What the hell is going on?"

He shook his head and said, "What…you thought that I was just some brotha from the hood? Some thug? Maybe a gang-banger?"

"What? Huh? Ummmmm…I don't know what I thought."

"You saw a brotha on a bike and thought that he didn't have nothing going for himself? Never crossed your mind that I possibly owned the store that I was walking into…did it?"

He had me all messed up. "No, I'm sorry, but I didn't."

"Why? Cause I'm Black?"

"No…no…well…" I was winded. I felt so stupid and ashamed. "I'm sorry, but when you see so much negative shit on TV and around you, you start to believe the hype."

"And it's tragic…'cause you're Black too and you believe that shit about your own people."

"Damn…I don't know what to say."

He waved his hand. "You wouldn't be the first and you won't be the last."

"I feel terrible…"

"Don't…the world wants EVERYONE to believe that we're all a bunch of illiterate, gang-banging, rapping, pants sagging, murdering thieves, and rapists." He sighed. "They are so good at stuffing that propaganda down our throats that we swallow it without asking where the crap came from."

"Wow…" That's all I could say.

He continued. "My family own a lot of the stores in the neighborhood. You heard of the Ramseys…"

I interrupted him. "The furniture store?"

"Among others…"

"Yes…yes…that's your family?"

"Yep…unfortunately."

"Unfortunately?" I asked.

"Clearly, you don't watch the news."

"I do, but I've been in school…my head has been in the books."

"Well, you ever heard that phrase 'mo' money, mo' problems?'"

"Yes…" I said, taking in Chicago's beautiful landscape.

"Well, after years of making us what we are…the weight of carrying everything on his own shoulders became too much for my father to bear…" He looked out of the window. "He's dead."

I touched his hand. "I'm so sorry to hear that…" I asked.

"Bullet to the head," he confirmed. "He killed himself."

"Oh man…that's terrible…I'm sorry."

"Why? Did you kill him?" he asked.

"No…" I said, frowning. "It's just that…you know…that's what people say when people die."

He laughed. "They say that shit because they don't know what else to say. The words 'I'm sorry' are safe…relieves them of any guilt or any sense of responsibility they may feel, but are they really sorry? You can only be sorry if you actually did something to be sorry for…other than that, it's just lip-service."

"Well…I do feel bad that you lost your dad."

"Why? He was an asshole. You don't get as rich as he was being nice…believe me."

I looked at him.

He smiled. "It's okay. I'm glad that he was an asshole. We never had to suffer. We never struggled and although we made our money in the 'hood'…we lived in a neighborhood where Black boys didn't get shot for wearing a hood."

"Black boys should never worry about that…"

"But, sadly, they do…"

"So you're a rich kid…damn…that's cool."

"Yep…I guess…"

For a moment, we both stared out of the window. He broke the silence. "So…you're in college?"

"Yeah…" I said, turning to look at him.

"For what?"

"I wanna be a doctor," I said.

"They use the word 'wanna' in college?" he teased.

"Until those student loans are paid off…"

We both laughed. He looked over the front seat. "Let's stop by the house…"

"Yes, boss…" he said.

While we drove around, we talked about all of the things that we'd been up to since we last met and when we didn't talk, he would reach over and touch my hand. It was nice being with him. It was another thirty minutes before we finally pulled up in front of a gate. The driver hit a remote and we pulled in. We drove around a circular driveway until we landed in front of two large gold doors. The car came to a stop. Instinctively, I opened the door. The driver jumped out and said, "You're trying to get me fired?"

"No...no...no," I said, nervously.

He laughed. "I'm just teasing...people do it all of the time...until they get used to it."

"I wanna get used to it..." I mumbled under my breath.

He walked around and opened the door for Isaac. The driver ran and opened the front door. They both waited until I walked in. I looked around and suddenly, I felt underdressed. I began to straighten my clothes. He walked up behind me and whispered, "You look fine."

Suddenly, a figure appeared at the top of the stairs. "Isaac...you're home early," she said.

She looked like a queen as she proceeded down the stairs. "Hey mama…"

"We're not on a plantation, Isaac…"

"Yes…mother…dear…"

When she placed her foot on the bottom step, Isaac ran up and grabbed her hand. She stepped off of the last step and walked toward me. She looked me up and down. "We prefer that the 'help' enter through the back door…"

"Mama…" he said.

She frowned. "I was just joking. You can take a joke right…ummmmmm????"

Trying to erase the scowl on my face, I extended my hand. "It's Peaches."

She looked down at my hand. "I don't do 'hands', honey…you'd be amazed at what folks do with their hands."

Isaac cleared his throat. "Mother…you look tired."

She laughed and leaned into my face. "That's code for 'get out.'"

I didn't laugh.

"Okay, Big Boy...help mother to the library...and you two...be good." She began to walk away. "It was nice meeting you...ummmmmm???"

"Peaches," I said, reminding her.

"Whatever..." she said, letting me know that she didn't give a shit.

As they walked down the hall, I heard her say, "Check her pockets before she leaves..."

He looked over his shoulder to see if I heard her. I guess by the look on my face he could tell that I did. He shook his head. A few minutes later, he returned, apologizing. "I am so sorry...she's old...don't pay her any mind."

"Yeah...if she was younger and talking that shit, she'd be getting her ass-whooped, right now."

He laughed. "I bet..."

He took my hand and led me into a room that had more gold and bronze in it than the Treasury Building. "Wow...this is beautiful."

He plopped down onto the couch. "This is a rich person's way of trying to separate themselves from regular folks…by surrounding themselves with all of the money that they've ever made. It's gaudy and sad…" He looked up and saw that I was still standing by the door. "It's okay…this stuff won't bite you."

I walked in. He patted the seat next to him. "Come on…you can do it…"

I sat next to him. He hit a button on a box on the table next to him. "Can we get some snacks, mama?"

A voice responded. "Yes…I'll be in there shortly."

I looked around the room as he spoke. I still couldn't believe what was going on. Moments later, a woman walked into the room. "I got your favorite," she chimed. "PB&J…" She sat down a tray that had two plates and two glasses a milk on it.

He rubbed his hands, excitedly. "You are the best…thanks, mama."

Confused, I asked, "I thought that the other woman was your mother."

Taking a big bite out of the sandwich, he said, "She is…she made me…carried me…but this woman raised me."

She smiled. "And who is this beautiful young lady?"

"This is Peaches, mama…"

She walked over and extended her hand. "It's so nice to meet you, Peaches."

Trying to chew the peanut butter and talk, he said, "She's really my grand-mama…I call her mama because that's who she is…to everybody."

"And she serves you?" I asked, taking her hand.

"Yes…" He swallowed some of the milk. "You better not go in her kitchen…no one goes in grand-mama's kitchen."

She rubbed her arms. "It's chilly in here…start a fire, Isaac…"

"I will, grand-mama…thank you so much for the sandwich."

I looked up. "Thank you…"

You're both so welcome…" She turned to walk out of the room. "It was nice meeting you, Peaches."

"You too…" I said. "What do I call you?"

She stopped at the door and smiled. "You can call me, mama…just like everyone else." She closed the door.

"She's so nice…" I said, spitting crumbs at him. "I'm sorry…"

"You say 'sorry' a lot…nobody's that damn sorry."

I picked up the crumbs.

"Say it enough times, Peaches, and it starts to lose its value."

I took another bite out of the sandwich to avoid saying it again. He stood up and walked over and placed a few logs of wood in the fireplace. He lit a fire. "I take it you've never seen one of these before either…"

"I see fire all of the time…" I thought about it for a second and said, "On the stove, when

424

someone's house is on fire, or when my car over-heats."

He looked at me. "I owe you an apology…"

I looked at him.

"I know what I said about that, but maybe I did mislead you…while you were opening up to me, I was keeping all of this from you."

I swallowed, hard, trying to get the peanut butter down. Sucking my teeth, I said, "We were both young…I shared with you because I never thought that I would ever see you again."

"Dang…"

"I'm just being honest and you had your reasons for keeping your secret…"

"But it was wrong…"

"Look…I was in such a bad place…I couldn't see past my pain and my own indignation."

"I like that. A big word. A college word. Impressive…"

I tapped his arm. "You're silly…I was in a bad place, but I thought about what you said…I was so knee-deep in my own shit that I didn't see that the only person who could save the both of us...is me. And I know that she's still alive. Twins just know…"

"You're still looking for her?"

"I tried and this is going to sound terrible, but I barely knew her. She slept across from me her whole life and I didn't know her…"

"That's not terrible…you got folks who don't even know themselves…let alone someone sleeping across the room from them…"

"You're right and since no one looked for her in the beginning, any trail has since been erased, but I'm not giving up hope. One way or another, we will be joined together again. I know it…"

He raised his glass of milk for a toast. "To bringing your sister home."

I smiled and tapped my glass against his. We finished eating. He stood and grabbed my hand. We walked over to the fireplace and sat next to it.

"This is nice…thank you." I said.

"No problem…"

I stared into the flames.

"You miss her?"

"More than life," I said.

He grabbed my hand. "She'll be back…"

"Thanks…"

There was a moment of silence. I stared at the ambers as they flickered from the flames. He broke the silence.

"Peaches, do you believe in love at first sight?"

Trying to lighten the mood, I said, "Yeah…I felt that way about a donut once…then, I ate it." I looked over at him. He had a serious look on his face.

"Peaches, I'm serious…"

"Isaac…we shared a bottle of water one day…"

"And yet, here we are…" He smiled. "I'm a true believer in destiny. Do you believe in destiny?"

I shrugged. "Never really thought about it."

"I believe that you and I are destiny."

"And what made you feel that?"

"I'm going to keep it real with you, Peaches…can I keep it real?"

"Ummmmm….sure…"

His tone grew serious. "I've had a lot of girls."

"A lot?"

"A lot," he confirmed. "I've been having sex since age 10."

My eyes widened. "10!!!! Dang…"

"When you're wealthy, you can have anything you want…you don't even have to ask for it. People just give it to you. After 'fucking' for so long, it gets boring. It has a diminished return…it's kinda like what you said about addiction and what you used to do to yourself…after a while, it wasn't even about the pleasure, anymore…it was just a process…a means to an end. I can't even remember any of them…not even the one that I gave my virginity to."

I thought about Carlton.

He continued. "They meant nothing to me, but after I met you…even though our meeting was short, I never stopped thinking about you. That's how I knew…and I knew that's why I would see you again…because you're the one."

"You sure that it wasn't pity that you felt?"

"I know the difference, Peaches and that's why I was there tonight…I was looking for you."

"I have to admit something…I was looking for you too."

"And you found me…" He wrapped his arms around me.

"Yes, I did…" I spent the rest of the night being grateful for destiny.

I didn't realize it, but I'd fallen asleep. When I awoke, I found his grand-mother standing over me. "Good morning..."

I looked around. "Wow…where's Isaac?"

"He needed to take care of some things…he'll be back. He told me to give you these."

I looked at her hand. She had some clothing, some shoes, some underwear, and some toiletries in her hand. "How did he know…?"

"He had me check your clothing while you slept and he sent one of the assistants to one of our clothing stores last night."

I kinda felt violated, but when she held the clothing up, she said, "You like it…right?"

I smiled and said, "Yes…"

"Good…now, come on before the wicked witch of the south-side brings her grouchy ass in here."

"Okay…"

I followed her down the hall, pass ten rooms, before we landed in front of a door that led to a room full of black marble. "I'll be back to check on you shortly…okay?"

"Thank you…"

She turned and closed the door. I stood in the middle of the room for about five minutes, trying to digest all of this. I removed my clothing and jumped in the shower. As the water ran over my skin, I looked at the scars on my arms. I couldn't help but think about Grace and wonder where she was, wonder what she was doing, and hope that she was as happy as I am right now.

After I was done and dressed, I opened the door to find the wicked witch of the south-side standing in front of me.

"Good morning," she said. "Ummmmmmmm???"

"Peaches," I said, reminding her, again.

She ignored me. "I see that you found the bathroom…"

"Yes…thank you so much for letting me use it."

"You can thank my mother-in-law…she's down the hall…where you should be."

Suddenly, she appeared from a room that was a few doors down. "Don't you have a date with Jack?" She shooed her away. "Jack Daniels…that is," she said, grabbing my arm and pulling me down the hall. "Ignore her crazy-ass…that child is one plum short of a fruit basket."

We walked into the dining room. The room was so big, you could fit my whole dorm-room in it. "Where's Isaac?" I asked.

She took my dirty clothing from my hands. "I will take care of these for you…he'll be with you shortly…now, sit…I'll have someone bring you your breakfast."

I sat down and seconds later, a woman walked in and handed me a plate. She poured a glass of juice and quickly left the room. As I ate, I couldn't help but notice the photos on the wall. I stood up to look at the photo. It was his mother, a man, Isaac, and one other person.

"That's my family," he said, from across the room. "You like the clothes?"

"Yes…I love them. Thank you…"

"You're welcome…"

I pointed at the photo. "Who's the young lady?"

"My sister…the lucky one."

"Lucky?"

"She got out of here…young…I'm left here to pick up the pieces…to run things."

I walked back over and sat down. "Where were you?"

"I had some business to take care of…"

"Well, I have to get back to school…" I smiled. "I really had a wonderful time."

"I'm glad…" He stood and took my plate.

Suddenly, the door flew open. "What did I tell you about that?" She smacked his hand and took the plate from him. Then, she, quickly, exited the room.

He smiled and shook his head. "I can't ride back with you…the driver will get you back to your car safely. When you get to school, I want you to call me…just to let me know that you're okay."

I smiled and said, "Okay."

He walked me to the door. His grand-mother handed me a bag. "Here's your clothes, sweetie."

"Thank you," I said.

Isaac opened the door. The driver was waiting for me. Over my shoulder, I heard, "Bye….ummmmmm???"

"Peaches!!!!!" *Bitch,* I thought to myself.

"I hear, Jack, calling you!!!!" His grand-mother said.

He kissed me on the forehead. "I'll talk to you later?"

"Definitely…" I turned and walked out into the sunshine. The driver opened the door. I looked back and waved at him. He smiled. When I got into the car, I watched him through the back window.

An hour later, we were back in front of the store. I looked around for my car. When I didn't see it, I jumped out. The driver shook his head.

"Where is my car?"

The driver handed me a set of keys. "That's it right there."

"Where?" I asked, panicking.

"Right there…" he confirmed.

I hit the lock button. When the lights flashed on the car in front of me, I fell to my knees. "No way…"

"Yes way…" he teased.

I ran over to the silver Benz that had replaced my hooptie. "Ain't no way…"

He smiled. "All of your belongings are in your car…Isaac donated your car to charity."

I paused for a moment. "This is too much. I can't take this and wait a minute…what gives him the right to get rid of my car?"

The driver pointed at the window. "He left something for you."

I reached in and removed the envelope. I opened it. It was a card. *Please, take my gift. I want to make sure that you get back to school safely. Enjoy it…have a good day.* ☺

I looked at the driver. "Is it okay?" he asked.

I thought about it for a second and said, "I guess…"

"You'll get used to it…" he said, before walking away.

Grace

Chapter 35

I'd stopped counting the days. I'd completely given up hope that anyone would find me. I'd adjusted to the new world that I lived in – in all of its brutality and ugliness. They've done things to me that should only happen in nightmares. As each day passes, I've made it a point, every day, to try to forget the events of the day before. Holding on to the images, the memories, will only make things worse. The pain was more than enough to bear, I just wanted it to end.

There were times, when I thought about that day – thought about what I could have done differently, but I'd come to the conclusion that what happened was supposed to happen and although painful, the reason why I was strapped to this bed would one day become clear to me.

Until then, if death was my fate, it couldn't come soon enough.

I'd spent so much time on my back that I began to develop bed sores. They had to start taking shifts getting me out of the bed to let me walk around to do some chores for them. I enjoyed the moments of freedom – fleeting as they were, those moments would come at a price.

And he was getting crazier. They both were, but he was gone. He used to be the calmer of the two, but now it didn't take much to upset him. He would go from zero to crazy in 1.0 seconds at any given time of the day.

"Don't I take care of you, Peaches?"

"Yes, you do…" I said, as he trimmed my pubic hair. It was something that he loved doing – prepping me for the videos.

"I would think that you would be a little more grateful…"

"I am, but…"

"But…but…ungrateful ass…that's just like you…you got a roof over your head…somebody taking care of you and all you can do is bitch…"

"I didn't bitch…"

"Sounded like you were bitching…"

"But I didn't…?" I asked, confused.

He looked at me. "Look at your face…fix it."

"Excuse me…Fix my what?"

"Fix…your…face…"

"What is my face doing other than looking at yours?"

"You wanna get hit?"

"Do you?"

Before I knew it, he grabbed my arm and twisted it around my back until my fingers were touching the back of my head. I screamed in pain. "Owwwwwwww!!!!"

"Let's get things straight…you're in my house."

"Don't…stop…" I said.

"You made a mistake and now is a good time to remind you of what happens when we make mistakes."

"What happened? What did I do? Let my hand go."

"I will when I think that you've learned your lesson."

Frustrated, angry, and tired, I said, "You know what? Fuck you and your lesson...kill me and get this shit over with," I said, exhausted.

"You would like that wouldn't you? You selfish little bitch."

"What?"

"And then, what about me?"

"What about you?" I asked.

"Exactly...what about me? What about me? What about me? What about me? What about me? What about me? WHAT ABOUT ME???!!!!"

"Ummmmm...okay?"

He released my arm, took a deep breath, and said, "Okay...now, about dinner."

Rubbing my arm, I said, "What...you wanna talk about food now?"

"Let's go…" He dragged me down the hall to the kitchen.

Quickly, I prepared him something to eat and sat the plate of food in front of him. I was leaving the room when he said, "Now…how was your day?"

Holding my arm, I asked, "My what?"

"Your day?"

"What?"

"You don't want me to ask you again."

Aggravated, I began, "It was…"

He looked up and looked at the door. "Bye."

His response startled me. I don't know what I expected him to say, but I didn't expect "Bye." Weird, but I actually expected him to say "Thank you, bitch, for the food", but we were beyond any form of "thank yous" and it was times like these that he reminded me of that. I ran down the hall and into my room. I climbed on my bed and sat there. Moments later, they walked in and slammed the door behind them. Charlie locked the door.

I didn't bother fighting them. I just assumed the position.

"Good doggie…" she said.

"Good what?" I mumbled.

"You heard me…" she laughed.

Something in me snapped. I ran up on her and hit her in the face. We started fighting. He ran up and tackled me. While on the floor, she balled-up her hand and hit me in the face. They picked me up. Kicking and screaming, I said, "I got your dog, you He-Bitch."

They threw me on top of the bed and began to tie me down.

"This is why she has to be kept on her leash," she said as she held my feet.

The chill of the room woke me up.

"Say cheeeeeeeeeeessssssseeeee," she said.

444

The flash from the camera hurt my eyes. I turned my head. "Get out of my face with that thing…"

"Looks like somebody needs a spanking or how about a week without food, water, light…would that make you more photogenic?"

"Taking the food away would not be a punishment…it would be a blessing."

"You would think that after all of this time, you would be a nicer person…maybe you need a little more 'get-right?'" she said.

"You need some 'get-right'…believe me…because your shit is all wrong."

She rolled-up her sleeves.

"Leave her alone…" he said. "I know that this has been horrible for you…It happens to the best of us. You meet a good looking guy. He treats you well and then, one day, you wake up tied to a bed….happens to a lot of people, but look at us. I know that it's not the fairy tale that I promised you, but every night, there's been a 'happy ending'…wouldn't you agree? Well, at least for us, it has been…"

"You're insane…" I said.

"Now, you know…that hurts my feelings…"

"This is why you can't be nice to people…" she said.

"Fuck you…" I said.

"If only you could…" she said.

"Does he know that you're a man?" I asked.

She giggled. "I hope so or Houston we got a problem…shit he knows this dick better than I do…don't you sweetie?" She rubbed his head. "He looovvveess entering places that are normally marked 'Exit only.'"

"We all have our vices…" he said. "And I know that this is all confusing to you…"

"Why do you care? You brought me here to live-out some sick fucking fantasy with you and the chick with the Adam's Apple…"

"You're just mad because my eyebrows look better than yours…"

"Bitch, please…"

"You know…I could take offense, but I know you love this dick too…you scream and holla' and now, you wanna act funny."

"Are you serious?"

"Shit…when a bitch is thirsty, you can't be choosey about the glass that the drink came in…you just gotta quench that thirst…" She made her Adam's Apple jump up and down as she pretended to drink from a glass.

"You fucking disgust me…I don't give a fuck what they say about it being about control…a normal person wouldn't fuck you, so you snatch innocent people off of the streets…"

He frowned. "Innocent?"

"Yes, innocent…I haven't done anything to you or the bitch with the five o'clock shadow…"

She frowned. "You know…people like you piss me off. You criticize what you don't understand. I'm a man…"

"You're a sexual deviant who likes to wear women's clothes…"

"You ever heard that clothes don't make a man?"

"And having a dick don't make you one either. Clearly, it doesn't."

"Now, why is it that when a man dresses like a woman, he's a freak, but when a woman does it, it's normal, vogue, or chic? No one says a word?"

"Maybe, it's because you make one ugly-ass woman…which means that you're probably one UGLY-ass man. Must be fucked-up to realize that you're the kid that no one wants on their team…"

"You might want to tape her mouth…" she insisted.

"That tape is drying the skin around her mouth. It looks nasty on camera…" he said. "Stop provoking her…and to be honest…she's telling the truth…you could see your beard under your foundation…"

She grabbed her face. "Why didn't you tell me?"

"Shave all you want…ain't gon' change shit… and you can hit me, rape me, tape my mouth, and you will still be a fucking crazy bitch in a skirt.

Oh, I'm sorry…I meant, a crazy bitch with a dick in a skirt…a little dick at that."

She lunged at me. "I will kill you!!!!"

"GO AHEAD!!!! KILL ME!!!! I DON'T CARE!!!! YOU WOULD BE GONE. HE WOULD BE GONE AND THIS SHIT WOULD BE OVER WITH!!!! KILL ME, YOU PSYCHO MAN-SHE!"

He grabbed her from behind and pushed her towards the door. "GO!!!" he yelled.

"Why do you let her talk to me that way?"

"Because it's funny…you have to admit, the shit is hilarious…"

"NO!!! NO!!! Fuck that. She said I have a little dick. This shit ain't for play…this shit is real." She paced the floor and then walked back over to the bed. "She needs to kiss it…"

"Get out of here, Charlie…" he said.

"No…she need to kiss it and make it better…"

"GET OUT!!!" he yelled.

"No, fuck that…" she said.

"I ain't kissing shit, Pickles…" I said.

"Oh, you ain't? And what did you call me?" she pulled down her skirt. "You gon' kiss this, bitch, and apologize…"

I turned my head.

"Will you please kiss it so that she can leave the room?" He said.

"You're asking her? Make that trick do it," she demanded

He grabbed my face and she climbed on the bed. "Kiss it!!!"

I turned my head. He grabbed me again.

"Kiss it or I'm going to show how big it really is."

I closed my eyes, took a deep breath, and kissed it. She smiled and climbed off of the bed. She started laughing. "I need to get you some lip-balm, before those crusty-ass lips cut my dick off."

I spit on the bed. "Yet, I kissed it and you're still a fucking toad and I ain't sorry…"

"But you will be…keep fucking with me." She handed him her earrings. "Hold these…this bitch wants me to break-off one of these finger nails in her ass."

He pulled her arm. "You have all the time in the world to break nails off in that ass."

He dragged her to the door.

I laid there until, I heard the "click-click" of the door, again. They both walked in.

Charlie walked in wearing a long red negligee with matching red heels. "You didn't shower? You knew that I was coming back. I like my pussy 'shower-fresh.'"

I didn't respond.

She looked back at him. "We're just going to have to tape it anyway…" She turned up her nose. "I hate smelly fish, but that's what you get when you leave it sitting out all day." She removed her robe.

He sat in a chair across the room and turned on the camera.

Charlie turned to him. "Shoes on or shoes off, Sweetie?"

"You know that I like it when you keep your shoes on."

They laughed and looked at me. She walked over to the bed and began to look around. "Oh shit…I forgot the extension cord and the duct tape…"

He sighed. "You know what they say?"

"What?" she said.

"Life favors the prepared…"

"Bruh…you are so right…good looking out. I really need to get my shit together."

"It's okay…that's what I'm here for."

"What would I do without you? Okay…I'll be right back." She ran out of the room and returned holding the cord and the tape. "Ready…"

I cringed and turned my head.

She grabbed my face and began to apply some makeup. "Don't play hard to get. It's exhausting and I've been messing with you all day…I had to get my nails done…do my hair…"

"You need to fire the bitch who did your hair…looks like you had a fight with a lawnmower and the lawnmower won," I said.

"I know what you're trying to do, but it won't work…"

"Get away from me…"

She sighed. "You're so adorable…can't wait to cuddle with you…"She laughed and turned to him. "You wanna get it right the first time. I'm not as young as I used to be. I can't promise more than one 'take.'"

"Don't forget your angles, honey. Your fans want to see it all."

"I know, right…gotta keep my fans happy."

I started to cry. I was so tired.

She waved her arms. "Cut! Cut! Now, look at her face. She can't go on looking like this. They can't smell her through the camera, but they can see that mascara running down her face." She grabbed her make-up bag. "She has to look good…she's the star of the show."

REMY

Chapter 36

I miss my babies. I have to admit that I was glad that they were gone, but that didn't stop me from missing them. We had some good times, but probably more bad times than good. I spent so much time frowning that the only time I smiled was when I watched them walk out of my house. I spent so much time raising them that I think that I forgot to love them and now, that they are gone, I may never get that chance again.

I think about them all of the time. It's weird. You get so used to the dysfunction that you don't know what to do with yourself when it's gone. For months, I would stand in their room and look at their beds. I would smell their blankets – hoping to get one last 'whiff' of them. I know that it's weird, but a parent never forgets that smell. That baby smell. Even as they get older they still carried a trace of it - the "before they grow-up and start smelling their own asses" smell.

They were so much like their mother. There were days, when I would think about her and cry. Sure, I moved on to another, but there's nothing like your first – your first kiss, your first real hug, your first true love. She gave me the greatest gift that anyone could have given me and I threw it all away. My own anger and frustration about my life prevented me from giving them the love that they deserved. Sure, my kids messed up, but that's what kids do, but I was so busy wallowing in my own bullshit that I didn't see that. While I, desperately, wanted perfection, all they wanted was to be my baby girls. By the time I figured the shit out, I'd dug a hole so deep I couldn't climb out of it. I just sunk deeper and deeper and deeper.

It's funny and I don't mean that in a good way, but after they were gone, I quickly realized how much I didn't like Mabel. I mean, I cared about her, but she was only a distraction. A distraction from the loneliness that became a "wall" between me and my girls. I was so busy chasing the "pussy" that I didn't realize that my girls were raising themselves. I was a provider, but not a father. I was unable to care for or protect them because no one cared for or protected me. My dad was the same with me. He put food on the table, a roof over our heads, and then closed the door and covered his ears as his kids cried-out to him.

And we cried. We cried every day. People say that whatever doesn't kill you only makes you stronger. That shit is only for super heroes and only works in comic books. Children are not "made of steel". They are fragile and breakable and once broken, even if they're "glued" back together again, there will still be cracks. They say that kids are resilient. They bounce back. Humans don't bounce back – balls bounce back. We never forget the pain. We may grow up – move on, but we never forget the pain. Sure, we can try packing it away and storing it in the recesses of our minds, but even when it's out of sight, it's never out of mind.

My past and my present became one. Every woman in my life has either hurt me or left me. The first woman in my life, abused me. The second woman, my sister, abused me. The third woman, Peaches, loved me and then I abused her and then came Mabel. This is going to sound terrible, but I didn't love her. It's not that I didn't try. I just didn't know how to and I'm sure that for most people, loving someone is probably not a difficult thing to do, but for someone like me, it was hard. I didn't trust her, because I couldn't trust her, so I decided to hurt her before she had a chance to hurt me. Maybe I should have sat her down and talked to her. Maybe, I should have been honest with her about my past, but I saw what that did to Peaches. I didn't want another woman to have to shoulder that pain or be forced to live with my horrible memories.

So instead of calling her, sending her a text, or an email, I decided to invite her over and just tell her, but she wanted to have sex first and no man rejects sex even when they know that accepting it will come with grave consequences. And it was good. Something about the kids being gone, brought out the freak in her. She fucked me like she was auditioning for a role in a porn flick and I enjoyed every stroke even though I knew that I was dumping her.

And I did. I dumped her during the after-glow. At the time, I didn't know that fucking someone and dumping them as soon as you "pull-out" was a bad idea, but she quickly showed me that it was.

Slowing my breathing, I rolled off of her. "Mabel…you know…I've been thinking…"

"About what, honey?" she asked, as she grabbed my arm and wrapped it around herself.

"Now, that the girls are gone…"

She sat up on one arm and with a curious look on her face, she said, "Yes?"

"I was thinking…"

She sat up on the bed. "Yes, baby…please, ask your question…"

"Well, now that they are gone…maybe you could…"

Jumping up and down on the bed, she said, "Yes, Remy…YES!!!!"

I sat up and looked at her. "Yes, what?"

"YES...I WILL MARRY YOU!!!!" She threw her arms around my neck and hugged me. "Yes, yes, yes...!!!"

The fuck? I pushed her back off of me and said, "Nooooooo...I was thinking that you could move out."

Now, frowning, she said, "Move out?"

Now, I was frowning. "Marriage? What would make you think that I would want to get married?"

Her tone changed. "Wait one fucking minute...Your daughters move out and then you put me out? The fuck?"

"I was going to talk to you about this earlier, but you started kissing a brother's neck and shit and you know what that does to me..."

"So, wait a minute, wait a minute, wait minute...all this time, you knew that you were going to dump me...and you still had sex with me?"

"That doesn't affect an erection...this head was thinking about dumping you. The other head...well, it had other plans."

Her eyes grew so wide that I thought that they were going to pop out of her head and hit me in the face. She flipped on her "Nay-Nay" switch. She rolled her neck and her eyes and continued, "Wait a minute…wait one motherfucking minute. I know that you didn't just fuck me and dump me."

"What were we just talking about, Mabel? I swear that we've already gone over that. And I thought that that would be nice…we make love one last time…before…"

"The hell? Are you serious, dude?" She huffed. "Not if you're the only motherfucker in the room who's aware of the plan…"

"Don't act like this, Mabel…"

"Like what, Remy? Like a motherfucker who just got fucked and dumped?"

"I didn't know that we were committed to each other…"

"Motherfucker…my clothes are in your closet…"

"I know and wasn't that nice of me?"

"Your ass is crazy…" She stood to put on her clothes. "Look at my ear…your daughter did this shit…I didn't press chargers because I love you."

"And what does your ear have to do with this?"

"How am I going to date again?"

"I got passed it…"

"Your daughter did it!!!"

"I'm just saying…you only need your ear for listening…doesn't get in the way of anything else."

"Are you serious?" she asked. "You sound like your damn daughter…"

"Mabel…everything has an expiration date…we had a good time…I didn't promise you anything more than that."

"So you just fucked me…now, you want to leave me."

"I'm not going anywhere…you are…"

"You son-of-a-bitch…I wasn't fucking playing house. I wasn't practicing. I was 'in it to win it.'"

"Win what? A husband?" I frowned. "You women are all alike…using your pussies to trap a brother…"

She walked over to where I was standing. She stuck her finger in my face. "The fuck you just say?"

"You heard me and get your finger out of my face."

"I don't need to trick a motherfucker into doing anything and I'm not someone you just use, Remy…"

"Mabel…some advice…you want a husband? Get the ring, first. You stick your finger out and he's either going to put a ring on it or walk away. You open your legs and you're only going to get one thing." I paused for a second and continued, "Well, maybe four things, but ain't none of them a ring. You open your legs and think a man is going to stick a ring in it? Not unless it's wrapped around the tip of his dick."

"Asshole…" She was breathing so hard, snot flew out of her nose. "I see why those girls were so fucked up. That's 'cause you're fucked up. You've been hiding this crazy shit this whole time because you knew that once exposed, no one would fuck you…even if you paid for it."

"If I paid for it, the hoe wouldn't be all up in my face…talking about marriage."

"Are you calling me a hoe?"

"No, I'm just saying…"

"But I love you, Remy…we just made love…"

"And look how fast we went from making love to making hate…"

She shook her head. "I just don't believe this shit…"

"You know what you need, Mabel…"

"Don't tell me what I need…your ass needs a colonic because you are full of shit."

"You make it seem like I said or did something to deceive you. We had sex…I wasn't the only one screaming…you screamed a few times too…I would say that we're even, but you slept in my bed…ate…enjoyed the heat…washed your ass..."

She opened her mouth to say something, but then she stopped. All of a sudden, the look on her face changed. She cracked her neck and she cracked her knuckles like she was about to do something, so I braced myself for whatever was coming, but then she just smiled. She turned and put on her clothes.

"I'm really sorry, Mabel"

"Fuck you, Remy and fuck the horse that your low-down dirty ass, rode in on…"

Damn…the horse too? I thought to myself. "If I hurt you, I'm sorry."

She turned and looked at me. "If…motherfucker, did you just say, 'If?'"

"Yes…I really am sorry. Look…let me help you get your things together…"

Her eyes grew dark. She slipped on a pair of shoes, grabbed her keys, and her purse and said, "You can have this shit…"

"I am sorry, Mabel." I followed her down the hall and into the living room.

She opened the door. "No…you're not sorry, but you will be."

"Is that a threat?"

"No lover…that's a promise."

Chapter 37

The truth is, I was glad that she was gone and in her absence, I didn't lose one night of sleep thinking about her. The only time that I'd thought about her was when I had a hard-on and there were other ways to take care of that. Now, I was alone and it's when you're alone that the demons start to speak to you. When you're reflecting on all of the messed-up shit in your life is when you start to hear those little voices that call-out to you. And I did everything that I could to ignore them, but then I was looking out of the kitchen one day and I saw that patch of grass in the back-yard that seemed greener than all of the other grass in the yard and I thought about what lied underneath it – her little body and the lies that buried and kept her there. And just when I thought that that was enough to send me over the edge, I get one of the worst phone calls that any man in my position could get.

Ring! Ring!

When I looked at the caller-id, I sat the phone down because we were done. I didn't have anything else to say to her. Unless, she wanted to drop by for a "quickie."

Ring! Ring!

I walked away from it and decided to turn on the TV to drown out its sound. I must have drifted off, because a few hours later, I awakened to the sound of someone banging on the door. Groggily, I walked over to the door and looked through its peep-hole. *What the fuck does she want?"* I thought to myself. I pretended to not be at home, but then I looked down to find the doorknob *turning. Forgot to change the locks...SHIT!!!* Before I could do anything, I was staring her in the face.

"Why didn't you answer your phone?"

"When people want to talk they answer their phone...I didn't want to talk."

"Well...I need to talk to you about something."

"Well, what is it?" I asked, walking away from her.

"Well…I'm pregnant."

I stopped. It felt like someone had just thrown a shoe and hit me in the back of the head. At first, I didn't respond. I needed a minute to process all of it.

"Did you hear me? I said, 'that I was pregnant.'"

I still didn't turn around because facing her would be acknowledging her and her bullshit, so I kept walking. I walked over to the refrigerator and said, "Congratulations…who's the lucky guy?"

"You," she confirmed, following me into the kitchen.

"Well…that's tragic…"

"Why do you say that?"

"Cause…I don't want any more kids…"

"This is a sign, Remy, that we're supposed to be together. This baby is ours…to love and to raise together…"

"You see how the other two turned out…why would I want to do that all over again?"

"Well, maybe things will turn out different this time…"

"It won't…why? Because I'm fucked up and you're fucked up…and in this case, two negatives will not make a positive."

"Please, Remy…"

"Look…I'm not trying to be mean…"

"But you're being mean…"

"I don't mean to. I just know that I can't be a father again and I definitely can't be with you right now. I need to take some time and work shit out. "

She reached out to me. "We can work things out together…"

I slammed my hands on the countertop. "Kids should never be used that way. They shouldn't be the reason for love but the result of love…"

"Please…"

"You're trying to make me do this, Mabel. What do you think will come out of that? When you try to force a man to do some shit he don't wanna do…"

"But it's yours…"

"The jury is still out on that…I don't know what you've been doing since I've last seen you."

"Don't do that, Remy…I'm not a whore. I know who I've been with."

"And you want me to take your word?"

She walked around, trying to face me, but I turned my head to avoid her. "Remy, don't do this…"

"I can't, Mabel…I can't…"

"So what do you want me to do?"

"You're grown…figure it out."

"Figure it out? What do you mean?"

"I mean that I just can't do it…not now…not ever…"

"Well, you're going to…"

"Look, just like being a father is an option, being a daddy is too…I'm sorry that this happened, but I'm telling you that I can't be either one…I can't."

I walked over to the couch and sat down. "I'm sorry that this has happened to you…"

"You mean to 'us'…"

I sighed. "Okay Mabel…whatever…text me and let me know how things work out at the clinic…get a receipt and I'll reimburse you."

"The fuck? You're not going half on dinner or paying for gas…this is a child's life…"

I didn't turn around. "Lock the door on your way out and please…leave the key." For a moment, she was quiet. Then, I heard some footsteps, but they weren't heading towards the door. They were coming towards me. As I stared at the TV, I could see her reflection in it. Her arm went up in the air and when it came down, she hit me in the chest. Then, she did it again and again and again; smooth like a child banging on the table when their breakfast is late and before I had a chance to think – before I had a chance to move, she threw something in my lap.

"Reimburse that, you lousy piece of shit," she said, before turning to walk away. Suddenly, she walked back over and grabbed my mouth. Forcing it open, she said, "And here's your fucking key."

I spit the key out of my mouth and into my hand. At first, I didn't feel anything until I saw the silver thing sitting in my lap. Then, I felt something warm trickle down my chest. I looked down and saw red stuff staining my shirt. I grabbed my shirt and ripped it open. I looked down and there were bubbles coming out of one of the holes. I rolled onto the floor and crawled over to where my phone was sitting. I pressed 9-1-1.

A voice came through the receiver. "9-1-1, what's your emergency?"

"I've…been…stabbed…" I said, trying to stop the blood. "She stabbed me."

"Who, sir…where are you?" the operator asked.

"I'm on my floor…dying…"

"Okay…okay…we're going to get someone right over there, okay?" she said. "Are you there alone?"

"Yes…" I said, gurgling.

"Sir…hang on. Someone's on their way."

I fell back onto the floor. I was drifting in and out of consciousness.

"Sir, stay with me…now, who did this to you?"

"Mama? Mama?" The phone slipped from my fingers.

"Sir….sir…sir?"

Grace

Chapter 38

Smack, smack, smack...

My tongue was glued to the roof of my mouth. I looked around the darkness. I noticed that they'd untied me. I tried to move but with every movement came excruciating pain. My vagina burned as if it'd been dragged across a carpeted floor. I tried to move my legs, but realized that they were still tied to the bed – spread-eagle. I reached down and touched my ankles. There was something wrapped around them. I searched for the knots and untied them. I sat up and that's when I realized that there was something sticking out of me. I looked down. I couldn't make out what it was because the room was so dark so I, slowly, pulled it out of me.

I threw my legs over the side of the bed and limped over to the window and removed the coverings. I flinched because the sun burned my eyes. Once I was able to focus, I looked over at the bed. In the middle of it was a large cucumber covered in blood. I began to cry. I looked back at the window. Just then, I saw someone walking down the sidewalk. I began to bang on the window. I tried to cry out, but my mouth and throat were so sore that I was only capable of whispering. "Help…help…"

They looked up. I banged harder and whispered, loudly, "Help…help…"

They smiled, waved, and proceeded down the sidewalk.

"No…wait…please come back…come back…"

It was then that I heard a click-click sound. She walked in. "Good morning, Sleepy-head…"

I fell on all fours and tried crawling away from her.

"Don't be like that…" She stopped and looked at the bed. "You made such a mess last night…" She picked up the cucumber and took a bite out of it. "Absolutely delicious…" She looked over at me. "Now, what would you like for breakfast?"

I whispered. "I want to go home."

"You keep asking and I keep saying 'no'."

"And I will keep asking…"

She chewed and swallowed. "Home isn't on the menu, but we got some ham and eggs."

I crawled over to where she was standing. "Please, I swear…let me go…I won't tell anybody."

"I need you to wash your ass because you're starting to stink up the place." She stood to leave the room. "Tonight is going to be fun. We're going to have company."

"Please…why won't you tell me why you're doing this me?"

She stopped and looked at me. Her eyes grew dark when she said, "Because we can." She walked out and locked the door.

I crawled over to the bathroom door. Using the door-knob, I lifted myself. I limped over to the mirror and looked into it. My eyes were red and swollen. There were bruises on the side of my mouth. I looked down to find an imprint of something on my left breast. I examined it closely. *Teeth marks.* I grabbed my stomach. It hurt so bad. I sat down to use the toilet. The urine burned the folds of my skin. I grabbed the wall and sink and grimaced in pain as my bladder emptied itself. When I was done, I crawled over to the tub and turned on the water. Before the tub could fill, I climbed inside. I began to cry again.

The bedroom door opened. I could hear her humming and moving around the room. When she was done, she came into the bathroom and turned the water off. "Do you know how much we spend on water every month? Sprinkle some water and soap on that shit and let's go."

I looked at her and frowned.

"I made you breakfast. It's on your bed. Now, hurry up…I ain't got all day."

Slowly, I placed the soap on the towel and began to wash myself. Once I rinsed, I stood to dry my skin. Out of the corner of my eye, I could see her there – watching and waiting for me.

I wrapped the towel around me and walked out into the room.

There was some lotion, perfume, and some underwear sitting on the bed. "Put this on…I will be back to check on you shortly." She was about to leave the room, when she said, "Don't let me catch you banging on the that window again or I will toss you out of it…you don't want to know how concrete feels once your head hits the pavement…believe me…you don't want to know…it'll mess-up that pretty little face of yours and that'll be a waste." She walked out of the room. I looked at the plate of food and the other things on the bed and pushed them aside. I climbed into the bed and cried myself to sleep.

A few hours later, I was awakened by voices in the hall. The door opened. Several people walked in the room. Charlie weaved her way through the crowd and looked at me. She sighed, turned, and looked over her shoulder. "She's still in training…I'm sorry." She removed the plate of food. "Didn't I tell you to put this on?" she asked, angrily. I ignored her. She raised her hand and slapped me across my face. "When I tell you to do something…do it."

I licked the blood off of the corner of my mouth.

"Give us a second…she needs to get dressed."

One of the men said, "She won't need it."

The other men in the room began to laugh.

"She's going to make this up to you...to all of you."

Gage walked over and pulled-up a chair. "Let's get started."

Each one of them began to remove their clothing.

Charlie whispered in my ear. "Remember…hard or easy…"

I looked at her and then at all of the faces in the room. Defeated, I laid down onto the bed.

She looked over at them and asked, "Who's first?"

As tears rolled down the side of my face, I closed my eyes and tried to imagine that I was home.

The next morning, I awoke to him standing over me.

"You didn't eat…"

My mouth was so dry, I could barely open it. "I'm not hungry."

He sighed and sat next to me. "Peaches…I know that this may be hard for you, but a hunger strike isn't going to work."

I rolled over.

"Look, I know that you're hungry. You have food…you should eat."

I didn't respond.

"You take too much for granted…When I was young, we had so little. When there's no food…your body starts to eat itself… the pain that you feel when you're knocking on death's door….you can't imagine…that was my life." He rubbed my back. "It's almost over, Peaches. I promise you. Now, eat…"

Chapter 39

Every hole in my body was sore and swollen. I tried to move, but I was too weak. I was going to cry, but I'd cried so much, air replaced my tears. I turned over and moaned in agony. I crawled into the fetal position, closed my eyes, and waited for death to free me from this hell.

"She told me that you want to go home," a voice said, from across the room.

Whimpering, I said, "Hello?"

He stood and slid the chair across the room. He sat it next to the bed. He reached over to push my hair out of my face. He looked at the wall behind me and said, "We've grown so close these past few months...wouldn't you agree?"

I didn't respond.

"I feel like I can trust you, so I'm going to tell you a story." He walked over to the closet and removed a blanket. He placed it over me. "Peaches…when you saw me in the mall, you saw a young man who seemed to have a good head on his shoulders. A young man with his shit together. You looked in my eyes and saw a man that you could trust…that you could love…"

I was about to say something, but I knew that it would be a waste of time.

He laughed. "They say that the eyes are the windows to the soul. What do you see when you look in mine?"

"I see darkness…"

"My 'windows' must be dirty…" He laughed. "Parents should talk to their kids, more, about stranger-danger…"

I didn't respond.

"Did I tell you that I was adopted? In the beginning, they gave me all of the love and everything that I needed to grow up to be a healthy little boy. We were such a happy family and I loved them so much. What I didn't understand, at the time, was that they were grooming me…"

"For what?" I asked.

"That's a good question." He looked down at the floor and then back up at me. "This…"

"This?"

"The thing about families is that they all have their secrets and in the beginning, they were able to hide them from us, but once we got older…" He stopped to tuck the blankets underneath me. "I remember when he used to do this…"

"Who?"

"My father…" He sighed. "He used to tuck me in. He and my mother used to take turns checking on us. My mother used to say 'goodnight' to us every night and then he would come in behind her, and tuck us in. But then, one night, mama didn't say 'goodnight'. When we got up the next morning, we looked for her, but she wasn't there. I remember that he made us breakfast that morning….which was really strange because mama always made us breakfast." He paused and continued, "Burnt toast, burnt eggs, and burnt bacon. He would have burnt the orange juice too if he could have. We ate that every day until he could no longer afford the bacon. Next, it was the eggs and finally, it was the toast. We were so hungry – so cold. Soon they turned off our lights and our heat. Do you know what it feels like to be hungry and have no heat during one of Chicago's coldest winters? Of course, you don't…" He began to grind his teeth. "Sometimes, I can still taste that shit…like eating ashes…until nothing was left but air." And like a switch had been flipped, he snapped. "THAT BITCH! THAT BITCH!! SHE WAS SUPPOSED TO TAKE CARE OF ME! LOVE ME! BUT SHE LEFT US…SHE LEFT ME!"

I didn't respond.

He collected himself and continued, "He was too proud to beg and too afraid of going to jail for shoplifting, so we ate whatever he could find." He shook his head. "You never know how poor you are until you wake up one day and you wonder what it would be like to eat one of your siblings." He paused for a moment and then continued. "You see, he drank. He didn't have money for food or money for bills, but he found money for a bottle. It's amazing how people, who have so little, waste the little that they have on bullshit. I guess my mother got tired of listening to his excuses for not being able to do nice things for her and her children, because he didn't have any money, while guzzling down a bottle of bourbon or that he couldn't buy us shoes because he needed to get a bottle of wine. I guess it helped that he drank. Then, he couldn't hear or see her as she walked away from him and his children or see the trucks as they hauled all of our shit out of our house. You know what else alcohol does?"

"What?"

"Alcohol turns a man into the monster that he keeps trapped inside."

"Where is he now?" I asked.

"Dead, if he's lucky…" he said. "He refused to change…until, the bitter end…he refused to change. The sad thing is, he thought that she would never leave him, until she did…and left us too."

"And this is why you hurt me? You're blaming Peaches for what happened to you?" I said.

He sighed. "No…people are the sum of their choices. You didn't do any of this to me, but sadly, shit rolls down-hill…it all began somewhere else and it'll end here with me and you." He inhaled. "Take a deep breath, Peaches. You smell that? That is shit rolling…"

"But we've never done anything to you…"

"True…but like they say, 'No deed goes unpunished."

"No good deed," I said, correcting him.

He stood to leave the room. "I will share more of my story with you, later." He looked over at the nightstand. He saw the picture of my family and smiled. "You're really going to love the ending. I promise you. Now, get some rest. The next few days are going to be hell."

Peaches

Chapter 40

School was killing me. I had to keep telling myself that it was almost over. The only thing that kept me going was Isaac. He became such an intricate part of my life. He was always there making sure that I had everything that I needed. Every time, I looked up, he was sending me something. Having his driver arrive at my school with gifts and food was starting to make the other students jealous, but I didn't care. I was loving it. He made me feel like a queen and out of all of the women in the world, he chose me. I used to question how something so good could happen to someone like me, but it did. There were some days where it was too much to take in. He was so perfect. Almost too perfect.

And I was in love and when you fall in love, you become stupid. All sense of reason and logic ceases to exist. All you want to do is crawl up inside of them and leave the world and the horrors that exist in it, behind you. And Isaac did that for me. The thought of him made every cell in my body come alive and I think he knew it. If he didn't, it was because he wasn't looking or that he was blind, because no matter how I tried to hide it, my heart couldn't keep it a secret and I wanted to prove it to him.

The strange thing is, is that he never asked me for "it." Most guys would be begging for it or cheating at this point. Not him or at least that's what he says, but he was a man and I wasn't no fool. A man that looked that good and had that much money, could have any woman that he wanted, but he was waiting for me? *Yeah, right.* But I didn't want to lose him to someone who may be putting-out, so I needed to step up my game.

I wanted to prepare for it. Not like I did the first time. Like that old saying about "Fools rushing in"…this time I wanted to make sure that I did it right. I decided to ask my roommate some questions about her sex life. She was a girl who was very open about her wants, needs, and desires, so I knew that I would get the answers that I needed from her.

I was about to walk into our room, but I could hear her having a heated conversation with someone.

"Shiiiiiiiittttttt, who's that nigga? He's my nigga. Well, fuck that nigga and all of his nigga shit. Okay, then shoot that nigga. Why? Cause he's a nigga and when niggas do…niggas get done…when niggas get…niggas get got…nigga this…nigga that…nigga, nigga, nigga…that nigga's whack, heeeeeeyyyyyyy."

I thought that she was in need of assistance, but I walked into the room to find her dancing across the floor.

I tapped her on the shoulder and startled her.

She jumped and removed her headphones. "Girl, you almost got fucked up."

I laughed. "I thought that you were in here, already, fucking somebody up."

"Naw, girl…I was listening to this hot new track on the radio. It's a love song…"

I frowned and asked, "What? That's music?"

"Yeah, girl…that shit is HOT!"

"Sounds like a hot-ass-mess…" I sat down on my bed.

"Well, what do you listen to, Mother Peaches?"

"Well, I'm definitely not listening to that mess. You can't call me a nigga in the street without getting your ass whopped…so you're definitely not putting that shit to music and think that I'm going to dance to it."

She shook her head. "You know…that might be the reason why your dance card is empty…"

"Well, the shit can stay empty if I gotta dance to that mess."

She laughed. "You ain't gon' ever get laid with that attitude."

"Don't take much to get laid…believe me…" This felt like the perfect time to pop my question, but I had to wait thirty minutes for her to stop laughing.

"You're asking me about sex? How old are you?" she asked, wiping tears from her eyes.

I sighed.

"I know that you've fuck somebody. You have not gon' this far in life without dancing with the one-eyed dragon."

"The what?" I laughed.

"Never-mind, you're too 'green' to understand."

"I know what you're talking about and yes…I did something, but it was more like a drive-by than sex." I shrugged. "Can't really tell you anything else about it."

She fell on the floor, laughing. After she wiped her eyes, she said, "The fact that you don't know or can't remember or don't want to remember means that he didn't make a good first impression."

"Not even an indent…let alone an impression."

She started laughing again. "Well, girl, I've been having sex since I realized I had a hole and that it was good for more than just pee'ing…"

"Wow…that long?"

"Girl please….I'm thinking about doing it right now."

"Well, don't look at me."

"Don't nobody want you…" she laughed.

I laughed, again. "From what I can remember, it was horrible."

"Horrible?"

"Yeah…he was quick on the draw…is it always that way?"

She fell-out laughing. "Hil-ar-ious…I never had one of those before…I usually get the ones who get in and don't know how to get out. Gotta serve their asses eviction papers."

I laughed.

"Okay…" She balled-up her hand. "Maybe we need to start at the beginning…This is your vagina…"

"I know about that part…"

She pointed her index finger and continued, "Okay…imagine that this is his dick."

"Got it…" I said.

Then, she tried forcing her finger into her fist. She made an 'in and out' motion with her finger.

"This is sex…he's going to knock on your vagina's door with his dick until your vagina lets him in."

I frowned. "And what if it doesn't want it to come in?"

"Girl, you're crazy…anything that knocks long enough and hard enough, eventually, gets let in…" she laughed.

I laughed. "That illustration wasn't very academic…"

"Neither is sex…any layman can do it. But not everybody can do it right."

"What about oral sex? How soon is too soon?"

"Save that for the second or third time…you don't want to give him everything on the first go 'round'…they get spoiled…start acting funny when they don't get it…but he HAS to do you on the first date. That is a must…"

"Really?" I asked.

"A must," she confirmed.

"But is that fair?"

"Of course, it's fair. Men have the advantage in sex. They will get an erection and they will cum, no matter what. You could be ugly as hell…matter of fact, you don't even have to be human…it could be air…and the party is on and crack-a-lackin'. So you better get yours…'cause he's going to get his, no matter what…"

"Interesting…"

"You see…that's the difference between a man and a boy. A man won't even ask you…he walks in hungry…enjoys an appetizer before his meal…and THEN, he handles his business…a boy will climb on top of you…hump you like he's in a race against himself…bust a nut…and leave you pissed off and wanting to stab his ass in his sleep."

"That's what he did…"

"Those damn boys…" she confirmed.

"Does your boyfriend do…ummmmm, perform oral on you?"

"Girl, it's a requirement…he may not go to a restaurant every day, but he will be eating out… every day…that's for damn sho'…EVERY

DAY...and the only thing on the menu is me and what's between these fat-ass thighs."

I paused to process what she was saying. "Oh...okay...that's funny...and how do you do that...oral sex?"

"You ever had a popsicle? Same concept...the goal is to suck it, before it melts...'cause it's going to melt...probably faster than you'll want it to...if you know what I mean..."

"Got it...that should be easy." I laid back against my pillow. "I can't wait to have sex with Isaac...he's so good to me."

She walked over and sat next to me. "Never fuck a man because you feel like you owe him something. You start off acting that way and he's going to treat you that way. This is your first time...with him...since the other time wasn't good, it don't count...so you do it, because you love him."

"I do love him...he's a good guy. I know that he cares about me."

"Has he ever told that he loves you?"

"No...not yet, but he shows me."

"That's good, but get confirmation before you give up the panties."

I laughed. "I will…mama…"

"Do you talk about these things with your mother or your sister?"

"My mama is deceased and my sister is gone…"

"Gone where?"

"I don't know…" Suddenly, I became uncomfortable. "Can we talk about something else?"

She changed the subject. "So when do you plan on doing this?"

I jumped up, excitedly. "This weekend…I'm going to go shopping…get some lingerie…red…that's his favorite color and then, I'm going to put it on him."

She teased. "You gon' put it on him?"

"All over him…" I confirmed.

"Well, don't hurt him," she said, before climbing back into her bed.

"But I really want to..." I smiled and closed my eyes to daydream about my baby.

Chapter 41

After spending the whole day preparing for our first time, I called him and asked him to come and pick me up. For the first time, he didn't send his driver. When the car rolled up, it was him behind the wheel with a big smile on his face. When I saw him, I was so excited, I could hardly contain myself. After putting an overnight bag inside of the trunk, I jumped inside of the car. I was smiling from ear to ear. I kissed him and said, "I missed you."

He waited for me to buckle my seatbelt before saying, "I missed you too."

I hugged him.

"So how have you been?" he asked, as he pulled off.

"I've been good…passed all of my exams…going to be doing my residencies soon…really looking forward to getting some hands-on…"

He smiled. "Yeah…it'll be nice to have a doctor in the family…"

"In the family?" I asked.

"Yeah…you see a future for us, right?"

"Yes, Isaac…of course…"

"I'm glad that you said, 'yes.'"

"Now, that you bring that up…I was wondering…what do you think about…you know…taking the next step?"

He slammed on the brakes. "Next step????"

I looked back. "You're going to cause an accident…"

He looked around before pulling off. "You're talking about sex, right?"

"Yes…what do you think about that?"

"I think talking about it is a good start…discuss expectations…stuff like that…"

"Expectations?"

"Yes," he said.

"I don't have any expectations…I just want a man who will fight for me and not with me."

"That's not asking for a lot…"

"You'd be amazed…"

He reached out and touched my hand. "So when do you want to take that step?" he asked.

"Tonight…"

He slammed on his brakes again.

"Stop doing that, Isaac, before you get us killed."

He pulled off again. "So, you want to do it tonight?"

"Yes…" I confirmed.

"You sure?"

"I'm sure…"

He picked up the phone and made a call. "I should be there in thirty…yes, my regular suite…" He paused and looked over at me. "Make it special…" He hung up the phone. He reached over, grabbed my hand, and held it until we arrived in front of the Waldolf Astoria.

This hotel is absolutely beautiful - deep red woods, white marble, breath-taking views of the city, just absolutely beautiful. I was lost in its beauty until I heard the *ding* of the elevator door. As I watched the numbers light-up on the board, I became so nervous, I began to sweat everywhere. He could tell that I was scared, so he leaned over and wrapped his arms around me. As we walked down the hall to the room, I mumbled, "Don't fuck this up?"

The bellhop opened the door. He sat my bag on the floor and walked out of the room. Isaac tipped him with a hundred dollar bill. "See that we're not disturbed."

"Absolutely, Mr. Ramsey," he said, as he closed the door. A trail of rose petals met us at the door. We followed them to a king sized bed that sat in the middle of the floor. The covers had been turned back. A fire roared from the fireplace as its flame lit the room. He grabbed my hand and said, "You don't have to do this."

Nervously, I said, "No, I want to."

He smiled and said, "Okay…"

I grabbed my bag and went into the bathroom. I closed and locked the door. Once inside I sat on the side of the tub and tried to psyche myself out. I was about to take my clothes off, when I remembered what my roommate said, "Make sure that he loves you before you give up the panties." I stood and walked out of the bathroom. When I came out, I could hear him talking to someone. "Hey…" I said.

He turned and looked at me. "Isaac…I have a question…"

"Sure…what?"

"Do you love me?"

He smiled and touched my cheek. "I think I loved you from the first moment I laid eyes on you…I told you that."

I smiled. "Okay…I just want to make sure…I'll be back." I was so happy, I skipped out of the room. Once inside of the bathroom, I turned on the sink to freshen-up a bit. I took out my perfume and sprayed a little behind my ears, on my wrists, and on my thighs. I slid on the red negligee, that I'd purchased earlier, took a deep breath, and entered the room.

When I walked in, he smiled. He stood and walked over to me. He took my hands and asked, "Ready?"

"Ready," I confirmed, as my heart beat hard against my chest. He walked over and turned on some music. He turned back towards me and began to remove his shirt. When he revealed his chest, I saw the boy who'd convinced me that life was worth living. He walked up to me. I placed my hand over his heart. I could feel it beating against the palm of my hand. He took my hand and kissed it.

Suddenly, he picked me up and carried me over to the bed. He laid me down. I watched him as he removed the rest of his clothing. When he slipped off his pants, I blurted out, "Holy shit…!"

He laughed. "Too much?"

"What are you going to do with that?"

"Do I really need to answer that question...maybe we should wait?"

I could barely get the words out. "No, I'm sure I'll be fine, right?"

"I promise…I'll be gentle." When he was done undressing, he climbed on the bed and laid next to me. "You are so beautiful."

"You're beautiful too…"

He smiled and kissed me. He slid his hand under my gown and slowly removed my panties. My thoughts were racing. "Isaac…I have to tell you something."

Looking me in my eyes, he said, "Yes…"

"I'm afraid."

He looked down and rubbed his fingers over my legs. He kissed my hand again. "I won't hurt you…if I do…just tell me to stop."

"Okay…" I began to relax.

Slowly, he kissed my neck and I closed my eyes as he made love to me.

I was so tired that at first I thought that the voices that I was hearing were a part of my dream. I reached over on his side of the bed and realized that he wasn't there. Still dazed, I turned towards the bathroom door. I saw the light illuminating from under it. Sleepily, I crawled out of the bed.

"Isaac?" As I grew closer, I could hear him arguing with someone. "Isaac?" I walked closer and heard him say. "I love her."

I walked up to the door and placed my ear against it.

Isaac said, "She doesn't want my money…I won't let you come between us…."

I knocked on the door, interrupting them. "Isaac? Is everything okay?"

He turned on the water. As soon as it went off, the door flew open. "Sweetie, what are you doing awake?" He turned off the light.

Looking over his shoulder into the bathroom, I said, "Isaac? Who are you talking to?"

He grabbed my hand. "No one…now, let's go back to bed."

We walked over to the bed and climbed under the blankets.

"But I heard you talking to someone."

"I was, ummmm, singing. Yeah, singing."

"You were singing?"

"Yeah…now, come on…let's go to sleep."

Isaac wrapped himself in my arms and fell back to sleep while I spent the whole night staring at the bathroom door.

Remy

Chapter 42

I can't move my legs. I can't move my arms. Oh shit. Lord, I'm dead. The bitch don' killed me. I swear…this is why you can't turn your back on motherfuckers. Cut down in the prime of my life. I had so many plans. I was going to wear my new shirt, tomorrow, with my black jeans. I think the Bears were playing tomorrow. I had some leftover chili in the refrigerator. Damn, that chili was good. Wait…did I flush the toilet? I hope that I did. That would be embarrassing. I bet my daddy is going through all of my shit. A good thing that I have some life insurance. He'll probably still cremate my ass and spend the rest of my money at the casinos…dirty bastard. Ahhhhh damn, lord, I'm not ready. I'm too young and too good looking. Well, Peaches…I'm on my way, baby. I hope she didn't meet anyone new while up there. I wouldn't want to have to kick somebody's ass in Heaven. Wait a minute…what is that?

Beep, beep, beep…

What is that?

Beep, beep, beep, beep…

Is that my heartbeat? Lord, please let that be my heartbeat.

Beep, beep, beep…

Someone walked into the room.

Who is that? Hey, what's going on? Where am I?

They didn't respond.

HEY, WHERE AM I?!!!

They still didn't respond.

Don't ignore me…what's going on? What's happening to me?

I felt them touch me.

Why can't they hear me? I tried to move again, but couldn't. *What is this? What are you doing to me?* They turned and left the room.

Moments later, someone else walked into the room.

Hey, please help me!!!

"I'm so sorry, baby…" she said.

Sorry? Wait…I recognize that voice.

"You just made me so mad," she said.

Mabel!!! Holy shit! Get this crazy bitch away from me!!!!

Someone else walked into the room. "How is he doing?" she asked.

"He's on heavy medications for the pain…this way, his body has time to heal…" the other voice said.

Just sleep? Thank God…I'm alive! I'm alive! But wait…this bitch…Get this bitch out of here!!!!

"When will he be awake again?" she asked.

"He's going to be in and out for a while…one of the cuts just missed his heart…"

"I told him, doctor…you have to be careful out there…there are so many crazy people in the world…"

"What? It's you…crazy wasn't in the streets, it walked in my house…"

"Oh, thank you, doctor…I don't know what I would do without him."

"Well, I'll leave you here to visit with him…"

"Thank you, doctor…" she said.

Wait….noooooo…don't leave me in here with her!!!! NOOOOOOOOOOO!!!!!

When the door closed, she said, "Look what you made me do."

Wait…what?

"All you had to do was do right by me…"

Huh?

"I didn't want to stab you, but you wouldn't listen…"

Oh, I'm listening now…

"Now, God spared you because he wants us to be together…he wants us to be a family."

This bitch is nuts.

"I love you, Remy and I'm going to take good care of you."

Your 'taking care of me' is why I'm in the damn hospital.

"We're going to forget about this little misunderstanding and we're going to love each other...and we're going to be a family...we're going to be happy...okay??? Or the next time, I won't miss."

HELP!!!!!!!!

Grace

Chapter43

"What day is it?" I asked.

"Time…is just an illusion…" she said, removing the covers from the windows. "You shouldn't worry your pretty little head with such things." She turned and looked at me. "You are a mess."

I didn't respond.

"Guess what?"

I looked at her.

"I'm going to let you out of the room today…"

"I'm going home?" I asked, almost too weak to speak. I shielded my eyes from the burning rays of the sun.

"No, the house needs cleaning before the party tonight."

"Party?" I asked.

"Yes…" she reached for me.

I pulled away.

"I'm sorry…men…you can't live with them and you can't get fucked up the ass without em'…" She laughed and rubbed the hairs on her chin. "I guess you could, but plastic is just so…'plastic-iky' and lonely…wouldn't you agree?"

I begged. "Please kill me…"

"Soon…but right now, I have a list of things that I need done…"

"I'm begging you…"

"Your lips are moving, but it's only turning me on…"

"Please…where's your friend? Maybe he'll kill me…"

She shook her head. "He's out picking up a few things for the party…" She looked around the room. "He left some special instructions for you, so let's go…"

"Can I use the bathroom? Put on some clothes?"

"You can use the bathroom, but we've already discussed the clothes-thing…and you should be happy…not having to worry about what to wear…Personally, I think that clothes are overrated. I think that we should all go 'au naturale' like God intended…'"

"Wouldn't that be a problem for you? Especially, the 'au naturale' part?" I asked.

She frowned. "Fuck you…now, walk your 'au naturale' ass down the hall…"

I crawled out of the bed, and went to the bathroom. I didn't turn on the light because I didn't want to see my face. I started to use the bathroom, but the burning was so bad, I had to stop. I stood in the tub, turn on the cold water, and began to fill my hands with it. After filling them, I placed the water on my vagina in an attempt to put out the fire that was blazing between my legs. I screamed. "Shit!!!!"

She walked in and grabbed my arm. "I said, 'Let's go…'" She dragged me until we were in the kitchen. "Now…get over there and wash those dishes."

I limped over to the sink and began to fill it with water.

"And those dishes better be clean…" she said, as she sat at the table to watch me. When she saw me fill the other sink with water to rinse them with, she stood and walked over. "What are you doing?"

Exhausted, I said, "I'm filling the sink with water…"

She folded her arms. "I see what the fuck you're doing that's why I'm asking."

Confused, I looked down at the sink. "What's wrong?"

She grabbed a spatula that sat nearby and hit me across my back.

I screamed. "Aaaaaaaaaargh!!!!"

"So you're going to wash those dishes in soap water and then stick them in this water which is now going to be full of soap from the dishes and then what? Now we have two sinks full of soapy water. When or how are you going to rinse them? Because now they still have soap on them…you're either going to rinse them again…which means more water OR we're going to be eating off of dishes with soap on them…" She hit me again. "THINK!!!! That's like taking a bath…you bathe…now, the tub is full of dirt and soap…then what? You gone just dry off? Soap all up the crack of your ass…the dirt you just washed off is stuck to you…" She shook her head. "Just nasty." She hit me again.

"Aaaaaaaaaargh!!!!!"

"Now, let that water out of that sink and do the shit right."

"Okay…" I cried.

She walked back over to the table. "I don't know why he had to have you…can't even wash dishes…"

I began to wash the dishes and began to rinse them – one by one.

"Damn it!!!!" She slammed the spatula on the table. "Something is wrong with you…you know that?"

Before I could say anything, she'd hit me again. "Aaaaaaaaargh!!!" I collapsed to the floor.

"Bitch…you think water grows on trees?"

"Huh? No…."

"Wait until that sink is full and rinse them all at the same time…it's not enough that you're taking a shower once a week…now, you wanna waste water."

I climbed back up to the sink. In my weakened state, all I could think about was killing her or wishing that I was dead – whichever came first. I didn't care anymore. Whatever she was going to do, I wanted her to do it now and get it over with. I took a deep breath and said, "Don't get your pantyhose in a bunch. I'm going to wash the damn dishes."

She cupped her hands and blew into them. "Bitch, don't worry about my pantyhose. You better worry about those damn dishes."

"Wash your own dishes…" I said, bracing for the worse.

Frustrated, she said, "You know what? I should cut your tongue out, but you're going to need it later on…." She looked around the room like she was looking for something to punish me with.

"You know what? Bend over…" she demanded. She walked over and tried forcing me over the sink.

I put my hands behind me to block my butt.

"Bend your ass over…this shit is ridiculous…you got a whole house to clean and we are still fucking with these dishes. You have to learn."

"No…"

She looked at me. "Don't make me ask you again…"

This could be the end, Grace. I thought to myself. I took a deep breath and exhaled. I placed my hands on the sink and bent over. *I'm ready.* But she didn't want to kill me, she wanted to break my spirit even further.

She pulled up her skirt and tried to force herself inside of me. She couldn't and after four attempts, she became frustrated. "Now, look…my shit is limp…"

I closed my eyes and mumbled, "Our Father, which art in Heaven…"

She became angrier. "He ain't listening…"

And before I could think. Before I could move, I felt something cold being forced between my legs. Suddenly, I realized what was happening as I felt the handle against my thigh.

"The next time that I tell you to do something, get it right…"

My hands tightened on the sink. I felt the handle moving up my thigh.

"You're going to learn to do what I say…" she said, as she moved the spatula.

I felt the cold steel inside of me. Just then, I looked over and saw a knife sitting on the side of the sink. I grabbed it.

She stopped. "What are you going to do with that?"

I turned and the spatula fell out of her hand.

"So you're going to cut me?"

Through tears, I swung the knife.

"Oh, so you're going to cut me. Don't pull it unless you're going to use it."

"Like that limp dick of yours…" I said, pointing the blade at her.

"You better kill me or I'm going to kill you."

I lunged again, but she jumped out of the way. I fell to the floor. Suddenly, she was on top of me. We wrestled back and forth until she had my hand forced over my head. I took my free hand and began to pull at her hair.

She balled-up her fist and hit me in the face. "I…told…you…" She paused to hit me, again. "Not…to…touch…my…damn…hair…" She hit me one last time. She hit me so hard, I felt my neck crack and then everything went black.

"Arrrrrrgh…" I moaned. Dazed, I looked up to find them staring at me.

"Look at her face, Charlie…" he said.

"I'm sorry, but she tried to cut me."

"What did you do to her?" he asked.

"Well…" she hesitated.

"Come on…" he insisted.

"I told her to wash the dishes and she just couldn't get it right so…"

He shook his head. "So?"

"Soooooooooo, I might have stuck a spatula in her…"

"You might have?"

"The bitch made me limp, so I tried to teach her a lesson…"

"With a spatula?" he asked.

"Well, she was washing dishes…what else was I supposed to use? And look at my hair…I'm going to have to put on a wig, now."

He sighed. "Now, what are we going to do?"

"I could put some make-up on her…make her like new…"

"Like a new what? Can't no makeup fix that…and the party is tonight."

She began to pace. "I know, I know…I'm so sorry. They want her too…now, what are we going to do?"

He dropped his head and then as if a light bulb went off in his head, he said, "You know…she said that she has a twin."

Charlie walked back over and leaned over me. "Really?"

"Yep…" he confirmed.

"That's interesting," she said.

"Yep…" he confirmed, again.

She looked at him and then back at me. "Then, you know what you have to do. I'll go make some calls."

Peaches & Grace

Chapter 44

At first, I wasn't going to say anything about it, but I knew that if I didn't, I would be walking around all day questioning my own sanity, so over breakfast, I decided to talk to him about it. I was staring at him when he pulled out a bottle of pills, opened it, and removed one.

"Headache?" I asked.

"It's nothing…" He swallowed the pill with orange juice and proceeded to eat.

"Ummmmmmm, Isaac…about last night…" I began.

He touched my hand. "Last night was perfect…"

My thoughts drifted back to last night. "Yes, it was…" Snapping out of my daze, I said, "No…I was talking about you…and the bathroom."

Embarrassed, he said, "I'm sorry…I had some red beans and rice earlier in the day…"

I interrupted him. "No, no, not that…"

"Then what, sweetie?"

When he said that, my heart melted. I completely forgot what we were talking about.

"I was shopping, yesterday, and I picked something up for you."

Curious, I asked, "You did?"

"Yes," he said.

He reached underneath the table and when his hand came up, it was holding a small box.

"What is that, Isaac?"

"Just a little something to let you know how much I love you."

"Awwwwww…you didn't have to do that…"

"I wanted to…" He handed the box to me.

I stared at it for a minute before opening it. "It's a ring."

He grabbed my hand. "Peaches…will you marry me?"

I hit him in the arm. "Get out of here…"

"You want me to leave?"

"No silly…the ring…it's too soon."

"I know, but I believe that this is it…you and me…we're meant to be together."

"Wife, Isaac? Do you know me well enough to want to spend the rest of your life with me?"

"You can be with someone a million years and still never really know them, but what I know about you, now? Yes…I want you to be my wife."

"But I'm trying to finish school…"

"And I will support you…"

"Are you sure?"

"Peaches, why do you doubt this? Because we've only known each other for a short period of time? Think about it this way…it only takes a few minutes to make a baby and only nine months to bring one into this world…beautiful things can happen…in a short period of time."

I smiled. "That's true…"

"So let's do it…me and you…let's get married?"

I looked at the ring and then back at him. I thought about it for a moment and said, "Yes, Isaac…I will marry you."

I knew that once I said, "I do", I was saying it to his mama, his grandmother, and to everybody else who were a part of the Ramsey Empire and some of them weren't happy. They, quickly, made me aware of that.

Like a buzzard, she circled around me. "And what do you have to offer my son?" she asked, as she sipped from her glass.

"She don't have to give him anything, but her love," his grandmother said.

Isaac looked on without saying a word. You could tell that he's been raised to keep his mouth shut when these two got started.

"I know your type..." she said, slurring her words.

I frowned.

"You're a gold-digger..." she accused.

I didn't respond.

His grandmother spoke. "Like you?"

"Who?" his mother asked.

"You..." she confirmed. "Look, who's trying to call somebody out. Those who live in glass houses need to sit their butts down somewhere before they get cut."

"I don't think the quote goes like that, mama, but we get what you're trying to say," Isaac said.

"Don't call her, mama..." his mother spat. "I'm your mother."

His grandmother stood and walked up to her. "You're an over-paid baby maker who has worn out her welcome."

His mother's mouth fell open. "How dare you?"

"Trick, I'm just getting started. You flaunt around here like the Queen of Sheba when you ain't nothing but a hoe from the 'hood'. If my son was still alive…"

"Well, he ain't…is he?" his mother spat.

"That's 'cause your crazy-ass killed him. Don't no man kill himself 'cause he has too much money…he kills himself when he realizes that he has to share it with a crazy motherfucker who don't do shit but walk around all day with a glass glued to her lips. I don't even know why you bother using a glass…take that shit to the 'head' like you take the damn gardener."

Isaac stood. "Mama…I mean, grandmother…"

She pulled up her sleeves. "Naw…this bitch gon' learn today…it's time to call a spade a spade…cause you pick up some garbage on the side of the road and clean it off, don't mean that it ain't still garbage…"

She sat her glass down and then, quickly, picked it back up. She was about to say something when his grandmother said, "You better not open your mouth…the only reason why your crazy butt is not back on the streets is because I made a promise to your kids that I would keep you here…" She pointed at the glass in her hand. "And you better remember who buys that liquor in that glass…"

His mother opened her mouth, but then quickly closed it. She huffed and walked out of the room.

His grandmother laughed. "Whew…I've been wanting to do that for a long time…"

"Mama…" He shook his head. "Well, she deserved it."

"Oh, I know she did. Folks get grown and forget their place…that's what the elders are supposed to do…hand-out some grown-up time-outs."

We all laughed. She walked over to me. "For what it's worth…welcome to the family."

"Thank you," I said.

Chapter 45

We spent the whole day shopping. By the time night rolled around, I was ready to climb under a bed. Everyone had retired early, so Isaac and I stayed up to watch a movie. Twenty minutes into it, I was knocked-out. A couple of hours later, I was awakened by what I thought was the TV. With my eyes still closed, I reached for the remote and "clicked" the power button. I heard the sounds again, so I pressed the button again. When I realized that it wasn't working I opened my eyes. In the darkness, I reached out for him. "Isaac?"

"No..." he mumbled.

"Huh?" I asked.

"You can't do this..."

Groggily, I asked. "Huh? Do what?"

"I'm not going to let you do it…"

I wiped the crust from my eyes. "Isaac…what are you talking about?"

He pushed away from me. "No!!!! NO!!!!"

"Isaac…what is going on?"

"NOOOOOOOOOOOOO!!!!!"

Suddenly, the door flew open. His grandmother walked into the room. "Isaac…stop it. Stop it…"

"I know what you're trying to do…" he said, pushing her.

She grabbed him. "Isaac…calm down…now, take this." She managed to get the pills into his mouth. "Now, come on…get in the bed."

"But I told her not to…" he said, as he climbed into the bed.

"I know…I know…she just won't listen…I know…" she said, as she tucked him in. She stroked his face to calm him.

He began to calm down and moments later, he was fast asleep. I looked at her, then at him, and then back at her.

"I guess he didn't tell you…" She stood. "Come on…let mama make you some hot chocolate."

I looked at him. "Is he going to be okay?"

"Until tomorrow…" She took my hand and led me into the kitchen. I sat down at the counter.

She walked over to the refrigerator and took out a carton of milk. "Marshmallows or no marshmallows?"

I looked back over my shoulder.

"Awwwwww, it's okay. He's going to sleep all night."

"I'm not afraid of crazy…me and crazy are cool…but what's wrong with him?"

"I don't know if I should be telling you this…"

"Please tell me…"

"Isaac suffers from auditory hallucinations…"

"He's crazy?"

"No, he just has moments…trauma triggers the voices…"

"Okay…"

"Did he tell you that his father died?"

"Yes…"

She poured the milk into a pot and turned on the stove. "He's fine…and just like any storm, there's the calm…before and after it." When the milk was hot, she poured it into a mug.

"How long?" I asked, as I poured chocolate in the mug.

"Well…it started when he was young. When bad things happened, the voices helped him to cope…like having an imaginary friend, but it started to affect the relationships that he had with real people…"

"Awwwww, not my Isaac…" I said, blowing to cool off the milk.

"Yep…it became so bad, we had to take him out of school."

"That's so sad…"

"Yeah…I know…"

"Is he the only one…you know…who suffers from the illness."

"You make it sound like he has something terminal. You don't have to be crazy to hear voices…if that's the case, folks walking around swearing that they talk to God and that God talks to them, are all nuts…we all talk to ourselves….just some more than others."

"I mean…"

"I know what you mean…" She paused for a second and said, "In case you haven't noticed, I'm surrounded by 'special' people."

"His mother too?"

"Yes…but hers is a little more serious. She won't take her meds. Instead, she gets drunk, then all of the voices are drunk, and then I'm stuck in a house full of drunk people."

"Is he…is he…dangerous? Not that I'm worried about it."

"Are you? And no, he's not dangerous. He's the sweetest person on the planet…"

"He is," I confirmed.

She continued. "That's why he's been alone and that's the real reason why my son killed himself. He couldn't take it…it was too much to see his wife go through it and then to have all of the money in the world and you can't stop your son from suffering…"

"Was he 'sick' too?"

"No, honey…you don't have to be sick in the head to kill yourself…sometimes, it's the sickness of the heart that convinces you that you can't go on…"

"So…I'm okay?"

"I don't know…are you?" she laughed.

"I mean…"

"You're fine." She sat down at the counter next to me. "He's no more crazy than you and I…the only difference is, he's chosen to treat his crazy." She laughed. "He's not the guy who walks around normal and then one day, he doesn't have milk for his cereal and he goes and load-up a shot gun and kills every cow that he sees…"

I smiled.

"You don't have to worry about him…no more than you have to worry about me or the nutcase with a glass as a third hand…just make sure that he takes his meds and you both will be fine. He just needs someone to love him and care about him…you know? Like he loves and cares about you…" she grabbed my arm and looked at it.

We both looked at the scars. "He told you?"

"No, I saw them the first day that you came over here…and he wanted me to get you something to wear."

"Oh…"

"Now, go in that room and let him know that you're there for him…"

"Thank you for the talk…" I stood to leave the room. "And for the hot chocolate."

She stood. "Remember, we're all broken, Peaches…it's what we do with the broken pieces that defines us…"

Chapter46

The next morning, I awoke to find my Isaac – voices and all, lying next to me. When he sat up he smiled, unaware that he'd had an episode the night before. I turned over and kissed him. "How are you feeling?' I asked.

He smiled. "I'm good…how about you?"

"I'm good too…"

He looked at me. "What's up?"

"Nothing…"

He jumped up. "Good…I have a little business to take care of this morning and then, I can come and pick you up…we can do lunch…maybe go to the museum?"

"That would be great…" I patted the bed on the side of me. "Could you come and talk to me for a moment?"

"Sure," he said, as he crawled back onto the bed. "What do you want to talk about?"

He started to kiss me. I, gently, pushed him away. "Stop, Isaac…I think that we need to talk."

He sat down. "Okay…what's wrong?"

"Do you remember anything about last night?"

"Yes, I dooooooooo," he purred.

"I'm being serious…"

"Okay…what happened?"

I took a deep breath and said, "I heard you talking to yourself."

"What are you talking about, Peaches?"

"You were talking to an invisible person just like you're talking to me right now…"

He laughed. "That's crazy…"

I raised one of my eyebrows.

"I was talking to an invisible person…"

"Yes…" I confirmed.

Cornered, he said, "I'm sorry that you had to see that…"

"Your grandmother took care of it…"

He turned his back to me. "Peaches…I don't know what to say…I guess you want to leave me now?"

I thought about it for a second and said, "Please…do you remember who you're talking to?"

He looked at me and smiled.

"It doesn't scare me…hiding things from me, scares me."

"I should have told you, but I didn't want to run you away."

"Isaac…you ain't got nothing on me...believe me."

He grabbed my hand. "You know, I love you, right?"

I smiled. "I love you too…each and every one of you."

I thought that it would be cute to wear a pair of high-heels to the museum. They were cute for about five minutes. After that, it felt like my feet were in a vice-grip. On our way home, I was about two seconds from throwing my shoes out of the car window. I decided that I couldn't go another step in these things, so I begged him to stop by the mall so that I could pick up a pair of gym shoes or I was going to have to finish the day, barefoot.

We walked in and I hurried to the nearest shoe store. I was modeling several pairs for Isaac when a young man walked passed the store. He turned and came back.

"Damn…I don't believe this shit," he said, as he walked into the store.

Isaac and I looked at him. *Shit.*

"The heavens are shining down on me…don't I know you?" he asked.

Isaac stood. "Can I help you?"

"No, Bruh, you can't...I was talking to this young lady...standing right here."

"Who? My fiancée?" Isaac said, standing between us.

I could tell that something was about to jump-off, so I said, "Hey Gage..."

"You know him?" Isaac asked.

Gage's eyes widened. "Shit, she was telling the truth..."

"Who?" I asked. "How have you..."

"Look, I gotta get out of here...ummmmm, yeah...let's talk sometime...we definitely need to get caught up..." He ran out of the store.

Isaac looked at me. "What was that about?"

Confused, I said, "I have no idea."

Chapter 47

That night, Isaac was restless. He'd taken his medicine, but it made him extremely nauseous and irritable. He curled up in a ball and laid on the bed.

"This is why I hate taking that medicine," he said, holding his stomach.

"Tell me what to do to make you feel better…"

"Could you go and ask mama if she has anything to help settle my stomach?"

"Which mama?" I asked.

"My grandmother…" he said.

"Okay…I stood to walk out of the room. "I will be right back."

"Okay…" He grabbed the blankets and threw them over his head.

I walked down the hall to the kitchen, looked around, but no one was there. I didn't want to call out to her for fear of the wrong 'one' answering, so I went back to the room.

"You don't mind if I take your car? I can run to the store and get you something…"

He looked over at the dresser. "There's the keys, sweetie. Go by one of our stores and you won't have to pay for it."

"I don't mind paying for it…"

"Please, Peaches…just go to one of our stores…then that I way, I know where you are and that you're okay."

"Okay, sweetie…" I grabbed the keys and headed for the door. "I'll be right back…"

"And I'll be right here…" he said.

I walked out of the house and into the night air. I hit the remote, opened the door, and jumped in. Once out of the gate, I walked back to close it. When I got back into the car, I looked down the street and noticed a white van sitting on the side of the road. I looked at it for a second, but then blew it off because I was on a quest to help Isaac. Once in the car, I turned on some music. I rolled down the windows, to take in more of the night air. As the car hugged the road, all I could do was think about Isaac and our wedding day. I was concentrating on our 'colors' when I noticed bright lights bouncing off of my rearview mirror. The light hurt my eyes, so I tilted the mirror upwards to protect them. Then, I heard their horn blow. I sped up to get out of their way. This didn't satisfy them. They blew their horn again. I placed my foot on the accelerator. I looked at my side mirror and saw the van pull up on me. They blew their horn, again. Then, they took their van and rammed it into the back of the car. *BANG!!!* I looked down at the seat, and grabbed my phone. I dialed the first number that popped-up on the phone. It rang. "Hello," he mumbled.

Panicking, I said, "Isaac…Isaac…????"

Afraid, he said, "Babe…where are you?!!!"

"Isaac…someone just hit your car. I think that they're trying to run me off of the road.

"Stay on the line…I'll call the police." He moaned as he walked across the room. "Stay on the line, baby…"

They rammed their van into the car again. *BANG!!!* "Isaac!!!!!"

"Hello…my fiancée…look…listen…I'm trying to tell you that my fiancée is in trouble…" I heard him say.

BANG!!!! The van hit me again. "ISAAC!!! ISAAC!!!!"

"Baby, where are you?"

"ISAAC!!!" *BANG!!!* The car swerved off of the road.

"PEACHES!!!! TALK TO ME, PEACHES!!!!!"

When the car came to a stop, I said, "Isaac…I'm okay…they pushed me on the side of the road…"

"Peaches…look…lock the doors…see if you can pull off…do not open those doors…"

Just then, I turned. Something hit the window and shattered pieces of glass flew into the car.

"Peaches, what's happening? Peaches!" I heard him say, before I felt something hit me, hard, against the side of my head. "Isaac…?" I mumbled. "Isaac…?"

"PEACHES!!!!!!!" he screamed.

Chapter 4.8

"**M**ove!!!!" he ordered.

Holding my head, I asked, "Who are you? What are you doing?" Everything was so blurry.

"Shut up and get out," he ordered.

I stood, but my head began to spin. I fell down.

"Didn't I tell you to move?!" He ordered again.

I stood and grabbed on to him. When I was able to focus, I saw him standing in front of me. My hands were on his breasts. I removed them to rub my eyes. I was so confused. Her voice was deep like Barry White's, but he looked more like Vanna. I thought that I was seeing things until he opened his mouth again. "Let's go…"

She dragged me into a room. I was so dizzy, I collapsed onto the floor.

"Say 'hello' to your sister," she said, before closing the door.

The room was dark. I could barely make it out, but there was something on the bed. I crawled over to it. I climbed up and saw her, lying unconscious. "NO!!!" I screamed.

She didn't answer.

I screamed again. "Oh, my God…Grace!!!"

I tried to stand. Once on my feet, again, I stumbled to the bathroom. I soaked a towel in water and walked back into the room. I placed it on her face. She moaned. I began to cry. "Grace…Lord, Grace…look at you…you're alive…thank God…you're still alive."

She moaned again. "Peaches?"

"What have they done to you?"

She moaned. I tried lifting her. "Grace, look at me…" Every time, I touched her, she moaned again. She rolled over and wrapped her arms around me. "Come on…I'm going to take care of you." I dragged her into the bathroom and turned on the water in the shower. I lifted her leg and placed it into the tub. I did the same for her other leg. She sat down and let the water run over her head. I grabbed a towel and began to wash her. She screamed as the soap touched her wounds. "I'm so sorry, Grace…"

She grabbed my arm. "Turn off the water…" she mumbled. "Please, turn off the water…"

"Why?" I asked.

"Just turn it off…"

I turned off the water. She looked up at me. Her eyes were so swollen, she could barely see my face. "I'm going to get you out of here…you hear me?"

She looked down into the tub. Helping her to her feet, I wrapped her in a towel and took her back into the room. She sat down on the bed.

I pulled the chair around and pulled her close to me. "What is this place?"

"Hell…" she mumbled through a crack in her mouth.

"We have to get out of here…"

"Peaches, do you know these people?"

I sighed. "Yes…"

"Peaches…look what they did to me…because they thought that I was you. What did you do to these people?"

"Nothing, Grace, I swear…"

"Peaches…every time you do nothing, someone gets hurt…"

"I'm telling you, Grace…I don't know what the hell is going on. Gage was my boyfriend…"

"Which one is Gage?" she asked.

"The man…"

"They're both men," she confirmed.

"No, the other person is his sister…"

"They're both men, Peaches…believe me. I know…"

"Damn…"

"And that's not his sister…"

"Who is she?"

"Your guess is better than mine…"

"Damn…it was all lies," I said.

"Yes…" she confirmed.

I began to examine her. "What did they do to you?"

She exhaled. "She…he…she…he…he-she…"

"Please, Grace!!!!" I screamed.

"Peaches…it's too complicated and we don't have the time…okay?"

I stood and walked over to the window. "There's has to be a way out of here…"

"If there was a way, Peaches, I would have been gon'…you think I stayed because I like the damn food?"

"I'm trying, Grace…" I walked back over to her and held her. "Oh my, God…you're alive…I can't believe it."

Just then, I heard a "clicking" sound. Gage walked into the room and locked the door. I ran up to him. "You son-of-a-bitch…what did you do to my sister?!!!!"

He grabbed my hands. "Peaches?"

Grace mumbled. "I told you."

He stepped back. "You have to be shitting me…"

"Gage…why???!!!" I asked. "Why am I here? Why is she here? What is this about?"

"Oh…she didn't tell you about that yet…"

"About what?" I asked.

He grabbed another chair and sat across from us. "You know…now, is a good time to finish my story…"

"What story?" I asked.

"Oh…I was telling…damn, this is so fucked up. I don't even know your name." He looked at Grace.

"Don't tell him shit…" I said.

"Yeah…don't tell me shit. Won't matter in the end anyway. I was telling, Whatchamacallit, the story of my life…but instead of going back to the beginning, I will give you the 'Cliff Notes'…"

"What the fuck are you talking about, Gage?" I asked, frustrated.

"I looked for you…well, not you in particular. I looked for my mama and the trail led me to you. After I found out that she was dead, I almost just walked away, but the anger wouldn't let me…"

"Again…what are you talking about?" I asked.

"I'm getting there…if you give me a minute…"

"Fuck you…let us out of here…"

"Not going to happen," he confirmed. "Would I go through all of this just to let you go?"

"You're crazy…"

"Don't be mean, Peaches." He smiled. "In a way, this is your fault."

Frowning, I asked, "My what?"

"Yes…here, I thought that I was torturing you and I was torturing your sister. I blame that on you."

I shook my head. "This is insane…"

He looked at Grace. "I guess you have to thank your sister for this…"

"Fuck you," Grace mumbled.

Gage shook his head. "Not that again…"

"Gage, I swear…" I said.

"Peaches, calm down. I know that you can't wait to find out what's going on, but 'good things come to those who wait."

"I'm not waiting for shit." I frowned. "My fiancée has already called the police…"

"You got a damn fiancée? Damn, that hurts…" He laughed. "And, in a strange way, I loved you…'

"You what?"

"I did love you…almost like a…like a sister-girlfriend…if that makes sense…"

"It doesn't…"

"So I guess it's over now…between me and you?"

"You don't have to guess, asshole…it's definitely over."

He sighed. "Interestingly, I get that a lot…but I wasn't always this way. That bitch did this to me…"

"What bitch?" I asked.

"HAVE YOU BEEN FUCKING LISTENING? MY MOTHER! SHE DID THIS TO ME!"

I yelled back. "WHAT THE FUCK DOES THAT HAVE TO DO WITH ME AND HER?!"

He took a deep breath and said, "You're being rude, Peaches…"

I frowned.

"Any-who…" he leaned over and picked up the photo of my mother and her sisters. "You know…I've always wondered what she was like."

"Who?" I asked.

"My mother…my birth mother…"

Grace looked up.

"I wondered if she loved me…you know? Did she care about me?"

We listened, quietly.

A tear rolled down his cheek. "Maybe if she'd kept me, I could have had a better life, BUT SHE LEFT ME! WHAT MOTHER DOES THAT? LEAVE HER CHILDREN?"

"I would have left your crazy-ass too…" I was growing impatient.

"I always wanted to know why? Why didn't she keep me?"

I was growing more annoyed by the minute.

"Then, I found court records that showed that I was the result of a rape…a rape…that's terrible…you think that's why I'm fucked-up?"

"I don't know and I don't care…"

"Peaches, don't trivialize the horrors that made me the man that I am today…" he said.

"Man? That's a stretch…you're about as much of a man as your girlfriend."

"So, Whatchamacallit, told you about, Charlie… she's a sexy beast, isn't she?"

"You got the beast, part, right…"

"Careful…"

"I'm just trying to understand what's going on here. Your life was messed-up…you couldn't turn lemons into lemonade and decided to become a psychopath instead?"

He frowned. "Look at you girl with the big scientific words."

"I was gonna say 'asshole', but why tell you what you already know. Also, you know that most children of abuse don't turn into psychos…"

"For the record, I wasn't abused. I was neglected…but it still hurts the same," he began. "And I didn't hurt her. Charlie did all of that. She has a problem managing her anger, but we're working on it. Plus, I just couldn't bring myself to hurt my family…"

"Family?"

He ignored my question and looked at the picture. "You guys look just like her."

"Who?"

"My mother," he confirmed.

"Your mother?" I paused and stared at him.

"My mother…" He pointed at a face in the picture.

"Holy shit, Grace…"

She looked at him.

He smiled and threw his hands in the air. "Guess who?"

"What does that mean?"

"Say 'hello' to your long-lost cousin…"

"But I kissed you…" I said.

"I guess that makes us, *Kissing Cousins*…"

I wanted to vomit, but this wasn't the time. "So we're cousins?" I asked.

Grace sat up. "Wait…what? So you're saying that we're family?"

"One big happy family…I told you, Whatchamacallit, that you were going to love the ending."

"I'm so confused…so you're getting back at your mother by hurting us?"

"You're the only ones left…and somebody has to pay."

"But what do we have to do with what happened to you?"

"Nothing, but somebody needs to feel my pain." He stood to walk out of the room.

"This doesn't make sense…you don't have to do this. We can fix this…"

He frowned. "How are you going to fix this? Erase fifteen years of my life? Rewrite my story…add in some different characters? Throw in some rainbows…more sunshine? It's done and soon, it will all be over."

"What are you going to do to us?"

"Well, now, I don't know…what I wanted to do, I've been doing it, but to your sister. I could start all over, but it would take too much time and energy. I need some time to rethink this."

"You're a sick bastard…"

"I know…your sister told me that. She's just like you…completely had me fooled." He placed his hand on the door. "Now, you need to get her ready for tonight."

"Ready for what?" I asked.

"Ask your sister…" He opened the door. "I'm so glad that we're finally all together…like a family."

I tore up the room, trying to find something that I could use to make a weapon.

"There's no use…" she mumbled. "They took everything…"

"There has to be something…"

"When they come in here…they, usually have a knife."

"Really?"

"They'll be in here in a minute to make sure that we're clean and ready…"

"Clean and ready for what?"

She looked down at the floor.

"Fuck that…" I walked over to her. "You better get your ass up and help me find something. I be damned if I'm going to be here pass tonight…"

Immediately, the door opened. "Well, look at you two…they are going to love you."

"Charlie…" I said.

"Hey Peaches…long time no see…"

"What the hell is going on?"

"I just came in here to give your sister something for the pain." She had the knife in her hand.

Gage walked in the room. He kicked me in the back of my knees. I fell to the floor. He grabbed my arms and tied them together. He sat on my back. "Now, watch this, Cuz'…you're going to love it…they call it 'Cunt Odyssey'…it is the best way to administer a drug…she's going to feel so good in a minute."

Charlie grabbed Grace by the arm and led her to the foot of the bed.

Gage said, "Wait, let me get the cameras…I wanna take a picture. It'll be our first family photo."

"Hurry up before my shit go down!" she yelled.

He was gone for a minute, but, quickly, returned. He climbed back on top of me.

"Go," he instructed. "Don't forget your angles…I want to get all of this."

She hog-tied Grace's hands to her feet. She sprinkled a white substance on her penis and climbed on top of her. Grace screamed.

"Don't do that to her…leave her alone!" I shouted.

"In a minute, she won't feel a thing…" he said.

With each stroke, she screamed.

"I'm so sorry…" I whispered. She looked at me as only a big sister could. All of a sudden, she stopped screaming. Her eyes rolled into the back of her head and then there was nothing.

"Noooooooooooooo!!!!!" I screamed.

She climbed off of her. She checked Grace's pulse. "She's just sleeping…she's fine. She's on cloud nine." She took her hand and wiped the tears from her face. She walked over and forced her hand in my mouth. "A souvenir…" She fixed her clothes. "I'll be back to give you a little something, but you have to give a lady a minute to get hard again."

I crawled over to her. "Grace…Grace…speak to me."

She didn't respond.

I whispered in her ear. "That bitch is going to die."

I removed the ropes and quickly, removed my clothing and began to dress her. I sat her in the chair and proceeded to look around the room. When I saw it, I looked at it and smiled. An hour later, I heard a "clicking" sound. I laid across the bed and pretended to be asleep. Charlie walked in. "Hello…ready or not…here I come." She walked over to the bed and tapped me on the back of my leg with the blade of the knife. "Now, how did you get out of those ropes?" Stroking my leg with the blade, she said, "Wait a minute…I don't remember you having a birthmark."

Just then, Grace mumbled. "Surprise…"

Charlie turned to look at her.

I jumped up and said, "Hello Charlie…" Just then I reached out for her. Shocked, she looked at me. I lunged at her and she fell to the floor. "Let me go!" She dropped the knife. We wrestled for it. I got behind her and pinned her arms behind her back. Grace crawled over and picked the knife up.

I turned to Grace. "Help me! We have to tie her up…get those ropes…"

We tied her hands and feet. I began to pace back and forth. Grace mumbled. "You know what we have to do…"

"But you know that once we do this, there's no going back…"

"Look at me, Peaches…" Shaking, she pointed the knife at me. "I want to cut that bitch's dick off and shove it down her throat…"

I put my hands up. "Okay…okay…let's do this…"

She stared at her for a moment. "Help me get her in the bathroom…this is going to be messy."

"Wait….noooooo….please. I'm begging you…" Charlie said.

Before picking up her feet, Grace said, "This can be hard or easy…either way, I'm still going to enjoy it…"

"PLEASE!!!! I will give you anything!!!! No, please….I will let you go."

Grace frowned. "Ain't that some shit…NOW, a bitch wanna let somebody go…"

I laughed. "But I just got here," I said. I grabbed her hands and we dragged her into the bathroom. We dumped her into the tub and stood over her.

I looked at Grace. "What do you want to do first?"

Grace didn't look at me. Instead, she stared into the tub. "Leave and lock the door behind you…"

"Are you sure?" I asked.

Finally, she looked up and smiled. "Yes…"

I walked out of the bathroom and closed the door. I stood by the door and listened. There was some wrestling and several loud thumps. Charlie screamed. Then, the door opened. Grace walked out of the bathroom and handed me the knife. "Hold this…I'll be right back." She was walking towards the door when she turned and said, "Don't open that door."

A few moments later, Charlie tapped on the door. Crying, she said, "Peaches…please…Peaches."

Grace returned with something in her hand. I looked at it.

"Grace…is that a spatula?"

She looked at me. Her eyes were dark. She didn't respond. She took the knife and walked back into the bathroom. There was more wrestling and screaming. It seemed like it went on forever, but then, there was nothing, but silence. Suddenly, I could hear the water running. Grace walked out holding the ropes, and wiping the knife with a towel, she looked at me. She closed the door behind her. "You just can't fix those types…"

"Is she dead?"

"If not…her impersonation of being alive is 'bout as fucked-up as her impersonation of a woman…" She looked at the door. "He should be walking in shortly…"

"What did you need the spatula for?"

"I needed to flip a bitch…" She sat down on the bed. "How do you want to handle this?"

"I'll leave that up to you," I said.

I laid on the bed with my legs wide open as Grace lied motionless on the floor. The door opened.

"Charlie…what are you doing?" he asked, as he entered the room. He kicked Grace in the side. "Come on, Cuz'…you have work to do."

As he walked towards the bed, Grace reached out and grabbed his legs. He fell forward – hitting his head on the footboard. His eyes closed.

I crawled over. "Let's get him on the bed."

We lifted him. "Hurry…get his clothes off." Frantically, we removed his clothing. "Tie him up…"

Slowly his eyes opened. He tried moving. He looked at his hands and said, "Let me go."

"Sure, fam'…" I said, pointing the knife towards him. "But first let me tell YOU a story…"

"What?" he asked.

Grace walked over and sat in a chair that sat next to the bed. I sat on the bed next to him. I exhaled and said, "This is the story of a young man and his…" I looked at Grace. "Were you able to find out who she was before you killed her?"

Grace shook her head, "No."

His eyes widened. "Wait…Charlie…you killed Charlie? She's dead?"

"Well…yes and no…No, I didn't kill her. Grace did and yes, she's very dead."

"Damn…that's fucked-up," he said, shaking his head. "Now, what am I going to do?"

Grace stood, grabbed the knife, and walked into the bathroom. When she came out, she was holding something in her hand. "Here…she would want you to have these…" She took the object and said, "Hold his mouth…"

"Wait…the fuck are you doing?" he asked.

I walked over and grabbed his head. "Grace, what is that?"

"A souvenir…" she said. "NOW, EAT IT!"

"No, bitch…I won't…" he said, tightening his lips.

"You're going to eat this shit and you're going to like it…now, open your fucking mouth."

He struggled for a moment. Whatever it was, she shoved it into his mouth. "Swallow it…"

He began to gag.

"Swallow it, you bastard…" She placed the knife against his throat.

His eyes widened.

"I'm waiting and I can do this all night…since there's so much of her left…"

Slowly, he began to chew. Choking whatever it was, down, he swallowed. She patted his forehead. "Good boy…"

Pleadingly, he looked at me. "Peaches…"

Grace placed the knife between his legs and said, "Peaches…you were saying?"

"Now, back to the story…One day, I was in the mall…dealing with a lot of shit and a young man walked up to me…"

"Please, Peaches…I'm sorry…" he said.

I continued. "This young man seemed so nice and he came to me when I was at one of the lowest points in my life…"

"Please…" he begged.

I continued. "He was so persistent…so charming…earned my trust. I let him in, but he lied to me…that dirty motherfucker had an agenda…."

"Peaches? Can we talk about this?"

"…Now, he's tied to a bed and he's going to die…"

"WAIT!!!!! NOOOOOOO!!!" he screamed.

"It's a fucked-up feeling…being at the mercy of another human being…it must be so scary being so helpless…the fear…and the pain that you're going to experience…" He began to drift off. "Am I boring you?" I looked over at Grace. "What was that you gave him?"

"His girl's nuts and a little something to keep him from screaming like a bitch when it's time for him to get what he deserves. Now, enough talking…it's time to get him ready."

"For what," I asked.

"He has work to do…"

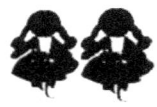

"How do he look?" she asked, brushing the wig that I placed on his head.

"Girl, in this lighting…he looks good enough to fuck."

"How's his makeup? Is he pretty?"

"Pretty as a 'peach'…" I looked at him. "The blush is a little heavy for my taste, but his eyeshadow is perfect."

"Really? I wanted to make his eyes pop…" She stood back to examine him. "What about his lips? Do you think that he needs more lip-gloss?"

"Girl, you put any more lip-gloss on his lips and those guys are going to slide right out of him." I stood back and examined him. "You know…there is a resemblance…especially, in the makeup. He looks just like, auntie."

Grace frowned. "Fuck him…now, turn off the lights and let's get this party started."

I walked over and flipped the switch.

"Now, let them in," she said.

I opened the door and several men entered the room.

"I hear you've come to party," she said.

"YES!!!" They screamed.

She grabbed the camera and asked, "Who's first?"

Two of them began to unzip their pants. The rest formed a line behind them.

He began to stir.

"We have something special set-up for you...have any of you been to prison?"

You could see their excitement even in the darkness.

"Then, you're going to love this..."

"Wait...hold-up you guys..." she said, as she walked over to check his mouth. She kneeled down and whispered in his ear. "Welcome to the family...Cuz'."

I checked to make sure that the restraints were tight. She turned on the camera and said, "Don't forget your angles, Cuz'…your fans are watching."

The sun was saying 'hello' as they all said their "Goodbyes."

As I pulled back the curtains, I looked at him. "Damn Bruh….you don't look so good." Grace was removing the tape from the camera. I looked over at her. "We can't leave him this way."

"You're right…" she confirmed. She picked up the knife, walked over, and stood over him. She raised her hands over her head.

"Wait," I said. I ran out of the room and down the hall. I looked through the drawers until I found what I was looking for. I ran back into the room. I walked over to the bed. "Let's finish him…together."

She looked at my hand and with tears in her eyes, she smiled. "Okay…"

We both raised our arms and at the same time, we lowered them, plunging the knives, deep, into his chest. The first blow left the walls decorated in his blood – over and over and over and over, again, we stabbed him, until there was nothing left of him, but the look of shock on his face.

"Look at his face…" She wiped the blood from her hands onto the sheets lying next to him. "I don't think he believed that we would kill him…"

I looked at him. "And some folks don't think shit stinks until they smell it..." I looked at the mess that we'd made and continued, "Now, what are we going to do with him?"

"Let's leave him right here…" She walked over and covered the window. "I want him to know what it truly feels like to be left in the dark."

We walked out into the hall and closed the door.

"Wait," she said. She ran back into the room and when she returned, she was holding something. "Mama's picture…"

Through the blood, that stained their images, I could see them smiling up at us. I smiled back.

"We should get cleaned up…" I said, looking at myself.

"Charlie has some clothes….upstairs. She won't be needing them…"

As we walked out into the moonlight, we barely said a word to each other. After walking around for an hour, she broke the silence. "Peaches, where are we going?"

I looked at her and smiled. "Let's go say 'hi' to our dear ol' dad…"

The End? 🎎🎎

Coming Soon...

Six Degrees of Separation

Spring 2017 in paperback

A preview of my next novel,

"Six Degrees of Separation (also referred to as the "Human Web") refers to the idea that, if a person is one step away from each person they know and two steps away from each person who is known by one of the people they know, then everyone is no more than six "steps" away from each person on Earth." -- Frigyes Karinthy

So now we must ask ourselves, "Where the hell did he come from?"

Prologue

Excuse me sir, do you have any change?" she asked, with the most beautiful blue eyes I've ever seen. I looked into my pocket and retrieved some small bills and handed them to her. It was cold out. Her teeth 'clicked' together as she thanked me. I had to admit that I felt sorry for her.

"Look, let me buy you a hot meal," I said.

"Oh, thank you, that would be nice," she responded.

We walked down to the corner diner. From the moment we entered, all eyes were on us. I ordered us some coffee to get us started. While we waited, the woman went on and on about the road that led her to this place — this moment in her life.

"He was a football player," she said, as if I gave a shit. "Yeah, he even went pro," she continued.

I looked around the room for the waitress who was taking so long to bring us our coffee that I was beginning to think that her ass took a trip to

Columbia to hand pick the beans herself. The woman sitting across from me was still rambling.

"I really loved his ass too…for real…no kidding. Everybody thought that I was only with him for his money, but I ain't no gold-digger.

No matter what they say," she spat through the gap in her front teeth.

The people in the diner watched and whispered as she took me down memory lane. She noticed it. I couldn't tell if she was embarrassed or not because her face was hidden under several layers of dirt. When the waitress finally arrived with the coffee, the woman excused herself, went to the bathroom, and when she returned it looked like she tried to clean herself up. She had pulled her matted hair back and she tried to wash her face. It was evident that she scrubbed really hard because now her pale skin was even redder than before. As I ordered, I could tell that the waitress was staring at me.

I didn't acknowledge her because I wasn't interested. When she realized that I wasn't going to give her the attention that she was seeking, she took the menus, placed them under her arm, rolled her eyes at the woman sitting across from me, huffed, and then walked away.

Still talking, the woman said, "That motherfucker even had the nerve to be on the down-low. Man, I heard she cut the shit out of his ass."

Now, she had my attention. "She who?" I asked.

"The bitch he dumped to marry my fine ass." She smiled. "Then he dumped me to get back with her. That's why I'm glad that he's dead...with his triflin' ass," she said, like a person who was trying to make Ebonics a first language.

Curious, I asked, "So, she killed him?"

"Naw," she began. The waitress walked over with our plates. She paused and threw some fries into her mouth. "Like I was saying...naw, that motherfucker got him some 'jail-house justice.' They raped his ass to death. He was a loser in life. Now, he's a loser in Hell." She went on like this for another hour.

I watched her thinking about what she may have looked like when she was younger. She was probably really pretty 'back-in-the-day.'

Now, she was just an empty shell — one of life's walking dead.

When she finished, I paid the tab and then we left the diner. I was about to walk away when she said, "I really appreciate what you did for me. Nobody has been that nice to me in a long time. Let me do something nice for you." She looked down at my crotch.

Frowning, I said, "There's nothing that you could do for me. Just take care of yourself."

"Please let me do something…it's the least I could do," she pleaded. She began to lick her lips seductively.

What a waste. I thought to myself. "Look, I'm good."

"Well, I promise that I'm going to do something really nice for myself. I might even use the money you gave me to go to the clinic and get myself cleaned up. Wouldn't that be nice? Change my life…become respectable," she said.

I looked at her. "Take care of yourself." I turned and walked away.

Later that evening, I was walking back in the direction where I left the woman. I walked passed an alley where I could hear someone both crying and laughing. I walked toward the sound. In the dark, it was hard to tell who it was. As I got closer, there she sat with a rope wrapped around her arm and a needle sticking out of her vein.

"Hey, I told you I was going to do something nice for myself," she said, recognizing me.

I looked at her; disappointed and angry. It was disgusting looking at her lying in the alley like trash that someone had thrown out. I leaned over her and removed the needle from her arm. Lying on the ground next to her was a spoon, a lighter, and a couple of rocks that looked like heroine. I placed a 'rock' on the spoon and began to heat it. She laughed to herself. When the rock melted and became a liquid, I filled the syringe with it. As she mumbled and laughed to herself, I asked her for her name.

"My name is Sandy," she said, enjoying her buzz. I hit the syringe with my finger, found her vein, and then plunged the needle deep inside of it. Initially, she smiled and closed her eyes.

Suddenly, she looked at me as if becoming lucid just long enough to realize what was happening to her. I smiled at her. Before ramming the needle deeper into her arm, I said, "My name is Izrael. It was nice meeting you."

Other Books

Other Titles

- *Never What it Seems*
- *Autumn Leaves*
- *Fallen Angel*
- *Never What it Seems II – A Mother's Love*
- *Kiss My A@@ - This is Not Your Typical Self-Help Book*
- *Somebody Else's Baby*
- *Peaches – Always Kiss Your Baby Goodnight*
- *Officer Friendly*
- *Born-Again Hustler – From Pimping to the Pulpit*

Website:
http://dianemartin.weebly.com